CROSS COURT

VAI DENTON

Cross Court

Copyright © 2026 by Vai Denton

Editing: Rachel Bunner (@rachels.top.edits)

Proofreading: Miah Onsha (@miahonsha.author) and Laura Hartley

Cover design: Vic Cavalieri (@weirdowithluv)

ISBN: 979-8-9904429-6-2 (paperback)

ASIN: B0FQRN9XX7 (ebook)

First Edition: March 2026

10 9 8 7 6 5 4 3 2 1

content warnings

Cross Court is the second book in the *Off Court* series. It is recommended that you read this book after enjoying *Drop Shot*, the first book in the series. Otherwise, there may be some spoilers. That said, this book can be read as a standalone and will have no cliffhangers.

If you are of the belief that content warnings are spoilers, please feel free to jump ahead now. For those who are interested, please be advised that this novel contains: mentions of a back injury, brief mentions of childhood bullying, on-page consumption of alcohol, neglectful parents, an incident with water, on-page sexual content.

This one's for me and all the real-life "unlikeable FMCs"—you're my favorite protagonists

CROSS-COURT / Adjective

Describes a shot that travels diagonally across the net,
from one side of the court to the opposite side, often used
in a series to draw an opponent out of position over time
and wear them down.

WTA schedule

Name	Date	Location	Category*	Court Type
Indian Wells Open	March 5–16	Indian Wells, CA, USA	WTA1000	Hard Court
Miami Open	March 18–30	Miami, FL, USA	WTA1000	Hard Court
Charleston Open	March 31–April 6	Charleston, SC, USA	WTA500	Clay Court
Stuttgart Open	April 14–21	Stuttgart, Germany	WTA500	Clay Court
Madrid Open	April 22–May 4	Madrid, Spain	WTA1000	Clay Court
Italian Open	May 6–18	Rome, Italy	WTA1000	Clay Court
Internationaux de Strasbourg	May 18–24	Strasbourg, France	WTA500	Clay Court
French Open/ Roland Garros	May 25–June 8	Paris, France	Major/Grand Slam	Clay Court

*Number designations indicate points won by winner
(Roland Garros winner gets 2000 points)

one

The best and worst thing about tennis? Momentum can change on a dime. One well-placed shot, one second's hesitation, muscles springing into action a moment too late, and suddenly the tide shifts. A match you were losing by miles can be within your grasp in a few won games, your opponent's confidence ripped to tatters.

Unfortunately, I am the opponent today, and my confidence has dissipated into the stifling desert air of Indian Wells, California. After winning the first set handily, I went down in the second-set tiebreak. Knowing momentum would be on my opponent's side, I prepared for a battle in the third set, and that preparedness gave me a 5–2 lead.

Which I've now squandered.

Four games in a row lost, and the American crowd clamors for my American nemesis, Anya Morozov, stomping their feet and clapping with excitement that she's one game away from being crowned this year's Indian Wells champion. A title nearly as prestigious and coveted as that of a major.

The two towels I slung over my face at the start of our short break do nothing to drown out the noise, though I am thankful I got them on before the frustrated tears began.

Déjà vu simmers through me, reminding me of January of this year, during an unprecedented run to the final of the Australian Open before falling to the world number one, Emilia Kessler, in a third set I could have won. *Should* have won. Or last month in Doha, playing some of my best tennis before losing in the final to the world number three, Valentina Ortega.

"Time," the chair umpire calls, which only escalates the noise reverberating around Stadium 1.

"Anya! Anya! Anya!" The chant sets my teeth on edge. Ripping the towels off my head, I grab my racket and march to stand below my near empty players' box. I don't dare glance at Anya; I'm sure she's grinning like a Cheshire cat.

Karolína, one of few privy to how difficult I am on myself during matches, ensures her face is devoid of anything but pride, though as my coach, there are plenty of technical and strategic things she could tell me to fix. Things that will torment me if I lose this match.

Who am I kidding? They'll probably torment me even if I win.

"Play your game, Nic," she yells from the first row, her bright blue eyes focused singularly on me. Still, with a thunderous crowd drowning out everything my insecurities don't, I hardly hear her, forced to read her lips. "Be offensive. Four points to tie it. You can do this."

I'm not so sure. My aforementioned tattered confidence wanes with each passing second, replaced with self-hatred and anger. And while I'm sometimes able to harness that anger and channel it to play better, that hasn't been the case today.

It's been like this for a while, the defeat weighing heavily after years of hard work not paying off. The sport I used to love nothing more than a chore, a means to get the adoration of a crowd that rarely roots for me in big moments.

My coach claps a few times for my benefit, encouraging me to focus once more. Penelope, my manager and publicist, and Nora, my strength and conditioning coach, each give me a thumbs up beside her, their expressions less veiled. They may be the only three people in this stadium rooting for me.

I wonder if they think I've lost already.

Shoving the notion from my mind, I turn toward the baseline, stepping a foot closer to the deuce side service box than I have been the last few games Anya served. After shifting the strings of my racket so they're evenly spaced and slapping each of my shoes with the center of the strings, I glance up.

The umpire looks around, maybe shocked the crowd has yet to quiet. "Ladies and gentlemen, please."

Finally, my eyes land across the court, where I spot Anya's grin, wide and trained on me. Taunting me. My blood rises to an absurd temperature, my hand tightening around my racket. I jump once, twice, and drop my shoulders so my torso is nearly parallel to the court, bending my knees and moving side to side. Anya's serves are like bullets, and if I can get the center of my strings on the ball, I can harness her power.

The crowd quiets, silent as the dead, everyone's breath held as Anya tosses the ball.

Her first serve is an ace up the T. The stadium erupts like it's over. And maybe I'm a fool for believing otherwise.

My resolve slips, and I take a step back for her next serve, giving myself more room in case she tries to serve up the middle again. Though, based on the countless hours of tape I've watched on her, she won't. I adjust my strings again, tap the center against each of my heels, and get set.

It's a kick serve out wide, my backhand return sailing past her baseline.

"Come on!" she roars alongside the thousands of people cheering her on.

Helplessness eats at my nerves, my hands shaky. She's two points away now. Adjust my strings. Tap the center of the racket against both heels. Bend and move side to side.

Another ace. I might as well not be here. I'm letting the crowd in, letting them take away my chance at the fifth biggest title of the year, but I can't figure out what to do.

With one last chance, I return the ball to her forehand, and there's nothing to be done when she sends it perfectly down the line.

A triumphant shriek from the other side of the net.

It's over.

My ears ring. Like my body knows the last two grueling weeks I've spent getting to the finals have come to an end, it aches, every muscle in need of an ice bath and massage. My walk of shame to the net is met with a curl of Anya's lips and a sarcastic *"good* match," her snicker poorly concealed.

Do not rip her arm off her body, I tell myself, though no one can fault me if my grip is tighter than necessary when we shake.

"Good match," I pretend to agree through gritted teeth before turning to shake the umpire's hand. Anya begins hitting balls to fans and pumping her fists, basking in her win. Infuriating as always.

Outside of a title slipping through my fingers, the worst part of losing in the final is that I'm expected to sit here and accept the consolation prize. Any other round of the tournament, I'd get to walk off the court as soon as it's over, but for the final? Give a speech, take pictures, and act as though I want to be here when I'd rather be anywhere else.

I am so *sick* of losing important finals. Losing one was demoralizing enough, but three? In three months? Pitiful.

It's taken me seven fucking years to break inside the top ten, but no one cares about that. No one gives a shit about you unless you take home the big titles: Australian Open, Indian Wells, French Open, Wimbledon, US Open. There is no love for an almost winner. For someone who can't close.

There are winners and there are nobodies.

And I cannot afford to be a nobody. I cannot afford to continue reaching the finals only to fall to players like Emilia, Valentina, or Anya, younger and less seasoned despite their higher rankings and greater title achievements.

It's not long before the dreaded "and now, to receive

her trophy, Nicola Vassilakis" thrusts me from my self-loathing. And as if the disappointment of the loss isn't enough, I stand on stage, holding my sad, little trophy, telling the person I hate most on tour what a great player she is in front of thousands of her adoring fans.

A fate worse than death.

two

Hours later, after a cooldown stretch and shower, I prepare my socially challenged brain for a gory presser, wherein I will be asked a multitude of painful questions. Half of these journalists hope to elicit as much drama as they can, pressing on purpling bruises with the expectation that they'll get something salacious from it.

Karolína, Nora, and Pen stride with me down the hall toward the press room. Foreboding settles in my veins as we move past Anya's team, where they wait for her post-match press release. Pen shifts behind me before we pass Anya's parents—who speak to her quietly in Russian, brows furrowed—and her brother Aleksandr, who's been working as one of her strength and conditioning coaches for over a year. He steps between her and her parents, arm brushing mine in the process.

Aleksandr's unwavering blue eyes meet and hold mine for a second longer than they should before I look away, my arm white-hot.

I loathe him.

"Sorry," he murmurs. Refusing to meet his eyes again, I shake my head once. I imagine he's apologizing for being in my way, but there's something in the word that feels deeper. Not that I trust my ability to parse his or anyone else's tone.

When there's a safe distance between us and Anya's camp, Pen speaks softly. "Okay, Nic. If there's anything you don't want to answer, look at me. They're not going to let you get away without some rough ones, but anything that hits too close to home, I'll set them straight, alright?"

"I can handle them," I grumble, fixing the various gold hoops along my ears.

"We know you can. That's exactly why you can't be the one to say anything, because it never goes well when you do."

So I don't mince words. Sue me.

"Fine."

A staff member opens the door, and I step in, pasting on a wobbly smile—or my best imitation of one—as flashes go off. Pen and Delilah—my closest friend and former doubles partner—both, on separate occasions, told me my PR-friendly smile needs work. I believe the former's exact words were "twitching the corners of your lips isn't enough to make people believe you like them."

The table in front of me is long, with one lone microphone, and I take my seat as I have many times, tossing my thick, wet, chestnut-brown hair into a bun to get it off my neck. Four rows, each with ten chairs, sit before me, full of photographers and reporters chomping at the bit to rip me limb from limb.

I rub a finger over my mati pendant on one of my necklaces, sure I'll need its protection now more than ever. The ridges of the blue eye kiss my skin comfortingly.

A woman with short black hair from tournament staff takes a seat at the table, out of view of the cameras, smiling at me kindly before turning to the room. "Good evening. Welcome to the press conference for Nicola Vassilakis. Please raise your hand if you would like to ask a question."

Hands shoot up all over the room, and the woman points. "Federica."

I scan faces until someone calls for my attention. "Nicola?" I bite back a grimace at their use of my full name and the image of an empty home and a sharp not-so-motherly tone it produces, my gaze landing on the woman in a deep blue pantsuit. She's smiling, which I take as a good sign. "Hi. Obviously, this isn't the outcome you wanted, but looking back at your tennis the last couple of weeks, how proud of yourself are you for reaching this final for the first time?"

Using the training Pen has drilled into my skull, I reply, "I'm thankful I got this far." Pen's lips twisting to the side tells me I need to say more. "It's always hard to make it to the final stage and lose. There's a lot of disappointment, but yeah, I played great tennis, and I'm happy I made it to the final." I'm hesitant to use the word *proud*, not sure I've earned it after today.

The press staffer points at another woman with her hand raised.

"After getting to witness that level of tennis today, I can safely say we're all glad you made it to the final," the journalist chimes in, smoothing stray strands of her blonde hair behind her ear. She smiles sympathetically. "Are there things you think you could have done differently? Things you did throughout the tournament to get you here that fell off near the end?"

Digging the heels of my shoes into the stage, I stare her down. "Like what?" The woman falters, glancing around, but at the shake of Pen's head, I exhale. "There are always things you go back to that you wish you'd done differently. What if I'd served out wide a few more times during the second-set tiebreak? Would she have caught on or not? What if I'd deviated a bit more from cross-court shots, went to the net more? So yeah, there will always be things like that."

Things that won't allow me to sleep tonight, or for the next week. Reminders that after years of hard work, after years of chasing the love heaped upon me when I won two junior majors, I'm still right where I started when I aged up.

Struggling to get a 1000 title, let alone a major.

Papers flutter as they search for the next barbed question. A man seated in the third row stands and, like a bloodhound sniffing out my unhealed wounds, says, "Nicola, you won two junior slams. After all that success, people expected you'd carry on your mother's legacy. Carmen Aguirre spent months as the world number one, and won fifteen singles titles, including three majors."

I clench my teeth so tight, I'll be surprised if they're not reduced to nubs. As if I need my mother's accolades told to me. Like I haven't spent years agonizing over the fact that not only have I not lived up to people's expectations, I've failed to live up to my mother's name.

"Despite the injuries and losses you've suffered thus far, do you think you're capable of getting to that level eventually?"

Clearing my throat, I search the room, as if the right words will appear. All I've ever wanted my entire life is to win majors, to be heralded as one of the greats, to have the adoration of millions.

But nothing has gone according to plan. Pen glares at the back of the reporter's head, ready to address him, but I can handle this. I can only imagine what people are saying about me on social media: some variation of *anybody who ever believed Nicola Vassilakis was Grand Slam champion material, read 'em and weep* or *this has to be one of the biggest chokes in WTA Indian Wells history* since those are consistent in my messages and tags, so much so that Pen now handles my socials. The last thing I need is to look like I can't take care of myself during a press conference and add fuel to their fires.

I want to scream. Am I capable of reaching my mother's level? I've been working my ass off for years with little to show for it. The number of times I've considered quitting is certainly not zero, especially after these painful losses this year, but I'm clinging to the sport I used to love and the joy that once came with winning.

"There were a lot of expectations about what I'd accomplish by a certain age. Have I done that yet? No. But I've made it into the same number of big finals this year as I have in the rest of my career combined. I'm finally in the top ten." With more conviction than I feel, I finish, "So yes, I am capable, and I'd like to believe this season so far is proof I'm knocking on that door."

Murmurs float around the room, hopefully impressed. Pen has tried to instill in me the need to make jokes, get these people laughing with me, but I've never been able to do that. I was, I think, born without much of a sense of humor, and that makes me criminally unfunny to most. Rarely do I know what to say during any social or public interaction, and if I sound like I do, it's because I've been coached.

It's frustrating being so fundamentally different from people that I need all these pointers. Since I was young, I've recognized that something is wrong with me, that I never say the right thing or act the right way. That I lash out when I'm uncomfortable. That my silences make people uncomfortable. *"It's off-putting,"* my nanny Daphne once told my mother the day she and my father returned from a month away, right in front of five-year-old me.

If only I were naturally comfortable with people like Delilah, the tour's sweetheart, or Anya, who has tennis lovers eating out of the palm of her hand despite how juvenile and bratty she often acts.

If only I didn't care what people thought of me.

Another man stands. "Nicola, you've got a healthy rivalry with Anya. You've played her eight times now and won once, over a year ago. You had the opportunity today after winning that first set. What went wrong? And do you think Anya is an opponent you can't crack?"

It's a question I should have expected, and yet it irks

me. Nothing about our rivalry is healthy. Since she was seventeen, she's been the definition of a prodigy, winning majors and tournaments. We may both be legacies, but Anya is the one who's been able to find success in that legacy.

While I never particularly liked her or the way she forces herself into her opponents' heads, when I moved into the top fifty and we began meeting more often, she became insufferable in a way I could no longer ignore. Training at her parents' facility, while beneficial to my rise, has only served to make things between us more intense.

I wonder if this short, pale man feels my eyes stabbing holes in him like a voodoo doll. Pen points at her smile urgently, so I force the corners of my mouth to twist up. "Anya is a great player. She's tough to beat, and today just wasn't the day for me to do it. She played better." Swallowing over the bitterness of those words, I finish, "There are a lot of young girls coming in from the juniors who are bright and full of potential. I'm going to continue putting in the work so I can keep pace with them."

After answering how I'll handle another potential meeting with Anya this season (prepare until my body breaks down), what it's like being a perfectionist (at this level, who isn't?) in a sport where you can lose half the points even when you win, and what I'm going to do to celebrate getting into this final (go to the gym to get stronger, something the room thinks is a joke), Pen checks that there are no more questions and I thank them all before heading out.

It's getting late, but I'm not going to be able to sleep

tonight. At least we're flying home to Orlando tomorrow ahead of the Miami Open, where I'll have a couple of days to unwind in my own apartment for the first time in two and a half months.

I just need to get through tonight.

Despite the itchy feeling it produces, I hug Karolína and Pen. The former gives me a look and a muttered but firm "rest up, then" when I refuse their offer of dinner before we part for the evening. I grab my tennis bag, stomping my way to the players' gym, whipping out my phone on the way, and watching the messages from my closest friends roll in.

SAHAR'S BAD BERLIN BAGELS

MAYA

No matter the outcome, you are an absolute powerhouse, Nic! You played so well!!

HARPER

I've never been so proud of you!

SAHAR

No seriously. You were so hot out there. Next time Anya is toast

Separately, Delilah texted.

DELILAH

Please go easy on yourself tonight

You played so incredibly. This one match doesn't define your season. It's still the year of Nic!

The knot in my chest eases a fraction but not enough to go back to my dark and lonely hotel room. Dumping my phone and bag to the side, I shove earbuds in, yank out my resistance bands, and get to work.

three

Less than half an hour into my stretching and band work, Anya comes to the players' gym to roll out with Aleksandr, her voice loud and obnoxious as she, no doubt, prepares for a night of partying after her win. It becomes so irksome, I have to turn my music up to a near painful decibel to drown her out, and even then, her laughter pulls me ever closer to ripping out an earbud and yelling at her.

Aleksandr, on the other hand, has remained quiet, glancing over at me with pinched brows, his lips tilted down, which is rare for him. Not that I pay attention.

When the urge to strangle her becomes too strong, I pull out my earphones and put my more heavy-duty over-the-ear headphones around my neck, shoving my resistance bands into my tennis bag.

Sleek floors gleam under bright lights, and treadmills line the far wall, with windows that look over the darkened park, their digital displays blinking. Behind them stand rows of bikes and erg machines that gradually give way to a sprawling equipment area—cable stations, benches, racks, medicine balls, anything an athlete might need.

As I walk toward the treadmills, Anya heads to the door. She turns over her shoulder and calls, "Sasha, are you coming?" She and her parents are the only ones I've heard call him that, a family nickname I assume. Her grinning eyes slip to mine, brightening when she notices I'm watching her.

"I'll meet you in the hotel lobby before dinner," Aleksandr responds. I can't see him now that I've reached a treadmill, the roll out area cut off from my view.

Oh well. None of my business. Headphones on, music cranked up, I begin a cooldown walk that'll hopefully earn me a couple of hours of sleep tonight. The match replays in my head as I move, missed forehands flashing behind my eyes when I blink, double faults when I breathe in, failed return shots when I breathe out. My muscles ache with fatigue from the last two weeks, and yet no pain can match the defeat settling between my shoulder blades.

There's movement in my periphery. My eyes snap to it, finding Aleksandr standing beside my treadmill. His hair has grown out since he shaved it in November, light brown at the roots and blond near the top, locks curling softly over one another. His face is tan from his time on court, and his blue eyes sparkle despite those pinched brows hanging over them. Well-muscled shoulders stretch his stupid slutty workout shirt taut against his chest and biceps and ending just below the waistband of his sweatpants so that when he lifts his hand to wave at me, a flash of his abs is exposed.

Clearly it's been a while since I hooked up with someone.

I look away like I've been burned, zoning back in on the music pumping through my blood. I refuse to glance back; we have nothing to say to each other, no reason to speak. Plus, in about an hour, he'll be toasting to his sister's victory over me. That's enough to continue fueling my blank stare.

His large hand covers the speed controls, dropping my pace until I rip down my headphones and glare at him.

"Can I help you?"

"Why are you training right now? You should be resting." His lips are still turned down.

"And you should be worrying about your sister, not me."

His lips twitch. "As a strength and conditioning coach, I feel I am obligated to make sure you're not overtraining and hurting yourself for the future."

I roll my eyes, slapping his hand away from the controls and increasing the speed. I add an extra couple of taps to get it faster than before, for good measure. Aleksandr doesn't walk away like I want him to though.

The infuriating eldest Morozov played on the men's ATP tour for years, winning a few majors before he retired, surprisingly, on a high note as the world number three. He got his credentials to become a performance coach and joined Anya's team last year, traveling with her all season. When one of the head strength coaches left the Morozov Tennis Academy—his parents' training facility in Orlando where Delilah, Sahar, Harper, and I all train during the offseason—in October, he took over offseason strength and conditioning sessions.

Unfortunately, Nora was at home taking care of a sick family member in November, so I had no option but to join a couple of times a week. Since then he has, it seems, made it his mission to annoy me despite the few words I've spoken to him and how quickly I dismiss him.

"Is there a reason you're bothering me?" I ask when, two minutes later, he's still here.

This time, he grins softly. "Aren't I always bothering you?"

"Okay," I concede. "Is there a reason you're bothering me more than usual?"

"How about I leave you alone when you stop over-working yourself after two weeks of ridiculously high-level play and practice and a competitive finals match?"

"How about you leave me alone and I won't throw a dumbbell at your head?"

Aleksandr chuckles deeply, the sound a rumble as his head dips. "Now that I'd like to see."

I don't know why I allow him to burrow under my skin like this, but I genuinely contemplate hopping off the belt and grabbing something to chuck at his head. Pen would be none too pleased.

"You're seriously thinking about it, aren't you?" he asks around another laugh.

"Are you going to wait around and find out?" My eyes lock on his, hopefully a clear message that I'm refusing to back down.

"I think I am."

When he doesn't budge after another minute, a groan rips from my chest. I slam my hand onto the *off* button and jump from the treadmill, hurrying toward my bag. Throwing it over my shoulder, I trudge to the main door. My lower back twinges, an old injury that enjoys rearing its head here and there, but if Aleksandr notices my knuckle pressing into the muscle, he doesn't say.

"Wipe the treadmill for me since you're so intent on my leaving," I say over my shoulder.

Grabbing my phone and ignoring the pang of disappointment—but not surprise—at seeing no calls or texts from my parents, I dial the first (and okay, only) person I think of, putting it to my ear as it rings.

To Aleksandr, who has caught up to me in the hallway outside the gym, I respond, "Stop stalking me."

He shakes his head as I slow to walk behind him. "We're going to the same hotel."

After the fifth ring, Delilah's soft, soothing voice mumbles, "Hello?"

The slight garble in her voice makes me pull away to check the time. "Shit, Del, sorry." It's after eleven in Orlando. With all the traveling I do, my internal clock is ruined and I've completely forgotten.

A deeper voice grumbles from beside her, and Delilah hushes her boyfriend, Matteo, before the phone is shuffled around. "Nic, hi." The last dregs of sleep cling to the words.

"Go back to bed. We'll talk tomorrow."

"No, no. I'm awake." A door snicks shut. I picture her leaving her bedroom in our apartment across the street from the academy before shuffling to the couch and settling in beneath the odd mix of art on the wall. "What's up?"

My eyes flick to Aleksandr, noting he's still within earshot. Loudly enough for him to hear, I answer, "I was trying to get Aleksandr to leave me alone. Apparently being on the phone will do the trick." His chuckle drifts back to me. Grinding my teeth together, I drop my voice. "He's annoying the hell out of me. And the last thing I want is to be around any Morozov."

Delilah giggles. "What is he wearing?"

"What a bizarre question for you to ask about a man who is *not* the man in your bed right now."

"Oh, please. I'm simply trying to figure out if the reason you're calling me is because you're flustered by his 'slutty little T-shirt.'"

"I'm not flustered," I mutter.

"No," she agrees. "Just annoyed."

The cool evening air wraps around me as I cross out of the Indian Wells Tennis Garden and toward my hotel.

"You doing okay?" Delilah asks me quietly after a minute or so.

Sometimes I wish she didn't know me so well. It's been a year and a half since we began growing close, but playing doubles together last season, plus spending the offseason living together, sped the process up significantly.

When I first arrived in Orlando to train at the Morozov Tennis Academy, Maya, Delilah, Sahar, and Harper were incredibly tight. Sahar and Harper are like sisters, having spent their childhoods playing together.

Maya and Delilah were doubles partners for years and roommates to boot. I was sure there was no place for me, and when they began including me in outings, I felt like an outsider. A fifth wheel.

I pushed them all away, tried to keep to myself so I could cut those feelings off before they grew, but Delilah didn't let me. She took me in like a stray dog in the way only Delilah seems capable of, and for once, the loneliness abated. I finally felt the belonging I'd been chasing all my life. My free time was filled with movie and game nights with the girls, along with Delilah's childhood friend, Austin, and Sahar's coach, Noah. And when Maya left the tour due to a career-ending injury, suddenly I was living with Delilah and more entrenched in the group than ever.

"I'm okay."

"Nic."

Up ahead, Aleksandr has stopped outside the hotel to talk to a player on the men's tour. He's laughing and clapping the guy on his back like he never left the tour, though I can't hear what they're saying.

"You can tell me what you're really feeling, you know," Delilah murmurs.

I eye the side entrance. "There are so many points I would have played differently. To go from being up a set to losing…And *god*, don't even get me started on Anya."

"You played incredibly. I've never seen you like that. It was a tough match."

I sigh.

"Was Anya really that bad?"

"Delilah, she yelled, 'Let's go!' after I double faulted.

And again two points later when she won a point from a net cord. Who *does* that?"

Laughing, Delilah answers, "She does that to get under your skin. You have to ignore it. She doesn't do things like that to me because she knows it won't bother me."

"No, she doesn't do that to you because she likes you."

She makes an acknowledging noise, then yawns.

"I'll let you go. Crisis averted with the other Morozov, and I'm back at the hotel."

"Alright," she answers sleepily. "See you tomorrow?"

"Yeah, see you then."

As I duck into the hidden private entrance to the hotel, I wonder how different life would be if Delilah and I had continued to play doubles together. Karolína and I went back and forth for days until we decided it was best I focus my energy on singles, but maybe if we were still playing, we would've been here together, hoisting a doubles trophy at Indian Wells. Getting dinner together. Flying home together.

I'm *so* incredibly happy that Delilah and Matteo started playing mixed doubles together and then fell into their relationship. They make sense in that otherworldly soulmate way that few people do—to the point that, in the beginning, even *I* was able to tell when they needed a moment alone. But that doesn't prevent the prick of jealousy I feel at times, the loneliness that Delilah kept at bay creeping back in.

I want, for once, to be someone's first priority. Their first choice.

But there are pieces of me that are too worn or jagged

to fit together with anyone else's, and I've resigned myself to that fact. My minimal social skills and abrasiveness may make relationships off court too difficult, but no one cared about that when I was winning.

All the masses care about is who holds the trophies at the end of the day. And one of these days, it's going to be me again.

four

Two days and a quick stop off in Orlando later, I stand before the grand Vizcaya Museum, half an hour from Miami Gardens and Hard Rock Stadium. Delilah and Harper have made a point this year to put on tourist hats in the free time we get before and during tournaments, dragging me and Sahar with them.

Stucco walls give way to Renaissance columns and ivy-framed balconies. I haven't necessarily enjoyed all the museums I've been forced to visit this year, but I can certainly admit this one's quite beautiful.

I catch the end of Delilah's speech. "…and it was built during the Gilded Age."

Sahar nods, her red cowl-neck spaghetti strap dress providing a canvas of strong tan shoulders that her thick black hair spills across. "Mm-hmm, mm-hmm. And when exactly was that?"

"The Gilded Age," Delilah repeats, like that's enough information, and Sahar snorts.

"The early 1900s," Harper supplies helpfully.

"The whole thing is forty-three acres," Delilah continues. "Similar to Nic's parents' house," she jokes.

I roll my eyes, though her laugh makes my lips tip up. "They live on the Athenian Riviera. There's hardly room for that." What I don't acknowledge is the many properties they own across the world, which combined, sit on far more.

An incredulous knit of Sahar's brows. "Didn't you grow up with a clay court on the grounds?"

I sigh. "Yes. I'm not saying it isn't massive. It's just not a sprawling Venetian bayfront villa." Apparently, I retained more from Delilah's helpful informational than I realized. She grins, pleased.

"I'd kill for a house with amenities," Sahar answers, tucking her arm through Harper's as we walk inside.

"Trust me, most of the property and rooms are untouched." My parents spend less than two months at home and the rest of the year traveling the world. Before they moved me to New York, even I didn't live there much, and when I did, it was by myself, with a nanny, or with a tennis coach. Most of my memories of Greece are from my yiayia's house, and later, from a boarding school because it was "easier that way."

Falling into step beside Delilah, I finish, "If I could give it to you, I would. Or I'd turn it into a museum like this." At least that way, someone would appreciate it.

We pass through obscenely opulent rooms, most with painted ceilings and many with meticulous stained-glass windows. A music room with a harp, frozen in time. A drawing room with tapestries and oil portraits, air thick with memories the plaques and tour guides can't tell us.

At one point, Delilah points out the detail of the hand-tiled mosaic flooring and Sahar asks, "Babe, are you sure you haven't been here before? I didn't get a chance to listen to any of the audio tour, but if I had to wager, you'd have them beat."

"They should give you a job as a tour guide," Harper adds, piling her long dark brown hair into a bun on top of her head.

Delilah throws her arms out, basking in the praise, her blue eyes lit. "If I got to spend all my time in a place like this, with chandeliers bigger than my body and doors *carved* like this one"—she gestures to the one behind her—"I'd die happy."

"But then you'd have to live in Miami." Sahar mimics barfing, and the three of them laugh.

"And where would Matteo be in this fantasy?" Harper asks.

It's like a game of mental gymnastics trying to find a place to enter the conversation. By the time I produce a worthwhile thought, they've moved on. Outside of being asked direct questions, I'm practically hopeless.

"You think my very Italian boyfriend would mind spending his time in a Venetian estate?"

"He'd hate all the people though," I finally add.

Delilah giggles. "Good point. All in favor of me *not* quitting the tour to become a *tour* guide, say aye."

I roll my eyes again, but my indulging "aye" overlaps with Harper's and Sahar's, and we move into the next hallway.

A loud horn sounds from somewhere behind us, startling us closer to each other. For some reason beyond my comprehension, a child of seven or eight stands beside a horrified middle-aged woman, an air horn in hand.

"Tommy, I asked you to leave that in the car," she says urgently, looking around apologetically and hiding the horn in her purse.

Harper and Sahar exchange a glance, giggling.

"Do you remember the time we were eating dinner at that restaurant in Melbourne and Maya and Ryan were by the river, about to kiss?" Sahar asks.

Delilah joins them, holding her abdomen as her laugh grows quieter. "You mean when the boat horn scared him so badly, he jumped two feet into the air, nearly hit Maya and then yelled at the guy on the boat who was laughing?" she finally manages after catching her breath, wiping a tear from her eye. This must have been before I began training with them.

Harper's practically wheezing. "Yes! I've never seen him turn so red."

Sahar shakes her head. "God, he was the worst. I'm so glad that didn't work out."

"Sahar!" Harper admonishes.

"What? Did we want her to stay with that asshole?"

Delilah curls a strand of blonde hair behind her ear, taking stock of the guests around us and leading us into the next room. "Definitely not."

And I'm back. It's moments like these that remind me of eating lunch alone at my boarding school in Greece. Of feeling alone in a room full of my aunts, uncles, and cousins. Left out. Awkward.

Entirely superfluous.

The girls are still talking about another time Ryan did

something stupid when we step outside. Gravel paths curve between manicured hedges and fountains trickle into basins ringed with moss. The symmetry is breathtaking enough that I forget the painful tug in my chest.

Delilah nudges me, folding me into the conversation. "Ryan was Maya's almost boyfriend there for a while, until he decided he couldn't commit to her but could to Anya. It was years ago though. Obviously things have worked out for the best."

Sahar scoffs. "Yeah. Ryan's sad and alone and struggling to stay in the top two hundred and Maya is loved up and living her best life."

"As it should be," Harper agrees.

"Right," I add with a nod. Maybe not so superfluous after all. The painful tug turns to gratefulness.

We turn off the main axis to a smaller alcove, which Delilah tells us is called the Secret Garden, before she says, "Speaking of Maya, she told me she'll be in Charleston during the open. She wants to get food with us."

Harper claps once. "Oh, yay! That'll be fun. I haven't seen her in ages." She gets distracted by something down the path and excitedly gestures for us to follow. Delilah does so overzealously, like a puppy following after her, tail wagging and all. Sahar glances at me like we're sharing a joke, and while I'm not sure I understand, my lonely heart preens at being included.

My phone flashes with a call from Nora, who stayed back in Orlando for a few extra days to care for her mother. I show Sahar the screen and point with my chin toward Harper and Delilah. "Go ahead. I'll catch up." She nods and I swipe to answer the call. "Hello?"

"Hi, Nic. How are you feeling about the tournament?" Nora asks.

"Good." Putting Indian Wells behind me has been a challenge and a half, but Miami is worth the same number of points. It's another chance, and I won't squander it.

"Good, good. I'm glad to hear it." She's silent for a few beats, which raises my hackles. Nora has traveled with me to every tournament for the last year and a half, so it's odd now to be talking to her over the phone. Odder still that she called to check in.

"How are you?" I ask. "And your mother?"

There's a long sigh on the other end, then rustling. "Actually, that's why I'm calling. My mother's condition has worsened. She didn't tell me until I got here, but she received some test results last month and…I just don't think I can leave her, even with Julia here," she finishes, referring to her wife. "I don't know for how long, but I'm going to have to take time off."

"Oh." I resist the urge to do the sign of the cross, as my yiayia would when she received bad news, instead touching the mati pendant on my necklace.

"Nic, I'm so sor—"

"No, god, no. There's no need to apologize," I rush to answer, realizing how inconsiderate my one-syllable response was. "I completely understand. I hope her condition improves soon and she feels better."

"Will you be able to find someone on short notice? I don't want to leave you without a strength and conditioning coach."

I've already started trying to piece together where I'll go from here. Most performance coaches I know have been working with their player for at least a couple of months. "I'm sure Karolína and I will come up with something. I'll continue the exercises we were doing in California and hopefully come clay-court season, I'll find someone."

"If you want, I can train you remotely. I feel horrible."

"Nora, really. Take care of you and yours. The last thing you need while helping with your mother is hopping on a video call to tell me to straighten my spine during Bosu ball holds."

She laughs, though I was being serious. "You're sure?"

"Of course."

Another long sigh. "Okay. I'll be cheering you on from here. And if you need me for the offseason, call me."

"Will do."

We say our goodbyes and I type out a quick message to my coach. I know it's only been a few seconds, but I'm frustrated that I haven't found a solution yet. I pray Karolína will. She usually does.

Sidling up to my friends, I pretend to listen to Delilah lecturing about the five areas of the garden.

"Nic?" Delilah asks softly, like it's not the first time.

"Hmm?"

"Is everything okay?"

I glance up, realizing all three of them are watching me. "Nora won't be joining me for the rest of the tour. Her mother isn't well."

Hearing the words from my own mouth paints them into reality. I try not to panic. The work Nora and I do is incredibly important to my development on and off the court. We spend hours perfecting my form in the gym, on the field, and on the court to prepare my muscles to better withstand the aggressive level of play I've developed. Karolína is a genius when it comes to fixing my approach to a match, but that differs greatly to honing my body to improve my performance.

"Oh no! Do you think you'll search for someone else or go without for a while?" Harper asks.

"I'd rather not go without, but I'm not sure what my other options are. I texted Karolína."

"I'm sure the two of you will figure it out," Delilah reassures me, stepping closer without touching me.

"Hey, so don't get mad at me, but why not train with Aleks?" Sahar asks after a beat. "He told Noah that if the right player came along, he'd be willing to step away from Anya's training. It's not like she needs two performance coaches. Plus, he was helpful and knowledgeable when he trained us this offseason."

"Is that a joke?" I ask sharply. Delilah winces, exchanging a look with Harper.

"No," Sahar answers simply. "You know Karolína will recommend him first. Last season, Anya moved into the second spot in the rankings and won, what, like six titles? I'm not saying he was the sole reason but..." She shrugs. "And, if you want to be petty, you're also kind of getting in Anya's head by taking her brother *and* performance coach."

I blink, but Sahar doesn't back down. It's something I like and respect about her a lot: she's nearly as combative as I am.

"He might be the only performance coach willing to step up right now. If you start working with him during this tournament, you could be in a groove come clay-court season."

Her final sentence hangs in the air, mocking me. I grew up playing on clay, and it has always been the season I love most, even if it hasn't always been good to me. Clay is a slower court with balls that bounce higher, which is at odds with my aggressive and quick style of play. Still, clay feels like home, and it's the season I anticipate most each year.

But the concept of asking *Aleksandr Morozov* for help goes against everything I've worked so hard for. His youngest sister is quite possibly the worst person I have ever met. She smears me in the press and gloats every time she beats me. After I win a set during a match, she takes a long bathroom break to disrupt my rhythm. She always makes sure to take my favorite court (court fifteen, tucked away in a quiet corner of the facility), a grin pasted on her face when I walk through the gate and realize it's taken. The hitting partners Karolína lines up for me keep disappearing, only to appear on Anya's team, in her box. Through it all, her brother stands beside her, needling me with his faux boyish charm and comments he knows will piss me off.

And that's not the worst of it. No, because that would require examining the infamous post-match press conference Anya gave last year after beating me at Wimbledon.

When asked if she thought I could win if we played again later in the year, the she-devil laughed and said, "My brother pointed out that she seemed out of shape, so maybe if she works on that." And while one could make the argument that she has two brothers, only one of them trained and traveled with her to every tournament.

So the universe will have to forgive me if I'm not jumping for joy at the idea of working with the asshole.

Of course, my friends aren't privy to all this. When I saw the presser, I was too embarrassed to show them. What if it was true? And if I showed them and admitted it bothered me, then what? It wouldn't change a thing, and since none of them have brought it up, I'm not sure they've seen it.

To them, my dislike for Aleksandr probably begins and ends with the fact that he's Anya's brother. To them, perhaps I'm just petty.

I pull myself out of the anger-induced spiral Sahar's comment pushed me into, realizing the girls have switched topics as we stroll through the final section of the gardens and toward Biscayne Bay. Delilah stays close, her way of comforting me, I think. She and Harper trade fun facts they learned from the plaques inside, and Sahar mouths, "I'm sorry," before shooting me an apologetic smile.

I answer with what I hope is a reassuring nod.

A few hours later, as I sit in my hotel room watching the errors I made during my Indian Wells finals match, waiting for Karolína to let me know if she's come up with anything, the few group training sessions I had with Aleksandr float through my head. Each one pushed me exactly the way I like—to the point where I felt like my lungs might collapse—and my body was so sore the next day, I wasn't compelled to hit the gym.

But in no universe, on no planet, is that enough to convince me he's my sole option. Of that, I am sure.

SHOTS FIRED

AUSTIN

Nic, if it helps, I've taken it upon myself to send you a list of players whose performance coach you could poach

Hey! That rhymes!

DELILAH

She's obviously not going to do that

HARPER

Austin, what?? This is insane.

SAHAR LAUGHED AT "NIC I'VE TAKEN IT UPON MYSELF TO SEND YOU A LIST OF PLAYERS WHOSE PERFORMANCE COACH YOU COULD POACH"

NOAH

I'm with Austin. Poach a coach! Poach a coach!

MATTEO

I do not recommend this.

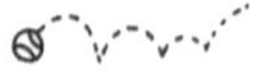

The next day, while warming up on a practice court in Miami Gardens with Delilah, the very person I've been trying to push out of my head appears, cones in hand. His hair is messy, and though I'm across the court, the blue of his eyes shines the way it always seems to. His muscles flex as he opens the gate, his biceps straining against his ridiculously tight shirt. When I drag my eyes from him, I find Anya's second performance coach, both her parents, and the woman herself, a smug smile on her face—still riding the high of being crowned the champion of Indian Wells, I'm sure. My blood simmers.

I told myself not to, but I looked through the draws and realized if we both keep moving on, we'll play again in the semifinals. My bye first round gave me lots of time with a physiotherapist, and it also means I have one less match I need to win on the way to being the Miami Open champion. If I can keep up my level of play through tomorrow's second-round match and over the next week and a half, I can win the same number of points here as I should have in California last week.

Watching Anya walk onto the court with her head held high, her light brown ponytail swinging, and a smirk as sinister as a predator's on her lips reminds me of California and all the other times I haven't been able to best her. It reminds me that, if I do have to play her in the semifinals, I'm not so positive I'll come out the other side a winner.

"Nic!" Karolína calls from where she sits on the bench beside Delilah's coach. "Down the lines," she urges, pointing to Delilah, who stands in the middle of the ad side of the court.

I nod. Ignoring Anya's presence, or at least trying to, I slap a ball down the line, then another and another until Delilah and I are both breathing heavily. Unfortunately, the anger that lives deep inside me has gone nowhere despite how much it usually helps to take it out on a tennis ball. It's not as fun as it should be, as it used to be, and that frustrates me more.

"I'm going to take a breather!" Delilah calls, walking to the bench to grab her water. Maybe I should join her, but as stupid as it sounds, it feels like showing weakness. Instead, I bounce a ball against the court four times, then toss it and slam it into the deuce side service box.

Out of nowhere, Aleksandr sidles up beside me, a grin lifting his lips. It's such a fixed presence, like he's forever holding back a joke. Or he just enjoys tormenting me. "You seem angry."

My eyes narrow. I pick up another ball, but this time instead of serving it, I maintain eye contact and slap a forehand as hard as I can. It slams into the metal fence with a loud *thwack*. "No."

He laughs.

"What are you doing here?" I ask when that's not enough to scare him away.

"Anya's training on this court," he replies, hooking a thumb over his shoulder at the court beside mine. It takes concerted effort for my eyes not to drop to the flash of his abs the motion uncovers, but I manage.

"Shouldn't you be training her in the gym, Mr. I Can't See Past My Muscles?" *What? What kind of insult was that?*

Another laugh, and I school my features so he remains unaware that it was a slip of the tongue. "I hadn't realized they were so large, but I guess if they're impressive enough for even you to notice…" At my rolled eyes, he continues, "Plus, after the few group sessions we had together last November and December, you know I like to do lots of court work." He says it like there's an underlying meaning. Like the few times I joined his sessions while Nora cared for her mother bonded us enough that we have some semblance of a relationship now.

"I hardly remember them. Must not have been very difficult or effective."

"I'm happy to give it another go," he answers.

The words burn like an iron on my cheeks and in my stomach. I wish for a bucket of ice dumped swiftly over my head. "I'd be happy to never talk to you again."

"Such sharp words from someone who couldn't take her eyes off me when I walked through the gate."

Leveling a glare at him, I answer, "Keep dreaming. I was more focused on the fact that your sister requires four people for her conditioning."

Aleksandr adjusts his silver chain, tucking it under his shirt collar, his grin faltering. "Yes, well, nobody can claim my parents are inattentive." He glances back, eyeing the way his father waves at the court behind him, speaking in Russian to Anya. His mother's hands are on her hips.

I don't know how to answer. Instead, I slap another

ball, ignoring the questioning gazes of Delilah, Karolína, and Delilah's coach, Francesca. "There are three free courts farther away from me," I say, changing the subject.

"You're right, I *could* move us to practice court five," he allows with a contemplative nod. "But how fun could it be to watch you try to break your strings with a ball from that far away? Nah, I'd rather see your power up close and personal."

"A kink of yours?"

"Absolutely."

Taking care not to grind my teeth, I grab one final ball and slap it across the court. "Whatever. I'll be sure to put blinders on so I don't glean anything from your training." I nod to where Anya sits on the bench, glaring at us. When his eyes follow mine, she gestures at him before crossing her arms. Not only does she need multiple performance coaches and her parents, but apparently, she needs their attention on her at all times. Such a brat. "Don't keep the world number two waiting over there," I finish, and it comes out far more bitterly than I'd like.

His smile drops again, eyes drifting over my features. I hate that it feels like my head is nothing but a piece of glass, the inner workings of my brain laid bare for him to read, when I try so hard to hide it from the world. "Oh, Nic. I'd tell you all about my training if you'd just ask," he murmurs. "I'd be happy to train you."

The need for that bucket of ice grows dire.

"That won't be necessary." I glance away, searching for another ball to smack the hell out of.

"No? Nora changed her mind and will be continuing with you this season?"

I whip around to face him. "How do you know about that?"

"She emailed my parents to get her access at the facility changed. They informed me in case you needed a training plan."

"How kind of them, but like I said, that won't be necessary."

"You don't even want to give it a shot?" His voice changes, his spine straightening. "I'm really good at what I do." Is that pride?

"That's okay. I wouldn't want to drag your average down with my poor fitness. You know, with how out of shape I am." The words taste sour on my tongue, and I wouldn't be surprised if it shows on my face.

A groove digs itself between his brows. "Huh?"

Rolling my eyes again, I take a step back. I need space from him and this conversation, so I ignore the stupid voice that told me drinking water during a break showed weakness and join Delilah. By the far fence, Francesca and Karolína are pretending to pick up tennis balls, heads bent close together. Gossiping, no doubt.

"Good talk?" Delilah asks, giggling.

"What's funny?"

"Nothing," she reassures me, though her smile hasn't gone anywhere. "I'm just proud that the couple of times his T-shirt rode up while you talked, you didn't look."

"I hate you," I grumble.

She hums. "I love you too."

THAT AFTERNOON, AFTER DELILAH LEFT TO SPEND TIME with Matteo, Karolína walked me to my hotel room with a not-so-gentle urging of "Rest your ass before your match tomorrow."

I'm, of course, not resting.

The Miami Open players' gym is crawling with players from both the men's and women's tour and their teams, machines overrun. With limited room for me to train, I find a quiet corner in the rollout area and pull out a balance board and tennis ball, wincing at the hint of muscle fatigue in my left quad.

It's not like I'm setting up at a rack or running on a treadmill. A little core work after a hitting session never killed anyone. I'll be in and out, my core stronger.

Body facing the clock on the wall, I plant my right foot on the highlighter-yellow board, right knee bent and left foot in the air behind me. I manage my breathing the way Nora taught me, but the clock slows as I close in on thirty seconds. I lose my balance right before I hit twenty-five, grit my teeth, and begin again.

I finish the first of four sets, nearly toppling off when I breathe a sigh of relief at the thirty second mark. Right as I'm switching to my other leg, a familiar (and very annoying) body slips from the masses. Aleksandr's younger sister, Natasha, walks in the other direction from him like they just finished talking and went their separate ways. Aleksandr has a weird look on his face, a knuckle rubbing against his sternum. His expression changes as he stops in front of me, his eyes taking in my area, from my tennis bag to the ball beside the balance board under my foot, then to me.

"Stop looking at me like that. It's unsettling." My focus shifts, my core disengaging, and I lose my balance. Crossing my arms, I glare at him.

"I get the feeling not much unsettles you," Aleksandr says.

"You're wrong." I step back onto the board, glancing away from him. "Can you stop bothering me when I'm trying to work out? Or all the time."

"I thought Karolína told you to rest."

"You talk to my coach without me now? Or are you stalking me again?"

He smiles and steps closer, his hand a foot from my waist. "She might have asked me a question or two and mentioned it. Indulge me for a second, will you?"

"I will not." I step off the board, away from him. I know Karolína was affiliated with his family's facility before I started working with her, so it's not crazy that they might have a professional relationship, I just hate the idea of him talking to my coach about my training at all, but especially without consulting me.

Aleksandr heaves a beleaguered sigh. "I understand if you hate me because of who I'm related to and what you perceive that means, but what I care about most is ensuring talented athletes like you don't get injured."

I nearly make another comment that his name and filial affiliation aren't the worst things about him but think better of it. He's clearly not going to stop, and if I'm truly doing something that might flare up my back injury or lead to a new injury, I *should* listen. I step back onto the board and nod for him to continue.

"Okay if I touch you?" he asks softly, and the question

is so startling I teeter. No one ever asks that. Even Nora took a few months to realize I dislike being touched without warning or when I'm overwhelmed. There's no way he's noticed my aversion, and yet…

I nod again, and one of his warm palms lands on my stomach, searing through the material of my tank top. The other settles on my back until I'm warmed on a cellular level. I have to look away.

His gaze blazing a hole in my face, he asks, "You had a back injury, right?"

I swallow over a dumb question, like *how did you know?* because said injury had me off and on the tour for a year at twenty-one, my rank dropping like a stone in water. "Yes."

"I've noticed that sometimes you overcompensate for it. Straighten your spine and take a deep breath."

Reluctantly, I listen.

"Good. Really good, Nic." He pulls his hands back an inch but doesn't step away entirely. "If you won't heed my advice about overtraining, let's at least make sure you're preventing injuries."

My eyes meet his finally, and they're so sincere, the words tinged with something I can't figure out. They bang around in my head, mixing with the expression he wore as he approached me, until I come up with a word: *guilt.*

But that can't be right. I shake my head, noting my thirty seconds are over and stepping off.

"How many sets are you doing?" he asks after he registers our proximity and takes his own step back.

"Four total."

"Then hand-eye coordination work with the ball?"

"Yeah," I murmur.

He claps once. "Alright, let's get to work. I want you out of here in under thirty."

"Or what?"

His grin is back, boyish and absurdly infuriating. "Or I'll annoy you relentlessly until your only option is to leave."

six

While I'm not one for press conferences, talking to Jackson at the Tennis Broadcast desk after a win never feels as stifling or hard to navigate. He allows me my silences, content to sit beside me until we're on air, and he does his best not to ask questions that dig a blade between my ribs. I settle beside him after my third Miami Open win, offering the best imitation of a smile I can muster.

"Hey, Nic," he greets me quietly, pulling his microphone toward him as the cameraman in front of us holds his hand up to let us know he's not ready. Jackson's hair is gelled back, a curl slipping free across his forehead, and he wears a dark blue quarter-button down with the Tennis Broadcast's logo on the lapel. I don't know much about him other than he grew up in Orlando, training at the Morozov Tennis Academy from a young age with Sahar, Noah, and Harper, who dated his younger brother. After a few years on the tour, he retired, switching to broadcasting.

"Hello."

"How come you never seem happy after wins?"

I shrug. "Just my face." Or maybe it's the fact that I don't allow myself to celebrate until I've won a tournament.

Or that I haven't enjoyed myself on court in months.

Jackson chuckles softly. "I'll try to be as unobtrusive as possible," he promises with a smile. I nod my thanks, glancing around. Sometimes the desk is indoors, and other times, like today, it's outside, allowing players to walk around nearby.

The bright Miami sun filters through the open roof of Hard Rock Stadium, casting warm light over the grass of the football field and the broadcast desk. Behind me, the tunnel to Stadium Court, where a men's match is being played, yawns open. To the right, beyond the towering bulk of the court seating, the rest of the arena's turf stretches out, scattered with players warming up, stretching, and quietly preparing for their matches, headphones over their ears to drown out the noise. Every few minutes, there's a loud hum of the crowd getting into the match, and my blood, which fails to recognize that I'm no longer on court, sings along with it, loving the sound of having a crowd behind me.

"Ready in three, two, one, go," a woman beside the camera calls, nodding for Jackson to begin. Pen, who stands beside her, points to her exaggerated smile as a reminder, and I paste one on.

"We're back on day eight of the Miami Open, Nicola Vassilakis here with us at our Tennis Broadcast desk. Nic, great to see you." It's a relief when he switches to my nickname. Another reason I don't mind him.

"Thank you," I respond. "Good to see you too."

"You always look like it's no sweat off your back during your matches, and today's was no different. You had to dig in the second set, but ultimately, you were able to pull out the win in straight sets. Tell me how you felt during the match."

An easy question, as promised. "Lina is a tough opponent, but I played loose today, and I think that showed in the score."

"It definitely did. Now, at the end of the match, you didn't even realize you'd won it. Is that right?" He chuckles. "You walked back to the baseline like you were ready to play another point until you saw Lina at the net."

I offer an embarrassed nod. "I was focusing on winning one point at a time. After the eighth game in the second set, when we went back and forth at deuce twelve times, I told myself to play each point like I was down a break. I didn't even know the score during that last rally."

"I love that. So you've been to the quarterfinals here a couple of times before, and you're into the quarterfinals again this year. What are you hoping to change going into this match?"

"Miami is always hard. It's the end of a long hard-court season, and it's a big tournament right after Indian Wells. I'm sure it's a matter of fitness, and hopefully I'm up to the task this year."

"Speaking of fitness, you've recently had a change in your training. Are you and Karolína planning on bringing in another performance coach, or will you be finishing out the year without one?"

That one isn't so easy. Because while I've spent the last

week explaining to my coach why I *don't* need to work with Aleksandr, she's spent the entirety of the week explaining to me why I do.

Namely the fact that over a third of my training comes from working with a performance coach, and that since Nora joined my team, I've consistently moved up the ranks. Also the fact that he's done so much for Anya's game and that his training in the offseason helped keep me in shape.

All good points, though I never admitted that to her.

If I can keep this run going here in Miami and prove to her that I can do this without a performance coach, at least until we can find someone else, it would make my life a whole lot easier.

"Right now, I'm trying to get through the end of hard court. Come clay season, we may reevaluate, but it's not a top priority."

"Of course. Clay season is your fav—"

"Nic!" a familiar voice calls. When I turn, Harper bounds toward us from the warmup area on the field.

"Oh, sorry, Jackson. I didn't realize you were live," she says with a laugh, tucking her dark brown hair behind her ears and giving the camera a winning smile. She waves at the viewers before turning back to us. "Just saying hi to Nic before I play."

Despite her claim to be talking to me, her and Jackson's eyes are locked on each other for a beat, then another, until finally Harper glances at me. "Great match, Nic. You played like the next Miami Open champ." She giggles, hooking her thumb behind her, where Sahar waves wildly from beside Noah. "Sahar and I are going on in a few."

"Good luck," Jackson and I say at the same time. Harper turns and heads back the way she came.

"What was I saying?" Jackson asks, dazed. He clears his throat when he notices me watching him, shaking his head. "Right, clay season. You grew up in Athens and trained on clay until you moved to the United States, right? You won the Junior French Open at seventeen before you aged up and began playing on the tour. Do you have Roland Garros in your sights again?"

The clay-court season spans April to the first week of June and features six tournaments. Roland Garros, the French Open, is the culmination of the season, the final tournament on clay and the second major of the year. A slam is always in my sights, especially the two I won as a junior. After my triumphs, I had so many new fans rooting for me to become something great. Many, I'm sure, have fallen away in favor of other players on the tour who've won slams, like Emilia and Anya. Young blood that have come in and followed through on their promise.

If I can get a big win this season, it might put me back where I was when I first aged up. People might root for *me* instead of Anya, even if she has the home court advantage.

And maybe I'll win the respect of my mother, if only for a brief moment.

My lips twist, hopefully hiding my grimace. "Who would ever say they're not hoping for a big title like Roland Garros?" I answer. "I'd love for my first major on the pro tour to be on my favorite court, but we'll have to see where clay season takes me." When I glance at Pen, she gives me a thumbs up and an enthusiastic nod.

Jackson smiles, inclining his head toward me. "Nic, congratulations on your win. You played really well today. We'll let you get some rest and recovery and hopefully talk to you again soon."

"Thanks, Jackson."

I set the microphone down and nod at Jackson once, pulling out my phone as I step away. Pretending I'm not disappointed by the dearth of messages from my parents, I scroll through the congratulations in the big group chat before heading to the players' gym, leaving Pen to take a call. It doesn't take long to get there, but a problem presents itself when Aleksandr pushes the door open for me, his face brightening.

"Happy Greek Independence Day!"

I blink, startled. "Oh…" It was heavy on my mind during the match, a small push on every strike of the ball so I could make my country proud on such a big day.

"Oh? I thought you'd be more excited."

"I didn't—" I clear my throat. He doesn't need to know he's the first to say it. "What's up?"

His head tilts, but he doesn't push. "I've got a cooldown workout for you." For the first time, I note the printed spreadsheet in his hands.

My eyes narrow. "You don't quit." It's been five days since our impromptu session, and I'd hoped he'd leave me alone after.

"You're the most tenacious person I've ever met. I figured I should take a page out of your book. Your talent and drive make your potential higher than virtually everyone else on tour. I want to be the person to get you there."

"Are you pitching yourself to me right now?" I ask incredulously.

"Yes." He flashes a smile. "Did I do a good job? I practiced it in the mirror this morning."

I can't contain my eye roll, grabbing the small stack of papers from his hand. He lets them go easily, grinning like he's won. I scan each of them. It's an entire training program for the next three weeks, my name at the top. Each box details the exact exercise with room for me to write in my weight or resistance level, and there are multiple options for pre-match, post-match, and rest and recovery days.

Brushing past him into the gym, I find Karolína. She smiles proudly. "There she is! Ready for cooldown and dinner?"

"Sure. Same as usual?" I ask, reaching for the set of resistance bands I keep in my bag, which lies at her feet.

Karolína glances at the papers still in my hand, then behind me, where I'm sure Aleksandr stands. "Or we could give Aleks a try," she offers. It's too coincidental for this all to be aligning so perfectly.

Turning around, I say, "Excuse us for a second." Aleksandr takes one look at my face before walking backward a few paces. When I gaze back at my coach, she's smiling innocently.

"Did you ask him to join us today?"

"No."

I cock my head, and she lets out a chuckle.

"Alright, sort of. He came to me while you were at the

broadcast desk and showed me his workout plan. It's even more tailored to you than the ones Nora has put together."

My temper flares subtly. "So, what? You asked him to hang out and wait for me to come back?" I don't like that one bit. All training decisions and concerns should be run by me before they're taken to others.

"He was here talking to some friends on the men's tour, Nic. I simply told him you'd be joining me in a few minutes."

"I explained why I don't want to train with him."

"And I understand that. You have your reasons, even if I don't agree with the—"

"He told his sister I was *out of shape*. And allowed that to be broadcast to the worl—"

"But right now, we have no other options. You are *so* close to a breakthrough. You need consistency in your training. Aleks has all the same certifications as Nora and has been training Anya for over a year now."

"That right there is another concern. He'd be leaving Anya to work with me—why?" And why would I agree to work with someone who, when I go head-to-head with his sister, will likely be rooting for her over me?

"That's a question you'll have to ask him. What I care about is that you're the most capable player here without a major under your belt. On your best days, nobody can beat you. If Aleks can do what he has for his sister, imagine what he can do to get you to your goals."

Crossing my arms stubbornly, I gaze at him over my shoulder. He's watching us raptly, his shirt caught in the waistband of his shorts like he stretched and it got stuck. I hear Delilah's teasing in my head before turning back to my coach.

"I need to trust the people on my team. You, Pen, and Nora are the team I built over the years. People I've worked with long enough that I can trust you with my life. How can I work with someone I don't trust?" Another thought occurs to me. "What if it's sabotage? That's the sole explanation for him wanting this so badly, right?"

Karolína smiles kindly, fondness melting the blue of her eyes. "Don't trust him with your life. Trust me instead. I'll check the plan and see if I can get another opinion. If they think it looks good and *not* like he's sabotaging you"—she chuckles like the idea is outrageous, which makes my eye twitch—"we should move ahead with it."

Maybe the idea of him sabotaging me *is* outrageous. We're both adults and despite how overeager he seems to work with me, he's also played his share of pro tournaments. Would he go so far to aid his sister?

I don't know. I don't know him.

Either way, I can't brush off the paranoia. Changing any part of my training could throw everything off balance. I'm somewhat on the up. I'm not sure I would survive whatever my subconscious believes Aleksandr could do to me.

"Try it out today," Karolina urges.

"Fine," I grit out. "But I'm not going to be nice."

"I wouldn't be your coach if you were."

I almost smile at that. When I spin once more and walk to him, shoving the papers into his chest, I say, "You may have convinced Karolína, but not me. I'll do your cooldown, but that's all. And stop going behind my back to my team. It's not doing you any favors."

"We'll see," he responds far too jovially for someone I've rejected no less than three times in the last week. "Let's have you do half a mile on the treadmill, walking pace."

I had a plan when I agreed to this, but it forms more fully now that he's telling me what to do. With a saccharine smile, I walk to the line of stationary bikes instead, changing the settings and jumping on the seat. I pump my legs, gazing at Aleksandr. Where I expected the smile to be wiped from his face, hoped for a furrow in his brow, there are only two little upticks in the corners of his mouth.

It bothers me.

"You're training your sister. Isn't that a conflict of interest?" I ask him. "Especially considering how much she and I dislike each other?"

"Focus on your breathing. We're in a recovery stage."

"That doesn't answer my question."

He sighs, the single indication that he's affected by my behavior. "First of all, if you agreed to work with me, I'd take a step back from her training. But either way, to me, this isn't about you versus her. It's about getting my players to their peak performance. At that point, may the best woman win. I want you to be the best version of yourself physically when you step on the court. I want the same for my sister. I think you do too. You'd rather beat my sister at her best than win because she's not in tip-top shape."

I hate that he's right, so I don't answer, focusing on my breathing and being slightly less childish than before. Because, honestly? That's the best answer I could've expected. Nora never made any promises about getting me to a point where I *would* beat my opponents. She focused on getting my fitness level up, week in and week out. If he's being honest, I can't ask for more from my next performance coach.

After finishing on the bike, doing some stretching—wherein I did the opposite of everything he told me, like a lizard stretch when he asked for pigeon, to Karolína's clear chagrin—and rolling out, I lie on the gym floor, thoroughly cool. Aleksandr squats beside me, handing me a sheet of paper that wasn't part of the original packet.

Confused, I ask, "What is this?"

"Look at it."

Upon closer inspection, it's nearly identical to one of the cooldowns he showed me. Except where he typed out *treadmill* on that one, he put *stationary bike* on this one. Where he had me doing pigeon stretch on that one, there was lizard stretch instead.

It's the exact cooldown I just did. The whole time, I was trying to show we wouldn't work, that I wouldn't listen to him, and in doing so, I fell into his trap.

"Stubborn as always. Luckily, I planned for that."

It's clear from the tilt of his lips (god, does it ever stop?) that he finds the situation amusing, but I feel exposed. Uncharacteristically so.

"Congratulations," I say flatly. "You figured out that I don't want to listen to you. Do you think that makes you special?"

Aleksandr laughs, as if my being laid bare for him is funny. It shoots me back to being seven years old, searching out people to be friends with at school, only to realize I was inadequate. Gangly, awkward, unable to navigate a social situation without the very people I sought to befriend making fun of me.

"I suppose not. Anya hates listening to me too."

My stomach roils at the idea that I'm anything like his bratty little sister, even if I did display a bit of childishness that has now backfired spectacularly. Suddenly, the noise in the room overwhelms me, and a familiar heat rolls over my shoulders. "It's not funny."

The mirth disappears from his expression, but it's too late. I knew this wouldn't work. I grab my bag, give Karolína a rough wave, and leave the players' gym as quickly as I came, in dire need of a locker room shower.

"Nic, I wasn't laughing at you!" he yells from the doorway I've left behind.

I don't care. I can do this without him.

seven

It's while I'm at the net, a passing shot hit by Daryna Ostapchuk whizzing by me, that I realize I'm going to lose this match. The ball is too far from my racket, perfectly down the line, and she's a point away from beating me in a second-set tiebreak.

A straight set loss in the Miami Open quarterfinals. Like last year and the year before and the year before. Because no matter how much work I put into this, it doesn't matter.

I toss a peeved glance to my hauntingly empty box, where Pen bites a nail anxiously and Karolína stands, clapping. The furrow in her brow is unmistakable: she also believes I'm going to lose this.

Get your shit together, I tell myself. *Why are you playing so poorly? Pull yourself out of this one. It's not that hard to hit a ball back onto the court until she messes up. So* do *it.*

As if this all hasn't been embarrassing enough, when I get to the baseline, serving to stay in the tiebreak, I hit a toss that's too far forward, and my first serve shoots into the net. I take a breath, bounce the ball once, twice, three times. The third bounces funny, so I start again. One, two, three, four. Look at the service box, where Daryna moves side to side, preparing to smash my slower second serve down the line for a spot in the semifinals. This time, my toss is perfect, but I'm too early, too eager to prove myself, and the ball sails outside the line of the service box.

I double faulted my way out of the match. A loss to someone I've beaten easily every time I've played her.

"Game, set, and match, Ostapchuk. Two sets to love, 6–2, 7–6," the chair umpire says into the microphone, Daryna's cry of excitement still reverberating between my ears.

Frustrated tears blur my vision as I shake her hand at the net, then the umpire's. I pack my rackets and bottles into my bag, throw it over my shoulder, and wave to the crowd as I disappear into the tunnel.

It's not until I'm alone in the locker room that I allow the floodgates to open.

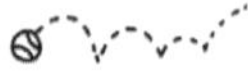

SAHAR'S BAD BERLIN BAGELS

MAYA

It was a great match, Nic! Still plenty of season left.

HARPER

Yes! Clay court is coming, and it's all yours!

DELILAH

I am so ready for the beast you're about to become on clay

AUSTIN

And if it helps, this gives you a few extra days to relax before Charleston

SAHAR

Dude, get OUT of here

SAHAR REMOVED AUSTIN FROM THE CHAT.

A FEW HOURS LATER, LONG AFTER KAROLÍNA AND PEN leave for our hotel, long after matches are done being played, I stand from a bench in the locker room. Normally, if I wanted to burn off this anger, I'd have to sneak past Karolína and Nora, who know that I tend to punish myself most after a tough loss. But, I suppose, lying on a bench like a zombie for hours, other women on the tour filtering in and out, was enough for the former to believe I could do myself no harm.

There's a cracking in my chest that feels more like defeat and less like the anger I'm so used to. I much prefer the anger to this, the edges of something far darker creeping in, seeping into the little crack, filling it till it shudders wider and wider and I'm exhausted and depressed and I just need to…

I don't know what I need. But the only thing that has kept the darkness at bay is putting my head down and getting back to my training. If I stop lying here and contemplating, if I spend all that time in the gym or on the court instead of wasting my time wallowing, maybe I'll see a sliver of progress somewhere. *Anywhere.*

Maybe I'll find something to latch on to so I stop hating the one thing I've ever loved doing.

Finding my way back to the gym, where only three people are cooling down after their matches, I pull out my boxing gloves and set myself in front of the lone punching bag in the far corner.

Punch punch punch punch punch punch. Until I'm breathing hard and the weight behind my eyes travels to the rest of my body, heavy with exhaustion from the weeks, months, years of training I've put it through.

Punch punch punch punch punch punch. Until all the mistakes I made today don't flash behind my eyes with each blink.

Punch punch punch punch punch punch. Until I hear the cheering of a crowd that loved me, rooting for me as I hoisted trophies that proved I was on the right path.

Punch punch punch punch punch punch. Until I hear the pride in my mother's voice after a junior French Open win, one of the rare times she's shown any emotion toward me. The child she didn't want to have, the obligation that ended her career early. The one that, if she and my father hadn't been swimming in money, would have caused far more problems.

Punch punch punch punch punch punch. Until I forget what it was like to be looked down upon by my peers growing up in Athens. Until I forget how the few social skills I developed in school disappeared while being home-schooled in New York, the rest of my free time spent on a court because it was the one place I felt connected to any member of my family in a new country I'd never wanted to move to. Because it was the place I felt powerful and in control.

Punch punch punch punch punch punch. Until I stop thinking about the fact that I have never, not for a second of my life, felt like a priority to anyone.

A moment before I begin another set of (rather weak) punches, the bag shifts out of the way. I'm so consumed, I don't notice Aleksandr, and when I overshoot, I topple into his arms, struggling to catch my breath. I can't pinpoint what happened, but I wasn't paying enough attention to the sensations in my body, and now I can't move.

"Hey," he says softly. "Come on. Let's get you on the ground." Gently, he sets me against the wall, out of view of the others in the gym. The black foam tiles beneath the punching bag stick to my legs, and my vision swims, so much so, I have to close my eyes and rest my head against the wall, still taking in huge lungfuls of air.

When I open my eyes again, Aleks is squatting beside me, a worried furrow in his brow. He points to my gloves, which are still wrapped tightly around my hands, and I give him a feeble nod. He rips the strap of Velcro off the right one, pulling it off my hand hesitantly, then does the same for the left one. A water bottle appeared beside me at some point. He cracks it open and hands it to me, and I gulp it greedily.

Finally, my breathing slows, and he glances at me meaningfully, just this side of chiding. "Nic, what are you doing? You're going to kill yourself." There's a hitch in his breath.

"I'm fine." I clamp my teeth together, glaring at the wall, refusing to meet his eyes.

"No, you're not. You're overtraining, as you have been for months. You just played a match after a long few weeks. What you need is to stretch, roll out, and sleep."

I roll my eyes. "Okay, Aleksandr. I'll take that into consideration."

"I'm not messing around. You have to stop this, Nic, or you won't have anything left in the tank and that'll be it. The end. The credits rolling on a promising career, thrown away because you didn't know when to quit."

My head whips around, eyes blazing into his. I've never seen him like this. He's dropped to his knees in favor of squatting, his light-brown-almost-blond hair tousled, brows nearly touching over narrowed eyes. There's no hint of his usual smile, his jaw clenched.

"Screw you. You don't know what it's like to feel like a fucking failure every time you walk off court. You don't know what it's like to labor under the load of everyone's expectations, to come up empty-handed time and time again until you're nothing more than a disappointment. You don't know what it's like to be so successful so young, only to lose your edge and find yourself at square one with people younger than you beating you when it should be *your turn*." I can't help the tear that escapes my eye at the words, embracing the anger it creates in me that *he's* witnessing this. I swipe it away. "You don't understand anything about my situation."

He's quiet for a few moments, watching me. It makes me angrier, that he's here, acting like he has any right to see me this way when his career was filled with so much success.

"Of course I understand. It's why I quit."

A request that he leave dies in my throat. I blink away the rest of the hot, angry tears. Blink a few more times until his lips curve into a kind smile.

Quietly, he adds, "Why do you think I've been watching you, waiting for you to show up at the gym and work yourself into the ground after every loss? Because I've been in your shoes. I've been just like you, and it almost killed me, no matter what it looked like on the outside."

"But you…you won so many titles. So many majors. Everyone loves you."

"It comes and goes. I'm sure you've realized that. They love you when you're winning, hate you when you're not. And while, yes, I eventually got to the point where I was winning, I was miserable. I got everything I wanted, and it still wasn't enough." He takes a seat in front of me, hands hovering around my ankles before they drop into his lap. "When does it end, Nic?"

"What do you mean?"

"When does it all end? When you win a 500 tournament? 'Cause you've done that multiple times. So does it end when you win a 1000? A major? Does it end when you win all of them? Does it end when you get to be world number one? When does it end? When do you stop pushing yourself so hard that you collapse? When?"

I have no answer for him because I don't know. I want to win a major, be a point of pride for my parents, and be lauded as a great by the public, but will I stop then?

No. I won't stop until I've put everything I have into this sport.

It's all I have. It's all I am.

Aleksandr seems to read this in my face. He sighs with a nod, like I'm a more advanced case than he thought. "You have to find a way to balance things out, solnyshko." If he notices my confused expression, he chooses to ignore it. "Killing yourself won't get you anywhere. Let me help you find that balance."

"I…What about Anya?"

He smiles wider. "I'm a professional. We'll keep her out of it. No talking about her with you, and no talking about you with her."

"But she's your sister. You'll have to spend more time with her and her team than with me and mine. I'm not sure how you plan to juggle multiple players."

"Not multiple players. Just you, if you'll have me. Anya has another performance coach, so even if I have to send her a plan here and there, she'll be the one to implement it. I'll be working with you in a more professional capacity, traveling with you to your tournaments."

"You'll still be rooting for her. What will you do when we play against each other? During warmups, will you be by my side? Will you sit in my box?"

"Of course I will." His head cocks. "I know trust and loyalty are important to you, and I'm committed to showing you I can give you that too. We can do a trial run for the next few tournaments, through the French Open, and see how you feel."

The most important argument I have sits on my tongue. I'm not one to shy away from confrontation, certainly not with Aleksandr, but for some reason, the thought of learning why he said what he did about me last year gives me pause. Soldiering on, I ask, "Did you mean it when you told Anya that I looked like I was out of shape after I lost to her at Wimbledon?"

Aleksandr blinks. "What?"

"In her presser after she beat me, she said, and I quote, 'My brother pointed out that she seemed out of shape, so maybe if she works on that' when asked if I would beat her later in the season."

He stares at me for half a minute before something in his face shifts. "That was…No. That's not what happened. If I remember correctly, I told her I thought your training could be more efficient because you're a strong athlete but sometimes Nora had you focusing on the wrong things." At my incredulous stare, he continues, "Nic, I'd never say that about you. It's wrong. You're very in shape, and you have been for as long as I've watched you. Anya is young and immature, and I'm sure she said it to get a rise out of you."

"So you didn't see the presser? You didn't know she said that?"

"Honest to god, this is the first I'm hearing of it. If I had known, I would have set the record straight with you." He places a hand on his chest, eyes holding fast on mine. "And before you ask if that's going to be an issue while we're working together, no. I can't control my sister and her behavior outside of tennis, but I can, in the future, make sure you hear any concerns I have about your training from me."

I sigh. I have no other reasons to say no. I need

someone to watch my matches, find where I'm struggling, and help me patch the holes in my game that Karolína can't. Do I want it to be him? No. But if he's experienced this, maybe he knows how to fight off the darkness. How to get me what I've been trying to find for years.

It's worth a shot at least.

"A trial run, then. But no more going behind my back to my coach."

The smile on his face could light the entire Morozov facility for weeks, the hint of a dimple carving itself in his right cheek. If I allowed myself to linger on his features for too long, I'd be halfway to admitting (only ever to myself) how unfortunately attractive it all makes him.

"First order of business is getting you to stop beating on this bag and delivering you to the hotel so you can rest." He reaches out a hand to help me up, and after staring at it for a moment, I slip my hand into his and stand. It's not as uncomfortable as I expected, his calluses melding with mine. I don't feel the urge to rip myself from his grasp. Still, as soon as I'm standing, I drop it, putting my things into my bag.

"Already telling me what to do?"

"Oh, did you believe you'd be the one calling the shots?"

Inexplicably, his words startle a small laugh out of me. He appears as surprised as I am about it, but his face lights further, if possible. And though I don't match it, some of my anxieties are assuaged knowing I'll have help for clay.

We amble to the hotel, side by side, more comfortably than the last time. The silence is nice, but Aleksandr is…

Aleksandr, and when we near the entrance, he says, "I have a question."

"Okay."

"Who are you without tennis?"

My nose scrunches. "What?"

"Who are you if tennis isn't a factor? What sorts of things do you like to do outside of tennis? What do you dislike?" He pulls open the door, and a gust of cool air hits me, smelling of lavender and warm cookies.

I blink at him.

"I'm going to take your silence to mean you don't know." He ushers me into the lobby and toward the row of elevators.

"Mou éphayes ta aftiá," I mutter.

"*What?*"

Sighing, I press the up arrow. An elevator opens immediately, and we step inside. I click the button for my floor. "It means you ate my ears. It's something my yiayia used to say when my cousins wouldn't shut up."

He hums. "I like that. But since you're either unwilling to cooperate right now or you don't have an answer"—he pulls a small notebook out of his sweatpants pocket, flipping past what looks like sketches and ripping out a blank sheet from the middle—"I have a request. Homework of sorts."

Aleksandr thrusts the paper toward me. "I want you to do one new thing a day, unrelated to tennis, whether that's trying a new food or watching a new show."

Accepting the paper reluctantly, I answer, "I don't watch TV." Besides the reality swill Delilah likes to watch.

"Exactly. Nic, you don't do anything besides workout,

play tennis, and watch film of yourself and your opponents. Your entire identity is inextricably tied to the game, and I suspect it has been for most of your life." The elevator slows, opening on my floor, and we walk to my room.

"I didn't realize I signed on a sports psychologist too." Glaring at him as we come to a stop at my room, I fold my arms over my chest. "And I do other things. I went to a museum with the girls. And when we're home, we have game nights and movie nights."

"Great. What's your favorite movie?"

My mind comes up blank, and he grins, nodding at the sheet of paper. "So we'll keep track of the new thing you do each day. And hopefully, in a couple of tournaments, you'll know a few things about yourself that have nothing to do with tennis."

I pull my key card out of my bag. "If I'd have realized you were going to cause this much trouble, I never would have agreed to this."

"It grows on you. Promise." He winks.

As I swipe my card, he holds out his phone. I type my number in and step inside my dark room, letting the door shut behind me without a word. He chuckles, the sound quieting as he moves back toward the elevator bank.

Tossing my bag to the floor, I flick on the desk light and write the date followed by:

Today, I agreed to work with the world's most annoying performance coach.

I take a picture and send it to the number that just texted me.

> There.

ALEKSANDR

> That's not unrelated to tennis, but I'll accept it for today.

> What did you learn about yourself because of that?

I scowl at my phone, then grab the pen and write below it:

I learned that I should not have agreed to work with him.

> 1 image.

ALEKSANDR

> Now we're getting somewhere! I'll think up ideas for things you can do this season. Come October, you're going to understand yourself better than ever.

> We agreed to a trial run, Aleksandr. Who knows if you'll still be around after clay?

ALEKSANDR

> I see you've outsmarted me.

> And call me Aleks. Only strangers call me Aleksandr.

By the way, you have beautiful
penmanship. I like that in a woman.

eight

Aleksandr's smirk when we get onto the clay courts in Charleston two days later worries me. I have no idea whether it's a *this is going to hurt* smirk, or, more distressingly, an *I know something you don't* smirk, but either way, I don't like it.

While clay courts tend to be made with the bright red dust most are accustomed to seeing, Charleston's clay is a dark grayish green, a product of crushing rock from nearby mountains. Though the surface is harder and faster than regular clay, a perfect transition between seasons, dynamic players find clay in general easier to navigate than power hitters like me. That's why Valentina Ortega, who uses heavy topspin and lots of variety in her play, has won the last two French Opens.

Even so, they were the courts I grew up playing on most in Athens. Nothing can beat the feeling of my shoes sliding on the red dirt, of being able to make it to a ball that would be too far away on another surface, the way it covers me in a layer of grime so it takes a few showers to feel clean. It allows me to be one with the court. One with the game.

There's nothing I love more than the red streaking my socks. Than taking part of the court home with me.

Though I've been away from Greece for the better part of thirteen years, over half my life now, stepping onto a clay court, no matter where I am in the world, is like stepping back into the place I grew up. The courts I lived on, because they were the one place I felt loved, and if not loved, respected.

"You look like you think I plan on torturing you," Aleksandr says as he sets up orange cones and highlighter-yellow agility hurdles, pulling three different long resistance bands from his bag.

Karolína sits on the bench, watching us, and Pen has her phone out, prepared to film. I'm wearing a new striped tank from Stratosphere, my biggest sponsor, and she's been adamant that we need to get footage of me training in it so that it takes off when they launch it in their new collection.

"More like I'm not sure you're going to work me hard enough." It's our first official session together, and I'd hoped he'd throw everything he can at me. But based on our conversation after my loss in Miami, it might be more likely we take things easy. Find balance and all that nonsense.

Another byproduct of our conversation Thursday is I find myself analyzing him and our interactions more. It's clear that there's more than meets the eye. I watch him now, placing four hurdles in a line on one side of the court, then four orange cones in a square. He's grinning at me, his eyes lighter than I've ever seen them.

Not that I've paid much attention.

"I will 'work' you plenty hard." His grin turns lascivious, a wink in my direction before he's serious again. Or his version of serious. "But I certainly won't punish you the way you do yourself."

There's a flash of something on his face, there for only a moment. It reminds me of what he said about being like me, punishing himself no matter his successes. I picture him in a locker room, barely holding it together after getting everything he wanted and it still not being enough. I don't remember his arc. When did he start winning? How long did he feel this way? Why wasn't winning enough? What made him quit?

And why do I care so much?

I assure myself that it's healthy scientific curiosity, wanting to know what my life might be like if things ever get better.

"You'd think the person who wants this job so badly would try to do things my way," I mutter.

"I want this job so badly because you're a phenomenal tennis player and I want to see you playing for as many years as your body allows instead of burning out at twenty-five."

Ignoring the fact that he either knows or guessed my age perfectly, I cross my arms. "I'll still be the judge of whether this lasts past June."

Instead of dimming, his smile brightens, which irks me. "Oh, solnyshko." He has yet to tell me the meaning of the word, and I'm too…something to search it up. Proud?

Maybe. Scared? Probably. "You're not going to want to get rid of me now that you have me."

"Cocky."

"Confident."

"Annoying."

He chuckles. "Persistent."

"*Annoying*," I emphasize.

"I believe that means you lose." At my questioning look, he continues, "You used the same word twice. If it was word play you wanted, you lose."

I resist the urge to stomp my foot. "Do you have a plan, or is needling me the only thing on the agenda for training today?"

"If you'll uncross your pretty arms for a moment, I can tell you what to do first." My eyes narrow at the compliment, but I comply. "Very good. Now come stand here." He points to the alley, away from where he set out all his equipment. I stand at the baseline of the alley, facing the net. Pen moves so she can get a good shot, whispering to my coach, whose eyes are fixed on the two of us.

"Are you warmed up?" he asks as he takes a step in front of me, then to the side so he's no longer in the alley. He already had me jog, roll out my lower back, do dynamic stretches and core activation—more than I'm used to.

At my nod, he gestures toward the net. "Lateral jumps with one-legged stutter steps." He demonstrates, pulling up the hem of his short shorts before jumping to his right and hopping on that leg twice. Then, he jumps to the left onto his left leg, hopping twice. "To the net and back twice."

I listen, trying not to glance at him for approval every few jumps the way I might have with Nora. When I reach the net, I turn around and begin again back to the baseline, then back to the net and to the baseline again. By the end, my breathing comes quicker, my heart pumping louder in my ears.

"Good. How's your back?"

I balk for a moment, forgetting his knowledge of my injury. Then remember the way his hands landed on my torso to straighten my spine in Miami. I'm warm, and it's not because we've started training.

"Fine."

He scans my face. Nods. "Now do two sprints to the net and back."

Again, I listen. "Put them together. Four sets. Lateral jumps into sprints."

By the second set, my chest constricts, my breathing heavy. My legs are jelly, and the "faster" Aleksandr calls after each set isn't helping.

As I finish my final sprint, Anya marches onto the court beside us, her hitting partner trailing her. Anya calls to Aleksandr in Russian, which he ignores. She tries again.

"I'm working," he answers without turning to her, his attention on me. "Two more sets," he says to me. I don't immediately begin, still processing the way he brushed her off.

Apparently, she is too. She steps onto our court, and speaks again, hands on her hips. Aleksandr sighs, turning around. "Anya, I told you I'm working." She looks ready to stomp her foot, but instead glares at me. I rub the mati pendant on my necklace between my thumb and pointer finger.

"Can't find any other performance coaches willing to work with you? That tracks." She scoffs.

"Anya," Aleksandr barks. "Enough. Get on your court."

She mutters something, turning on her heel. Seconds later, she's smacking a ball at her hitting partner, far harder than necessary for a half-court warmup.

"Ignore her," Aleksandr says, focusing on me once more. "She's upset she lost in Miami."

"And probably that she lost you," I point out.

He doesn't agree or disagree, instead gesturing at my feet. I do another set, more confident in my decision to work with him. After my final set, I bend over, clasping my hands behind my head and breathing deeply, in through my nose, out through my mouth. It hurts, and I love it.

"Good. Let's get water."

Pen and Karolína are sitting on the bench, so I grab my bottle and sit with my back in the net. Aleksandr settles beside me as I gulp down water. Anya slaps ball after ball at her poor hitting partner, a woman ranked in the upper thirties.

"You like the clay." It's said like a statement, not a question, pulling my attention to Aleks.

"It's what I grew up on. In Greece." Speaking it aloud instantly makes the nostalgia stronger. An ache for my yiayia's moussaka: delicious eggplant, beef, tomatoes, potatoes layered beneath a rich white béchamel sauce. For the tyropita my aunt used to leave at my grandmother's house when she dropped off her five rowdy children. For the way my yiayia would turn a blind eye to how much baklava I consumed because, by virtue of my not consistently trying to break a bone or a piece of her furniture, I was the easiest to deal with.

But thinking of home also reminds me of coaches terrified by my parents, who gushed about how amazing my mother was. "Why doesn't she coach you?" they'd ask, and I never had an answer. I think of quiet corners in my yiayia's house, tired of being left out and finding something of my own to occupy myself.

I adjust the gold hoops in my ear before doing the same to my necklaces, tucking the mati pendant under my tank.

Aleksandr observes me raptly. "You miss it." Another statement.

Swallowing over the memories, I nod once.

"So maybe your homework shouldn't be doing one *new* thing a day. Maybe it should be doing something for you each day. Like getting food that reminds you of home."

There's a humming in my chest. Nothing will ever come close to my yiayia's food, but it might ease the pain of the nostalgia.

I glance at him, take in the far-off look in his eyes and the way that, when he's not paying attention to it, his smile slips. Wonder what he wishes he'd done more of while on tour. "Do you miss home?"

Aleksandr shrugs. "Everyone but Dima travels the world with me, and even him I see often at joint tournaments."

"So family equates to home for you, then?" I ask quietly. I forgot he had a brother who played on tour too.

He opens his mouth. Shuts it. Hums. "I...I don't know. Both my parents were world number one players at one point in their lives, and that comes with a lot of pressure for their kids. I try to be with them, help them, as much as I can. I guess home as a concept is them because I'm so rarely apart from them."

His gaze slides to Anya, then to me, tracing my features, holding for a moment on my lips before jumping back to meet my eyes. I want to know more, want to know if being the eldest of four is as taxing for him as it has been for Delilah, but don't dare ask. It's not my business, and I don't want it to be.

Aleksandr blinks a couple of times, watching me, before his grin slides slowly over his face. He claps. "Break over. Back to work."

We stand, and he grabs the thickest of the three resistance bands from the ground. Whirling it over his head, he tosses it over mine like I'm a calf he's lassoing.

"My mom used to tell my sister if she scrunched her face like that too often or for too long, it'd get stuck that way."

My eyes narrow, flicking between Anya and him. "Talking about your sister is a breach of our agreement."

"You don't know which sister I'm talking about. I could be talking about Natasha."

Damn. He's right. Natasha Morozov, like me, often seems like the forgotten child. She's older than Anya by a couple of years, so closer to my age, and though she's in the top twenty most of the time, her parents are far more often found in Anya's player box than in hers. She's also Anya's doubles partner.

"Are you going to tell me what's next or keep talking?" I ask, hoping to divert the conversation.

His smile widens, and he tugs me closer with the resistance band around my waist, explaining what he wants me to do.

An hour later, when we've managed to use every piece of his equipment and I feel like I need to lie down, he says, "Done for today." I try to hold in the breath of relief, but he hears it. "Thought you were worried I would be soft on you."

"I told you I'm not worried about anything when it comes to you." Except for the fact that he's Anya's brother. But after today, that only acts as an irritant, not an anxiety. She's continued to pout, grumbling and smacking balls next to us.

"Right." We pack our things, and as we step off the court, my body covered in dark gray green dust exactly how I like it, he says, "I'll see you tomorrow."

"Tomorrow is my rest day."

Aleksandr gives me his dumb smile, like he's aware I won't be resting. But instead of saying that, he says something far, far worse. "I meant at brunch. Your friends invited me."

SHOTS FIRED

Who invited the oldest Morozov to brunch tomorrow?

AUSTIN

I wish I could take credit for this, but alas, I am in Monaco

DELILAH

Oh?? This is quite the turn of events

I would *never*

And Matteo (my honey bunny, who I love dearly) is also in Monaco

MATTEO EMPHASIZED "AND MATTEO (MY HONEY BUNNY, WHO I LOVE DEARLY) IS ALSO IN MONACO"

AUSTIN

I beg of you on behalf of the entire group, stop

The pet names must end

MATTEO

Are you upset that I don't call you honey bunny?

HARPER LAUGHED AT "ARE YOU UPSET THAT I DON'T CALL YOU HONEY BUNNY?"

HARPER

Rest assured, I have no idea who invited him.

(psst it wasn't me, but I know who did)

SAHAR

It was definitely Noah

NOAH

Damn it, Sahar

> Nic, please don't put me on your shit list. I
> have too much life left to live.

YOU REMOVED NOAH FROM THE CHAT.

SAHAR ADDED NOAH TO THE CHAT.

THAT EVENING, AFTER AN HOUR-LONG HITTING SESSION with Delilah, I settle into my hotel room, staring at the ceiling, awaiting a call that may never come. My fingers brush over the soft fabric of the blanket I travel with, thankful to feel it against my legs instead of the rough material of the one provided by the hotel. I reach over to check my phone again.

Nothing.

I spent the majority of my life trying my best to stay out of my parents' way. It was clear to me from the moment I could perceive much of anything that they wanted nothing to do with me, and if it was blatant enough for me to know it, it was obvious to the world too.

Outside of nannies, my yiayia took care of me during most of my early years, and even then, I was often over-looked for my other cousins. My many aunts and uncles sprawled across my yiayia's mansion on the Athenian Riviera, paid for by my pappou's shipping business. Younger cousins ran around the house, chased by each other and the matriarch of the Vassilakis family, while the older cousins disappeared into basements to partake in drugs and booze.

But not me. I sat primly where I was told and failed to interest any of my cousins enough to be invited to play.

Too quiet, too boring, too strange.

Same as in school. The problem wasn't that I didn't *want* to play so much as I wasn't sure how to be invited.

When I was six and my yiayia's health deteriorated, boarding school was the logical next choice. My parents certainly had no interest in shuttling me to and from school, so a British boarding school was the perfect solution. English became the only language I was allowed to speak. Greek went from my primary language to one I hardly used.

School was more of the same. More interactions I couldn't navigate, more teasing, more wishing to be anyone else, anywhere else. But when my parents realized professional tennis was a viable option—because, let's be honest, I spent all my free time on the courts running away from everything I could—being whisked to the United States didn't do me much good either. Home school for a few hours, tennis for the rest, minimal interactions with people my age. It didn't help that I had a slight accent I still can't seem to shake, no matter how much I try to shape my consonants the way Americans do.

My phone rings, and though the call was planned, it surprises me. "Weekly" calls with my parents usually devolve into one call a month, mostly with my mother, while my parents travel the world.

My wellbeing has never been their first priority.

"Hello, Mother," I answer after the second ring.

"Hello, Nicola," my mother's Spanish accent bleeds back. I bite back a cringe at the name. I doubt she knows how much I hate being called by my full name, especially since the reason I hate it so much is because it reminds me of her, nannies, and a dark, empty home.

It doesn't help that the name is the shortened form of Nicholas, and therefore only used for men in Greece. My parents couldn't even be bothered to give me a proper Greek girl name like Nikoleta.

"How are you?"

"Oh, you know. Your father and I are in Tokyo this month. Lots to do."

I hum in agreement. This call will only be a few minutes long, I'm sure. I'd have to win a tournament for it to last any longer.

Living up to the great Carmen Aguirre's name is no easy feat.

"Are you enjoying it?" I finally ask into the stilted silence.

"Of course. I went so many times for tournaments. Then we had you. So it's nice to be able to explore more."

If it's an insult, it's wrapped tightly enough in a layer of indifference that I don't recognize it as such. It's not as though their vacation plans were impacted much by me.

"I'm sure plenty of people take their children on trips with them to Tokyo."

"Perhaps. But you were so…peculiar."

I inhale sharply. There it is. The proof that my pieces are too fractured and jagged for anyone to want to hold on to them. Not even those bound by blood can stomach me, let alone love me. Why would I expect anyone else to?

"I wasn't sure how well you'd travel," she continues. "Daphne told us that you once spent an afternoon organizing your grandmother's spice rack while your cousins played. So strange. And at school, during assemblies, you threw fits. Covering your ears, causing a scene because you were too close to the speaker. She'd have to come pick you up and stay with you at the house. No, you wouldn't have done well on an airplane."

I could point out that the girls at school pushed me toward the speaker because they knew it stressed me out—fodder for their teasing. Or the glaring issue, which is that I travel plenty now without issue. Instead, I say, "Right." It's better not to fight her on this. She'll give up quickly and end the call in a matter of seconds after the matter is "settled."

It's her turn to hum. "Your father says hello."

"Hello." It's so absurd, saying hello to my father without hearing his voice. I can't remember the last time I did. If my mother is indifferent, my father is outright forgetful about my existence. The only thing he's grateful for is that his portion of his father's billions have somewhere to go when he dies. How horrifying it would be to donate it to charity or give it to his squabbling siblings he's constantly feuding with.

I haven't exactly told him I want none of it in the spaces of seconds we've talked over the years.

Physically, I'm pieces of them—my father's sharp cheekbones, nose, and thick wavy chestnut-brown hair (which I chemically straighten), my mother's gray eyes, bowed lips—and yet I have no idea whether I'm anything *like* them. Does my father feel alone in a room full of people? Does my mother react angrily when she doesn't understand something or is too hot, too overwhelmed, only to have remorse weigh heavily afterward?

I don't think so. They have so many friends, such rich social lives, that I have to imagine it's just me.

Just as it's always been.

"Alright, Nicola. Our friends want to get back to exploring, so I'll let you go."

"Oh. Right. Talk to you next week."

"Talk to you next week."

If I pretend it's true, I'll have something to look forward to. Maybe then I won't feel so alone.

nine

I'm not allowed *one* mimosa with brunch?" Sahar asks exasperatedly the next day. "On my *rest* day?"

"I literally haven't said a word," Noah answers.

"But I can tell by your pinched face that you think I shouldn't. Show of hands, who else can tell by Noah's face that he doesn't want me to drink this mimosa?"

At the glare she shoots all of us, we raise our hands, Aleksandr included. Delilah raises both her hands, and at our confused looks, says, "Matteo would agree with me if he were here. You know what? Someone else raise a second hand because Austin would agree too." Both are preparing for the ATP1000 tournament in Monaco, the latter of whom is playing in his first tournament since an injury benched him during the offseason.

Sahar raises a second hand, and Noah rolls his eyes with a smile. "Again, I haven't said anything. If you want a mimosa, have a mimosa. Just be ready for your match tomorrow."

The patio of the restaurant Delilah and Harper chose

—part of their *becoming tourists while on tour* bit—is sunlight dappled, filtering through wide leaves. Around us, cutlery clinks, mingling with laughter and the call of seagulls. Pitchers of cold water, sweet tea, and their less innocent afternoon friend, mimosas, make their way around tables by way of waiters skilled in the art of Southern charm.

And because I knew Aleksandr would be insufferable about the fact that I haven't been trying something new the last couple of days, I finally bit the bullet and decided to get the sweet tea.

Beside today's date, I'll be writing, *I do not enjoy sweet tea. It's too ungodly sweet for my tastes.*

Maya, who I haven't seen in nearly a year, sits across from me, her dark hair shorn at her shoulders. Though she left the tour injured, she's glowing. Likely a product of doing what she loves: heading and coaching for a charity that teaches tennis to underprivileged kids.

She looks around the table, making a noise of excitement, like she can't contain it. "I'm sorry. I'm just so glad to be here with you. I spend all my time with football players and children. I've missed this."

Delilah shoots up from beside me, walking around the table to sit in Maya's lap. Maya accepts her with a warm smile and open arms, and uncomfortableness flares in my chest. Not quite jealousy, but not unlike it either.

Perhaps envy that I can't so easily be part of this. That everyone seems to have their own favorite person and I'm just…here.

To the left of Maya sits Cooper, Maya's boyfriend and tight end for the Charleston Sabertooths, who does a phenomenal job of ignoring the glances he's drawing to our table, nodding along to the conversation Maya and Delilah have started about their time together on tour. His blond hair matches the straw cowboy hat draped over it, and his eyes never leave Maya. To my right, Sahar and Noah continue bickering, and Harper chimes in occasionally from in front of them, trying (and failing) to keep the peace.

I've been around these people for a while, and I still struggle to find my footing, knowing when and where to join in. Knowing what to say. I'm thankful they invite me and think of me as one of them, but in instances like this, it's so hard to feel like I *am* one of them.

The hint that I don't belong here presses painfully against my head, leading my thoughts to the gym. Would I have set myself up for more success if I'd stayed back to train?

I shake off the idea, sinking into the background, wondering if I'll go another twenty minutes without saying a word.

"The worst seafood I ever had while on tour was in Basel," Aleksandr says from beside Harper. While I spiraled, the conversation became tablewide. "I was sick for three days and had to pull out before the quarterfinals."

"Why would you think seafood in a landlocked country like Switzerland would be good?" Sahar asks.

He holds up a hand defensively. "I'd had it from another restaurant there before and it was good!"

"Wait, I know which place you're talking about," Noah says. "The one not far from site, right? With the amazing hand rolls?"

Aleksandr nods. "Exactly." He turns, eyes finding mine. Sahar speaks, but I barely hear it, locked on the sea in his eyes and the small grin on his face. He watches me like he can see in me what most can't. What I try so hard to hide from the world.

His eyes drop. It's only now that I realize I've been rubbing my arm with a finger, self-soothing. Immediately, I stop, shoving my hands under my legs. I've spent years working on my fidgeting while in groups, not wanting others to perceive how uncomfortable I am. So much so that Austin takes great pleasure in calling me the group's "ice queen," a title I'm more than happy to hold if it means they don't recognize I'm defective.

Over the years, I have learned that acting aloof forces people to keep their distance, from which point they can't poke and prod me enough to notice my nervousness. My inadequacy. And because normal people don't fidget when they're uncomfortable, I've exorcised the fidgeting from myself.

Or at least I thought I had.

"Which country has the best seafood, Nic?" Aleksandr asks after Sahar finishes speaking. All eyes turn to me, and I curse him, though I'm not certain whether it's for knowing me well enough to see I was drowning or because I've never been good as the center of attention.

Taken by memories of lavraki made by my yiayia, I answer, "Greece."

Harper points at me. "That's my second favorite! Madrid has had my favorite seafood yet." She rests a hand on her stomach like she didn't eat an entire platter of eggs and veggies. "I'd give anything for that right now."

"I don't think I've tried it there yet. We'll have to go this year," Aleksandr answers. Everyone agrees excitedly, but his eyes remain on mine, like he was speaking to me and me alone. I glance away, body warm.

The conversation slips elsewhere, and a few minutes later, when I'm sure I won't speak for the rest of our time here, my eyes focused on the table linen, Delilah leans over the table and asks me, "Nic! Do you remember that time we beat Ester and Valentina? What was the final score in the tiebreak again? Was it 12–10 or 13–11?"

"14–12."

"14–12! Can you believe that? Every time we thought we had it, we were *thwarted*. Nic had to put her backhand winners to good use for us to get the win."

"I hate being on the receiving side of her backhand," Sahar groans. "It's too damn good."

"You have to fuel your shots with anger," I answer. The group laughs, though I wasn't making a joke. Or are they laughing at me? I can't tell, but I don't think so.

Once we've paid, Maya checks the time, her lips turning down. "Oh my gosh, it's been four hours." She turns to Cooper, who nods. "Duty calls, my loves. We have to get going."

Delilah stands, pulling Maya into a tight embrace. "I'm not playing Stuttgart to give myself a breather before Madrid, so I can coach for the charity for a day or so before I leave for Europe."

My eyebrows come together, and I smooth them with a finger before anyone notices. I didn't realize Delilah wouldn't be in Stuttgart. It makes me wonder if I should be taking a breather before Madrid too.

But if I skip Stuttgart, I may not be warmed up and ready to go for Madrid. I can't take that time off. Plus, we have a week off between the Charleston Open and Stuttgart, when we'll be training in Orlando. That should be plenty of time off for me.

"I would *love* that. Text me the days so I can have everything ready," Maya says.

They're still squeezing each other tightly, and Sahar, who stands with the rest of us, jokes, "Okay, Delilah, we all want a turn too."

The pair separate, and everyone hugs Maya and Cooper. I'm last to wrap my arms around Maya, who whispers, "You've got an admirer."

I pull away enough to look at her, and her eyes flick to where Aleksandr stands behind me. "I'm not sure he's taken his eyes off you for more than a few seconds at a time today."

Rolling my eyes, I force a smile. "Right. He won't leave me alone. Very serious about my training. So much so, I can't enjoy brunch with my friends without him."

Maya smiles and hums. "Right." She squeezes my arms and pulls away, her side still pressed to mine.

Addressing all four of us girls, she says, "I guess I'll see you when I see you."

She's holding back tears, and Delilah, Sahar, and Harper rush forward to swallow her in a group hug that I'm now a part of. Arms wrap around me from all sides, and though I'm not entirely comfortable with all of it, my breathing is a little less forced than usual, a little less like someone's digging their knee into my chest.

After we finish saying our goodbyes, the rest of us

begin the walk back to our hotel. Shockingly, Aleksandr sidles up beside me at the back of our small group. His eyes burn a hole in the side of my face, and when it becomes unbearable, I whip my glare to him. "You have a staring problem."

He smiles. "Maybe."

"Not maybe. I'm diagnosing it."

"Okay, Doctor. What's the prognosis?"

"Not good. If you don't stop, I might finally throw a weight at your face. Or slam a tennis ball at you from close range."

"Hmm," he hums. "Not good indeed. What can I do to stop it before it gets to that point?"

"Find someone else to bother," I say like it's the obvious answer.

"Damn. Guess that's it for me. I'll have to bother you at least through Roland Garros. Will I make it without you breaking my pretty face or bruising me with a tennis ball?"

I bite back a small smile, hating how my body betrays me. "You'll be lucky to make it through the week at this rate."

He heaves a prolonged sigh. "Will you at least come to the funeral? Say a few words?"

"I think not."

"I love when you're mean to me."

I roll my eyes, noting that we've dropped away from the group, who are several yards ahead of us. Picking up my pace, I speed through a crosswalk in the hopes of losing him.

No luck. He's beside me on the other side in an instant. "Were you okay? At brunch?"

"We were eating with *my* friends. Why wouldn't I be?" With narrowed eyes, I finish, "I would think you, as the person who doesn't hang out with us much, would be the one struggling." The words taste funny on my tongue, tinged with regret. I've spent so long feeling left out, treating him like he doesn't belong makes me no better than my childhood bullies.

Aleksandr shrugs, unfazed. "I get along with anyone and everyone."

Must be nice.

I don't voice the thought, and because the man is incapable of being quiet, he asks, "Do you often find it difficult to talk in large groups?"

"Do you always ask such overstepping questions to people you hardly know?"

"Always. Though I wouldn't agree that we hardly know each other."

"I know exactly two things about you."

"Which are?"

"You're a Morozov. And you annoy me at every turn when you could be doing anything else."

His deep chuckle reaches low inside me. I hate it. "I thought I knew lots about you, but now I'm not so sure."

"What is *that* supposed to mean?"

"It means I thought you were just reserved. That the only thing you cared about was tennis and maybe, sometimes, your friends. But I was wrong."

I stop abruptly, though the hotel is visible ahead. If my body would let me, I'd disappear into my room and ignore this man and his discerning commentary. "Do you plan to do this with all your clients? Or is this just for me?"

Disregarding my questions, he adds, "You care so much, don't you? About what others think of you. About saying the right thing. About being included. About not fidgeting so people can't *see* how uncomfortable you are." His eyes drop to where my right thumb smooths a pattern against my other elbow, and I grimace. "You want to belong."

It's a knife to the chest to be perceived on this level. "Big fucking deal. I care about stuff. So what?"

"So I'm telling you it's okay to feel that way."

"Wow, I didn't realize you were the purveyor of what others are allowed to feel. Thank you, O wise one."

Another sigh. "Alright."

I charge toward the hotel, walking into the lobby to join my friends. The four of them are standing in a small huddle, discussing. When I get to them, Harper smiles at me, then behind me at Aleksandr.

"We're thinking about hitting the pool in a couple of hours. Meet you there?" she asks us both. At my nod, she, Sahar, and Noah wave goodbye and head toward the elevator on their side of the hotel.

Delilah bumps her hip against mine as we walk to the other side. "Want to come to mine and get ready?"

Aleksandr has put distance between us, thankfully, talking to Anya, Natasha, and his parents, who speak with their arms crossed. Most players and their teams stay here during the tournament, so it's not a surprise to see them. Anya catches me looking, her face contorting into a sneer. Still angry about Aleksandr leaving her team, I imagine.

I glare right back.

"Now?" Normally, I'd spend my off days with

Karolína and Pen, working through film or prepping for sponsorship work, but because I knew I'd be spending the day with the girls, they're exploring Charleston.

"I'm going to call Matteo for an hour. You're welcome to be there, but it might get inappropriate." She giggles. "I meant after. I feel like you and I haven't gotten to spend much time together recently."

My shoulders sag at the words. I thought it was just me who felt the growing chasm between us. Without doubles, we only get a couple of hours here and there, and often they're spent around other people. I can't remember the last time we hung out alone since the offseason.

"I'll be there."

ten

A few minutes later, I throw a thin sweatshirt over my cropped tank top and spandex shorts, in dire need of a workout to burn off the weird energy that's been hanging over me since brunch. I have at least an hour before I need to meet Delilah.

Charleston, while only a 500 tournament, is also the first tournament of the clay-court season, which makes it incredibly important. There's very little time to get acclimated, and the season is short enough as it is. If I win here, it will help my ranking, push me closer to making it to the finals at the end of the season, and, most importantly, help me prove that I'm ready to be formidable on clay. That I'm a top contender for Madrid and the French Open.

The best way I know to win? Put in more work. And with Karolína touring Charleston, she won't stop me.

I try to get my workouts done at players' gyms when I'm traveling, especially since hotel gyms rarely have the equipment I need. But this will be a short workout, a few sets of a few exercises.

The moment the elevator opens, I spy Aleksandr in front of the gym doors. His back presses against the glass, his head bowed over his phone, dressed exactly as he was at brunch, like he came straight here after talking to his family members. He glances up from his phone, and satisfaction settles in his features.

"You've got to be kidding me," I grumble.

"Somehow I knew you'd be here." He looks at me the way my yiayia used to look at my cousins when she was scolding them, eyebrows pulled over squinted eyes. "It's a rest day, solnyshko."

"Enough of that. What does that even mean?"

He pauses for a moment, eyes searching mine. "Little sun."

"Oh, ha ha. Very funny. I get it. Because I'm a ray of sunshine. Asshole." I step forward. "Let me through. I'm just going to stretch."

"You're not a good liar. How many years of your life have you spent overtraining?"

I want to scream.

"Ante pali," I murmur. *Here we go again*. A favorite phrase of my nanny, Daphne, when forced to pick me up from boarding school earlier than she was supposed to. Like after the headmaster noticed the teasing about my "boy's name" getting worse. As if time away from school did anything more than sharpen my peers' pitchforks. Aleksandr cocks his head, but I simply say, "You're annoying me."

"That's nothing new."

"Don't you think you got in enough of your antics earlier?"

"If we're going to work together, you have to listen to me. Rest days are integral to your growth. I know you know this. So what's the issue?"

"I think we've established that I *don't* want to work with you."

He's quiet, waiting for more. I sigh.

He's shown he understands me on a level few, if any, do. I'm not sure I can lie myself out of this one, and at this point, I'm not sure I want to anymore. Adjusting the hoops along my ears, I say, "I know rest days are important. But I also know any time I'm not working my ass off is time wasted. At brunch, I got an itch, like spending time with my friends takes away from my training."

Infuriatingly, he's still quiet, watching me. Making no move to speak. With narrowed eyes, I finish, "I need a major title this year or I'm not sure I can keep doing this. I'm tired of feeling like I'm not enough. Like nothing I do is enough. The world tells me I'm meant to be someone great, but with each passing day, I'm not sure if that's true anymore. Maybe I peaked at seventeen."

It's more than I've admitted to anyone besides myself. I can't figure out why *he* of all people is able to pull it from me, but I've become a wound ball of yarn, unspooled by a look from him. He's wrapped the end around a finger and pulled, unraveling every terrible thought I've had about myself and this sport for years.

"I didn't win my first tournament until I was twenty-four. I didn't win my first ATP1000 until I was twenty-seven. It wasn't until later that year that I won my first major. There's—"

"So you're saying I should just keep going and I'll win a major in two years?"

Aleksandr tilts his head. "You're being purposely obtuse."

"Am I? You didn't exactly resolve my concerns."

"If you'd have let me finish, you would've seen where I was going."

Crossing my arms to prevent myself from hitting him, I nod for him to continue.

"What I'm trying to tell you is there's more to winning majors than killing yourself on rest days. I'd venture to say that success is predicated upon rest. Only when I took a step back, started taking vacations, hanging out with friends, doing things for *me*, only then did I break into spaces I'd never been before. The answer isn't always to push harder. Sometimes the answer is to take a moment to breathe and give your body the rest it deserves."

"And you think if I take more breaks, I'll win Roland Garros? Hoist the French Open trophy?"

"There are a lot of factors that will go into you winning, but yes, I think it's the top thing you can change in your training to see more success."

I scan his features, including the smile that grows as he catches me watching it. We're closer than I realized, my body a few inches from pressing against his, so I step back. "And yet, here we are. You did all those things and you still quit. Maybe it wasn't the solution."

"I won the majors, didn't I?" He runs a hand through his hair, his eyebrows coming together again. "Nic, there's a lot about my life I would change if I could do it over again, and maybe if I had someone like me telling me to slow down, I'd still be playing. Maybe I'd still love the tour the way I used to. But if none of that changed and I felt the way I did that Sunday I won Wimbledon, I'd quit again. Despite the consequences."

This time, the guilt in his tone is unmistakable. Why does he feel guilty about quitting? What consequences? I'm positive there's much more going on in his head than I'm privy to, and I wonder if I should be paying more attention to him. Observing him the way he does me.

But it's not my place to pry, and if I were him, I wouldn't want me asking questions. I switch gears. "One day, I'm going to go to the gym during a rest day and you're not going to be able to stop me."

Aleksandr laughs, the tension leaking from his shoulders as he guides me toward the elevator. His hand never touches my back, again seeing me better than 99% of people I engage with, but I feel its heat from where it hovers. "I'd say over my dead body, but you don't need any more incentive to kill me." He presses the up button. "One day, you're going to believe that letting yourself rest is the best thing you can do for yourself."

After we enter the elevator, I turn to him, but as I open my mouth, he says, "I know. I'm annoying you."

Sighing far too dramatically, I cross my arms, staring at the numbers as they change on the screen near the top.

"What did you do for yourself today? You stopped

sending me proof after the first one, and I'm *sure* that doesn't mean you're not working on that list."

"I tried sweet tea at brunch today," I answer smugly.

"And?"

"Hated every sip of it."

Aleksandr laughs. "I could tell. Each time you drank it, your nose scrunched. You could have ordered a different drink, you know."

There he is again, seeing things in me no one else would notice. I turn away, frowning once more.

"You're cute when you pout."

"Are you flirting with me?" I ask him before I've had a second to filter the thought.

Aleksandr's grin widens. "Constantly. Glad you're catching on."

"That seems like a breach of contract."

"Really? I combed through it and didn't see a single thing about flirting." I peer at him out of the corner of my eye but don't respond, which makes him laugh again. "It's fun, Nic. It gets under your skin and you get all fiery. Did you know you play better when you're fired up? Makes you more creative."

"Your argument is that you flirt with me for the betterment of my tennis? Seriously? That's what you're going with?"

He shrugs. "Guess we'll have to experiment."

The elevator jolts to a stop on my floor, and I step out.

"I've got to help Natasha, so you be good. I'll see you at the pool," he calls after me.

I almost stop to ask what he's helping her with. Does it have to do with all the guilt he seems to feel? More and more, I wonder if it all boils down to him being the oldest of his siblings. But over my shoulder, I say, "No one invited you to that."

The last thing I hear before the doors close is his throaty chuckle. I pretend it doesn't stoke something deep inside of me.

eleven

I nod off watching film (both mine and Aleksandr's, but I'll take that to my grave), until Delilah finally texts that she's ready to go. The sun has begun to set when I show up to her room, pulling at the thin tie around my neck to loosen the knot of my bikini top. She opens her door, cheeks pink, her blonde hair in a bun, and a lavender polka-dot bikini strap poking out of her T-shirt.

"Hi!" she chirps. "Sorry that took so long, we haven't talked in a while."

That familiar bittersweet pang of knowing that, in many ways, I've been replaced.

"What, twelve hours?" I joke.

She snorts. "Probably less, but anyway. Ready to go?"

I nod. We're outside the pool room two minutes later. The sounds of splashing, Noah's booming voice, and Harper's laugh travel from inside. The glass doors glide open with a soft whoosh, the humid air hitting us with the strong scent of chlorine and the fainter smell of eucalyptus, as though all the oils from the spa next door have spilled into the pool. I'm lucky to be afforded luxury hotel stays during tournaments thanks to Pen's sponsorship work, and this one is no exception: vaulted ceilings with the last bits of sunlight spilling through the skylight and dancing on the surface of the choppy pool surrounded by curved loungers upholstered in plush white-and-cream fabric.

At first, I don't see Aleksandr. He's not on any of the loungers, and the only people in the pool are Sahar, Harper, and Noah.

Until a head crests the surface of the water and an admittedly glorious set of shoulders appear. His near-golden hair is darker, and I watch him push it out of his eyes with both hands, his corded biceps and triceps flexing. I can just make out the line of text over his heart, a tattoo. Below it is a perfect six pack, carved as though in stone, disappearing into the water along with a trail of hair—

"Nic, you're ogling," Delilah whispers as we approach the group.

A disgusted noise leaves my throat. "I am *not*."

"Wipe the drool off your face before he notices. Better yet, rip off your cover up so he can ogle you back."

"I will shove you in the pool."

She tsks. "Always threatening violence upon those you love."

"Sometimes those I love—"

I'm cut off by shouts of hellos from the group, who have finally noticed us. "Get in! It feels so good!" Harper calls. Her dark brown hair is piled in a knot atop her head, her dark green bikini top peeking above the water.

"What, like a five-year-old's pee?" I ask, dropping a towel on one of the chairs and forcing my eyes away from Aleksandr.

"So pessimistic. It's chlorinated to high hell. I promise you will not contract a virus," Sahar says. Her thick hair is blacker than night in the water, and she's wearing an identical bikini to Harper's but in red, like they went shopping together with the express goal of bringing us Christmas in late March.

"Can you really promise that though?" Noah asks, and she pushes him under water.

Delilah pulls off her T-shirt and shorts, cannonballing into the deep end. All but Aleksandr follow her there, heads bobbing near the far wall as they work to stay afloat.

I pull off my own long T-shirt, pilfered from one of my many hook ups' closets years ago that's gotten softer with age. When I turn, Aleksandr watches every movement, eyes meeting mine before they drop to where my hair coasts over my shoulders. I'm not sure why, but I toss it behind me, and the motion makes Aleksandr smirk. His gaze travels over my necklaces, then the little blue bikini top, eyes flashing as they take in the cut of my abs and the thin ties of my bikini bottoms.

Lust settles on his face. I can't tell when someone is joking with me versus laughing at my expense, but I've spent enough time with enough men to know desire when I see it. It sticks in his eyes and in the dimple in the corner of his smirk, egging me on. I'm not proud of the warmth that flares through my entire body, sinking low until it nestles in my stomach and between my legs.

I've spent very little time with men outside of the

bedroom. Any more than sleeping with them becomes a sticky business. Relationships don't appeal to me, and when feelings (always his) seem imminent, I end things. Less mess. And, I suppose, less worry that they might see something in me they won't like. Like the way I shy from touch once it's all over, or that I lack the ability to appreciate their humor, or that when I'm hot or overwhelmed, I might react in a manner they'll view as incongruent with the situation.

Slipping into the water slowly via the stairs, I allow myself one more second to take in his chiseled body up close before I glance across the pool.

"Never seen a woman in a two-piece before?" I ask him, leaning against the wall beside the stairs.

Aleks follows, his warmth mingling with mine. "Not one like you, no."

Remembering what he said in the elevator, I sink into this flirtation, refusing to give him what he wants. There's a reason I don't hook up with people I spend time with. Too complicated, I imagine. But this I can do. It won't go further than flirting, a battle of wits and nothing more.

It certainly has nothing to do with the pull to him I can't shake or the strange yearning to learn more about this man who is superficially happy but clearly dealing with something below the surface.

"Not one like me, hm?" I ask quietly.

"Is that your way of asking me to elaborate?"

"I was just repeating your words, Aleksandr."

He chuckles, switching so he stands in front of me. He's staring at me like he knows what I'm doing, his eyes lit as they search my face. "Of course. In that case, I won't elaborate, Nicola."

The image of a dark, empty home stabs behind my eyes, the sound of a mother's cold voice reverberating in the rare spaces of time when she felt like acknowledging her child. I try to hide my flinch.

"Nic," he corrects himself quietly. "I didn't get to tell you I'm proud of you for trying the sweet tea today."

"Do you realize how patronizing that sounds?"

His lips twitch. "Maybe. But I'm still proud of you. I think this is going to be good for you."

I only recognize that my bottom lip is sticking out when his thumb presses against it. It should be uncomfortable, should make me want to push him away, and yet…

"There you go pouting again," he grumbles softly. "You want to know what I find so fascinating about you?" He removes his thumb and laughs when my lip protrudes more. "You're so stubborn. That's reason number one."

"Says the man who steamrolled his way onto my team through sheer force of will."

"I'd do a lot more for a lot less."

"What does that mean?" I ask, hating the way my breath hitches in my chest. Even that, he takes notice of, his eyes dropping to the thin string lacing the twin triangles of my bikini together.

His pupils eat the blue of his eyes, and he takes a step closer, his right arm caging me against the pool wall, though he leaves room for me to exit on my right if I want. "That depends on what you want it to mean, I suppose."

"That's not an answer," I whisper. Somewhere far away, I hear my friends playing a game.

"No, it isn't, is it?" He sighs, glancing behind me. At 6'2", he's only three inches taller than I am, and yet he overwhelms the space. His chain dangles away from his chest as he leans toward me. "Let's just say I've spent a lot of time trying not to think too hard about what you'd look like in a swimsuit, and the few times I allowed myself to, well, I didn't do justice to you at all."

I gasp, and his eyes drop to my lips, where they rest for ages. The air is taut around us, and I'm drifting closer, my body betraying me once more as my chest shifts toward him, inches from closing the gap.

All at once, I realize I've been lying to myself. I want it. Want *him*. Want him to kiss me and take me in his strong, calloused hands and keep going until he's consumed me. Want him more than I've ever wanted any of the others I've been with.

The revelation shocks me enough that I slow my movement. He takes a step back. I don't have it in me to voice that I didn't want him to stop, glad that one of us ended it before it began.

"We're chicken fighting," Sahar sing-songs from nearby. It brings me back to where we are, and I realize they've moved to the shallow side, though they're near the opposite wall, giving us a wide berth. Sahar sits atop Noah's shoulders, her hands in his hair.

"Nic, hop on Aleks' shoulders," Harper adds.

"Ow! Sahar, that's too hard," Noah complains. His hair sticks up on the right where she pulled it.

"Quit being a baby."

"Let's go, solnyshko. There are games to be played."
Aleksandr beckons me, his hand held out.

"I'm not doing that."

"Come on!" Delilah exclaims. "It's not a fun evening
at the pool if there isn't chicken fighting."

"I think that's a stretch."

This time, Aleksandr does cage me in with both arms.
"This is not how I imagined my first time between your
legs, but I'm game. Get on my shoulders."

An affronted gasp leaves my lips. "That is an absolutely inappropriate thing for a performance coach to say
to the player they're training."

"I'll stop if it actually makes you uncomfortable. Say
the word." His voice drops, a grumble beside my ear, his
breath kissing the shell. "I think, though, that you're
starting to like it. Even if you hate yourself for it."

"You talk an awful lot," I answer, hopefully in a way
that doesn't belie the fact that my legs are pressing
together.

"You guys, come on!" Delilah says again. I'm definitely going to shove her this time. No threat or warning
beforehand either.

"All I'm saying is that I'm perfectly capable of being a
professional during the day and a delinquent with you at
night. Now, unless you're absolutely opposed, I'm going to
touch you so we can get you on my shoulders." He waits a
beat, and when I say nothing, drops so his head is all that's
above water, then turns around. He backs into me until his
head is against my stomach. I'm so shocked, my legs relax,
and he slides between, my thighs coasting over his
shoulders.

"Aleksandr!"

Warm hands I just imagined elsewhere wrap around my shins, and before I know it, I'm perched on his shoulders, my brain singularly focused on his head between my legs.

twelve

My time in Charleston moves quickly. I play my first match Tuesday and win easily, enjoying myself on court for the first time in months. In the spirit of letting loose and doing something for myself, I even go out to dinner with my and Delilah's teams, like old times. The next day, I don't bother to go to the gym outside of stretching with Aleksandr, knowing he'd stop me if I did. We haven't mentioned the incident in the pool, and though he still flirts during our sessions, it's never more than words. As if the moment of hesitation was all he needed to assume I'm not interested in him.

Which, of course, I'm not.

My match Thursday ends with a straight set win over another seeded opponent, and though my back injury flares briefly, I'm so glad to be in the quarterfinals that I focus on the cooldown Aleksandr has me do and listen when he tells me to see a physiotherapist.

I allow myself another dinner out that evening.

Though I'm reticent to believe his *try new things* list will help me, I order sea bass, which I've only had in Greece, and while it may not be as good, I like it enough that, when I get back to my room, I write

Eat more sea bass while traveling

beside today's date. I scan the last few days.

Went for a walk during sunrise. Work this into my days as often as I can.

Tried a piece of longan (fruit) that Harper got from the nearby Asian market. Didn't love the look of it (reminds me of a cyclops) but it was good.

I set the list down, restlessness zinging through me. Usually, I'd burn it off by going to the gym, but I'm trying to heed Aleksandr's advice, so I decide to go with an alternative: watching the match I lost to Anya in California. Settling under the blanket I brought with me, I watch my errors over and over again, promising myself I won't make any of them tomorrow when I play another seeded player in the quarterfinals.

The next day, I win my first set in less than forty-five minutes. The second, though, isn't so straightforward, especially when I hit a serve in the fourth game and my lower back spasms. I win the game, giving myself a 3–1 lead, but I approach my box after, hiding my grimace.

"Your back?" Aleksandr asks.

"Yeah."

"Do you want to play through it?" Karolína asks. "No one will fault you if you pull out. We can take a week or two off to get it rested. The last thing I want is for you to make it worse."

"No," I answer roughly, glancing across the court to where my opponent bounces a ball, walking toward the baseline to serve. "I can do this."

Her eyes narrow for a second, but she nods. "Then finish it quickly so you can have more of a break before tomorrow."

I do just that. Despite my limited range of motion and how exhausted I am after staying up too late watching the match against Anya, I win the next three games. And when my speech and press are over, I disappear in search of relief.

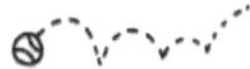

IT'S FREEZING. MY LIMBS ARE WEIGHED DOWN BY THE cold, and somewhere, distantly, I hear my name being called.

"Nic! Nic! Nicola!" Each shout is more urgent than the last until I open my eyes. My teeth are chattering and I'm dazed, confused by the man I'm seeing. The last thing I remember is my back getting tight during my match and wanting an ice bath. But by the time I got to the training room after press, I was too tired to put in the ice and just sank into the cool water, hoping a head dunk would wake me. Clearly it did not.

I'm lifted, weightless, out of the tub. The chattering of my teeth gets louder as I'm placed on my feet, a towel wrapped around me. The man pulls me into his body, his hands rubbing up and down my shoulders.

"A—Aleksandr?" I ask, unsure if I'm imagining things. If it's not him, I'm going to be very uncomfortable very quickly having this person's arms around me.

"I'm right here, solnyshko. Just…just let me get your temperature back up, okay? Help me get you warm."

I sink into him, closing my eyes, and instantly recognize I'm safe. "I—I didn't mean to…to fall asleep," I manage.

He smooths my hair, cupping the back of my head. "Shh, we'll talk about it when you're feeling better." The towel is soaked, so he pulls it off and tosses it away.

"I'm…I'm sorry."

He doesn't answer, picking me up and setting me on his lap on a bench, whole body practically wrapped around mine. I'm not sure how long we sit like that. I believe he has a short conversation, vaguely hear the person's footsteps receding.

When my teeth stop chattering and my shivering subsides, I whisper, "I think my core temp is good. You can put me down." I wait for a minute before I open my eyes and pull back enough to glance at him. "Aleksandr? I'm okay now."

He appears on the cusp of devastation, light brown eyebrows knitted together, a frown pulling at every one of his features. I've spent so much of this short relationship wanting to wipe the smile off his face, but now that it's finally gone, I hate it. I want his wide grin back.

Later, I will assure myself that it's the cold-induced confusion that has me smoothing the tension from his brow. The blue of his eyes seems to lighten a fraction, and I know I've lost it when I take his cheeks in my palms and pull the corners of his lips up with my thumbs.

"Something tells me you're not quite back to normal yet," he jokes weakly. "The Nic I know wouldn't deign to touch me."

"You're right," I'm quick to agree. "I must still be feeling the effects of the bath."

"I'll have to keep holding you. To keep you warm. Just in case."

"Alright," I answer softly. Though it's a physical intimacy I'm not used to, even with hook ups, I allow him to hold me in all the places my sports bra and spandex shorts don't, a warm palm resting against the outside of my thigh and the other on my waist. My head falls back into the crook of his neck lazily, and I enjoy the slowing of his heart against my shoulder as his breathing returns to normal.

"What happened?" he asks after a few minutes of silence.

"My back."

He sighs. "You played through it beautifully."

The compliment knocks me off balance. Aleksandr squeezes me once, and I remember I haven't explained fully. "I wanted to do a full ice bath after press, but I was too tired. I just turned the water on and got in."

"Why are you so tired? We had a short recovery session yesterday and your match was quick." At my silence, he pulls away, frowning again. Ruining my hard work. "You didn't go to the gym last night, did you?"

With a sigh, I admit, "I was up late watching old matches."

The disappointment is immediate, and it bothers me more than it should. "Nic, we've talked about this. You need sleep. You're playing a match a day at these 500s. Recovery is more important than anything right now, and that includes sleep. What were you watching? You've played a near perfect tournament."

"You think so?" I ask, hoping to divert his attention.

"Of course I do. You haven't dropped a set. It's like you've been playing on clay this whole time while people are still finding their sea legs." Right as I believe I've successfully distracted him, he asks again, with more force, "What were you watching?"

"The Indian Wells final, okay? I was watching myself lose to your sister again and again and again."

The tension in his face releases with his sigh. He shifts me so I'm on the bench beside him, and the loss of his warmth feels like a punishment. Hands resting softly on my shoulders, he turns me until they ghost over my back. A lingering shiver races through me. "Alright if I massage it?"

I nod, and he begins softly, then deeper until I can't help the moan that sighs out of me when he hits exactly where it's tight.

Aleksandr clears his throat. "This knot is like a rock."

"I'm an intense person."

A chuckle rumbles from his chest. "I like the self-awareness." His hands keep going until the knot weakens and the tension in my lower back dissipates. "Think you'll be okay for back-to-back matches tomorrow and Sunday?"

Back-to-back. He's assuming I'll win tomorrow. His confidence in me couldn't be clearer.

"I'll have a week at home to recuperate."

"Not what I asked."

I sigh. "I'll be fine, Aleksandr. Stop worrying about me."

"I find that to be an impossibility. You're constantly doing things that worry me."

Turning back to him, I raise an eyebrow. "Maybe that says more about you than it does me."

His small smirk is back. He starts pulling his quarter-zip off, and of course, beneath it, he's wearing his beefy boy shirt that barely covers him. The sweatshirt lifts his shirt up until I'm forced to see the cut of his abs. I don't look away quickly enough before he's holding the quarter-zip out to me with the holes for the arms extended, his smile growing. "You seem to like when I raise my arms. Fan of my hard work?"

I roll my eyes, shoving my arms into the sleeves and allowing him to tug the soft cotton over my head until I'm enveloped in both his warmth and his scent. Citrus and something spicy. "Tired of you inappropriately flashing me, more like. Do you own anything that isn't two sizes too tight and short on you?"

"I can't help being muscular. It's a product of the job."

"Is it?" I ask seriously. "You're training others. Not yourself."

He shrugs. "I'm in the gym so often, just makes sense to exercise too."

For maybe the first time in my life, I can read someone. Pick up on subtext that usually leaves me an outsider. Something about Aleksandr allows me to understand that there's more than what he's telling me. It's a rush. How embarrassing to be so excited to understand social interaction. "I don't believe you."

He exhales sharply, maybe surprised I've called him out. "You know how it is being the child of top players. There was a lot of pressure to be the best from the moment I was born, particularly as the oldest. They're great parents, but there was…an insane amount of pressure," he reiterates. "Four major titles wasn't enough to get them off my back. So I lifted to blow off steam and it stuck, an outlet when I'm frustrated."

"And I frustrate you *that* much?" I ask, gesturing at his bicep.

A gruff chuckle. "Sometimes, but no. I've been…" A beat as he collects his thoughts. "After I quit, my parents were more upset than I've ever seen them. They took that out on my siblings, ratcheting up the pressure on all three of them. Natasha is on the cusp of quitting because she can't stand it, and Dima and Anya are struggling. It's part of the reason I was working with them. So I could be there to guide them through our parents'…wishes. And while I'm not training them, you all play the same tournaments, which allows me to be available when they, Natasha especially, need me."

And suddenly it's all clear. The guilt I've noticed when he talks about leaving the sport has nothing to do with regretting it being over. He believes it's his fault his parents are pushing the other three so hard.

Before I can stop myself, I set a hand on his. "You shouldn't blame yourself for that. Their aspirations for the four of you are on them. The pressure on your siblings isn't your fault, Aleksandr."

There's an unconvinced tilt to his brows when he glances at where we're touching, and I snatch my hand back.

"And what about your parents?" he asks.

I'm not ready to leave the conversation behind, but I sense he's done. "I don't know much about parental pressure, I guess. The last time I saw my parents was"—I tilt my head, contemplating—"in Madrid two years ago. They happened to be there visiting my mom's friend. Didn't tell me until the day of, though I'm sure they knew I'd be there for the tournament."

"Do you talk on the phone much or…?"

I think of the last time I spoke with my mother, nearly a week ago. How they've made no effort to plan the next call and ignored the one text I sent to set it up. "We pretend we do. Claim we'll talk every week, but it's more like once a month. For a couple of minutes. Mostly about their trips." I lift a shoulder. "They don't have much to say to me unless I've won something."

"Jesus fu—" He cuts himself off with an angry laugh, shaking his head. "That's a different kind of pressure."

"Maybe." I shrug once more, feigning nonchalance. "I don't mind. What twenty-five-year-old needs to be talking to their parents all the time?"

"I would argue a lot of people in their twenties talk to

their parents often. More so for people born outside of the US."

"One more thing that makes me 'not like most people,'" I say sullenly.

"Do you have any other family you talk to?"

I clasp my hands. "It's been just me for a while now. It's not a big deal, Aleksandr. I have the girls and Karolína and Pen. Noah and Austin. I'm good."

"And me. You have me."

Scoffing, I say, "I don't have you. Who knows how long this will last? You're just here to help me with my strength and conditioning temporarily."

"Wow." His eyes flash. "And Karolína is *just* your coach and Pen is *just* the person who helps you with press and sponsorships."

"It's not the same."

"Why not? I've spent more time with you the last week than they have. Do they know about your parents? Do they know how much you miss Greece? How much you hate being touched without warning? Do they know that you have to bounce the ball four times before you serve, and if you mess up, you have to start again? Or that when you return, you have to fix your strings and hit both your shoes to feel prepared for the next point? Do they know that, when your eyes turn stormy gray, it means you're going to be at the gym, training when you shouldn't be?" At my shocked expression, he finishes with a, "That's what I thought."

"So just because I've been a little vulnerable with you a couple of times, you think that means 'we're...what? What do you think that means?"

"It means more than you're making it out to be, that's for sure."

"I..."

Aleksandr sighs, running a hand through his hair until the locks stick up at a funny angle. "I know it takes you longer to trust people, but I'm not sure what else you need from me to believe that I'm here for you. That I want to watch you succeed. That I want you to win a slam, not because it will get you your parents' attention or the adoration of the public, but because you work harder than anyone and you deserve it." He pulls two small boxes from beside him.

I eye them, one a glossy white with a gold foil tie, the other more unassuming, made of thick brown paper, the corners taped. I didn't notice them until now.

"What is this?"

"You talked about how much you missed home, so..." He nods for me to open them. I do, finding baklava in the first. Five pieces cut into neat diamonds, the top layers crisp and glistening with honey syrup that's pooled at the corners. Walnuts and pistachios peek through flaky phyllo layers, and the warm, sweet, and unmistakably familiar smell of my yiayia's house wraps around me.

Instantly, I regret my attempt to push him back into my mental box labeled *strangers*. I claim I want to be prioritized, but when someone finally does that, I don't allow them to.

"Open the other too."

I listen and find three golden-brown triangles nestled in the bag, the combination of butter and spinach enough to make my mouth water. Spanakopita. "Where did you get this?"

He stands. "Like I said, I know how much you miss Greece. Found a couple of places after dinner last night."

"Dinner ended at nine." I'm not sure there's a single Greek restaurant or bakery around this area, which means he took a rideshare. Probably far.

His right shoulder lifts. "I'm persistent." He starts to walk away. Sharp movements tell me he's upset. Over his shoulder he says, "See you at warmup tomorrow. I trust you can do your own cooldown today."

I stare at the gifts in awe, then obliterate half of each box. When I finish cooldown, half an hour of film with Karolína, dinner, and finally make it back to my room, I stare at my phone.

After changing Aleks' name in my contacts, I text him.

I'm sorry.

You're right. You are more to me.

You're my sweet treat delivery man.

ALEKS

Wow, three texts in a row and you made a joke?

I'm so capable of change.

ALEKS LAUGHED AT "I'M SO CAPABLE OF CHANGE."

He doesn't respond, and for reasons unknown, I'm desperate to keep our conversation going.

How did your night go?

ALEKS

Do you really care?

I frown, knowing it's my own fault that he would believe otherwise.

Wouldn't ask if I didn't.

ALEKS

It was good. Sketched. Natasha needed to talk so we went on a walk.

YOU LIKED "IT WAS GOOD. SKETCHED. NATASHA NEEDED TO TALK SO WE WENT ON A WALK."

Biting my lip, I type then delete three different messages. The first is a question about sketching, the second is to ask if his sister is alright, and the third is a frustrated string of letters that mean nothing. Before I can find the right thing to say or fling my phone at the wall, he responds.

ALEKS

I'll forgive you if you share.

Too late, I ate them all.

I include a photo so he can see the damage I've managed in a matter of hours. He never stood a chance.

ALEKS

Then you have nothing more to offer me for my forgiveness.

Drama king.

ALEKS

Says the woman who nearly drowned
herself in a non-ice ice bath.

Good night, Aleks.

ALEKS

Good night, solnyshko.

thirteen

Charleston's unique gray-green clay sticks to my sweaty body as I stand on the baseline, one game away from being this year's Charleston Open champion. I wipe a hand on my maroon split-skirt dress, then blow on my palm as Karolína yells encouragement from my box.

"One more, Nic! Right here." If I strain, I can almost make out which set of hands clapping is Aleks'.

After wiping away a bead of sweat traveling down the side of my face, I bounce the ball four times, toss it into the air, and slap it into play. Jenny Wooledge gets it back at the last second, an accidental drop shot that brings me to the net. A well-placed cross-court shot to her ad side. A ball slapped right at me that I volley cross court again, right inside the service line.

"Fifteen, love," the chair umpire says after its second bounce. The crowd cheers, loud whoops ringing out, and a quick chant of "Nic! Nic! Nic!" imbue me with an electric energy. Adrenaline and excitement course through my veins, where two days ago there was only exhaustion.

Three points away. I don't know if it's just that I'm winning or if I'm finally enjoying this sport that seemed a chore not so long ago.

Wipe away the sweat. Bounce the ball four times. Toss it into the air. Slap it into play. Ace.

"Thirty, love."

More cheering.

Wipe away the sweat. Bounce the ball four times. Toss it into the air. Slap it into play. She gets it back this time, and it's a backhand cross-court duel. Every time she thinks I might change it up, I keep it cross court, wearing her down until she makes a mistake, hits a ball a little too short, right in my strike zone, and I put it away down the line.

I barely hear the umpire's "forty, love" over the roaring crowd.

Grabbing my towel, I wipe away the sweat on my face and shoulders, trying to mentally set myself up for the match point. The media has accused me of not being the best closer, and I'm not going to be felled by that today.

"Thank you, ladies and gentlemen." It takes the chair umpire two tries to get them to quiet after I've lined up at the baseline. "Thank you."

My mind tells me to take it all in, look at the crowd and soak in what I'm about to achieve. But I haven't done it yet, so…

Wipe away a bead of sweat. Bounce the ball four times. Toss it into the air. Slap it into play. Her return slides into the net, and it's over.

"Come on!" I shout, pumping a fist as I find Karolína, Pen, Delilah, and Aleks all standing and clapping for me.

"Game, set, and match, Vassilakis. 7–5, 6–4."

I make the quick walk to the net, where I shake Jenny's hand. "Great match," we say in unison. I thank the umpire before I let my smile take over my face, basking in the crowd's praise. I wave to one side of the stadium, then to the three others.

The trophy ceremony and speeches move quickly, and before I know it, I've made it to the players' gym for my cooldown before press and photos. Karolína holds out her arms for a hug, and I'm excited enough, I don't mind. Another for Pen and Delilah, who squeeze me tightly.

"Told you you could do it," she whispers. "The season of Nic."

"Maybe."

She sets a hand on her chest, comically affronted. "Maybe? You just won the first clay tournament of the season! This is everything you needed to prove to yourself and the world that you're a force to be reckoned with on clay. Roland Garros, here you come!"

The words are so kind, I force a wider smile and squeeze her hand briefly. I try not to let my friends see how much I struggle with what the media says about me or the fact that I'm a disappointing failure when compared to my mother and my accolades as a junior. Telling them would serve no purpose other than bringing them down with me. But of everyone, Delilah has witnessed it up close the most.

My eyes slide to Aleks, who stands behind the rest of my team, leaning against the wall with his arms crossed lazily, a grin on his face. Like there was no alternative ending to this tournament in his mind.

I give Delilah another small smile. "You're right. It's good news for the season. It'll certainly help my ranking."

So why does the voice in my head keep saying, *Don't stop now. Keep the momentum. Get in the gym. Finish this.* It plays on a loop, and regardless of how exciting it was to hold up the trophy, how exciting it was to have the crowd cheering for me, nothing will quiet the sound. This is a small title, after all. I need bigger ones. WTA1000s and Grand Slams.

When does it end? When do you stop pushing yourself so hard that you collapse? When? Now Aleks' voice joins, tangling with mine, rattling so loudly, I have to shove my nails into my palms to get out of my head.

It's after dark by the time I've finished my cooldown, pressers, taken photos with the trophy, and had dinner with my team. As I pass the front desk of the hotel, a staff member flags me down, a large bouquet of flowers in his hands.

"Miss Vassilakis!" he calls, and I break away from my team, waving them to go ahead without me. Aleks eyes the man before disappearing into the elevator hall around the corner with Pen and Karolína.

"Yes?" I ask him.

The man holds up the vase. "These are for you. Delivered an hour ago. Should I have them sent to your room?"

I eye the muted pink and white roses, accented with other similarly colored flowers that I can't name. It screams my mother, and I take the glass vase. "I've got them, thank you."

Waiting until I get to my room to check the card proves difficult, so I hold the vase against the elevator wall with my hip and grab the small white cardstock in the middle.

Congratulations, Nicola. A job well done. Let's discuss this week. – CAV

The elevator jolts to a stop on my floor, and I grip the vase tightly, holding it to my chest as I make my way to my room.

My mother knows I won a tournament. She's proud of me. It's so shocking a sentiment that, when I get inside, I set them on a table and sit beside them, staring at the card until the words blur. Only when my cheeks numb do I realize I've been smiling. All the hope I've been hoarding that one day I'd get something, *anything*, out of my mom trumpets in triumph. It's not my first 500 win, but it feels significantly more important than the other three, which were met with silence, a text message, and a letter, respectively. Like each time I win one, I fall more and more onto her radar.

I'll have to find a way to get these to my apartment.

After sending a thank you text to my parents, I search the internet for anything about my win. About me. I click the first and begin getting ready for bed as it plays.

It's commentary over highlights from the match. In it, I'm hitting an ace. "Rising star Nicola Vassilakis takes home her first title of the year in Charleston today, and I have to say, she looked like she belonged there. Don't you agree, Gene?" a woman asks.

"Oh, absolutely," a male voice joins hers. "Vassilakis has struggled a lot since she aged up into the pros, with injuries and disappointing performances, but this season, things are certainly getting better. Her level of play has been spectacular, and though she didn't win them, her matches during the Australian Open, Doha, and Indian Wells have us all asking ourselves if she could be sniffing out a major title this year."

The screen cuts to a studio, where a middle-aged man in a suit sits beside a poised woman in a forest-green peplum top, match highlights continuing on the screen behind them.

The woman nods. "She's put herself in a great position for Madrid and potentially Roland Garros. Both tournaments will be big for her: she's the daughter of Carmen Aguirre, four-time Madrid champion in addition to her three major titles." I glance at the flowers on the table behind me, as if I need the confirmation once more that, though I've not done anything to live up to her reputation, she's proud of me. "And Roland Garros was the last major tournament Nicola won before she aged up."

The man, Gene, adds, "I've enjoyed watching her this season. This week especially, she's played some incredible tennis. For those who are unaware, power hitters like Vassilakis typically have more success on hard court and grass, where quicker points are favored. But she dug in this week and, I think, has proved to many that she's good on any surface. She's set herself up to be one of the, if not *the* favorite for both tournaments. I can't wait to see how the year goes for her."

"Me too. Now onto the men's tour…"

I click out of the video with a small, bubbly sigh, wiping off my makeup with languid strokes of a cotton pad. I should probably rest before our flight to Orlando tomorrow, but the boost my confidence received from the flowers and compliments is a high I'm desperately chasing. I find another video and press play, washing the rest of my makeup off.

Jackson and a sandy-haired man in his early thirties sit side by side at the modern Tennis Broadcast desk, a massive screen behind them cycling through match statistics and shot placement graphics for matches happening in Monaco. When the screen switches to highlights of my match, Jackson says, "As for the women, I think we can safely say Nicola is on her way to big things this year."

The sandy-haired man, who I'm remembering is named Sam—or maybe Dan—scoffs. "I'm not sure we can *safely* say that."

Jackson's frown matches my own. "What do you mean?"

"I mean, we've seen her get to these big tournaments and struggle in the ninth hour, right? A 500 is great, but she hasn't been able to close in bigger tournaments. You have to remember, she's never won a pro major or a 1000."

Toweling off my face, I peer at my phone. The difference between my and Jenny's first-serve percentages slide onto the screen, followed closely by our winners-to-errors ratios. The juxtaposition between this guy's words and what the screen says is enough to make me laugh sardonically.

"That may be true, but that's also true of plenty of players on the tour. She's won Charleston now, and she'll have lots of opportunities this year to win bigger tournaments. The fact that she's made it to so many big finals three months into the season is proof she's almost there."

"Sure, but she also lost in all three of those big finals. She'd been playing well at the start of all three tournaments before her level kind of fell off in the last couple of matches. And her semis match in Miami was abysmal."

"How many 1000s did you win?" Jackson asks. A joke, I think.

"None."

Jackson's expression remains open, like he's still joking, but with a bite, he answers, "Right. Nic is closing in on her first and has plenty of years left in the tank. I'm sure she'll get it figured out."

Sam/Dan shrugs, arms up in defense. "All I'm saying is I'm not sure she's cut out for a major title. More likely, I believe we'll see another major this year go to Emilia Kessler, one to Anya Morozov, and Roland Garros to either of them or Valentina Ortega."

Jackson stares at Sam/Dan for a moment before turning back to the camera. "Anyway…"

But I'm not interested in hearing more of this. I click out, swiping open the group chat that's been going off for the last few minutes.

SHOTS FIRED

SAHAR

Nic did the mf thingggg

HARPER

So proud of you! Can't wait to celebrate when we're back home!

AUSTIN

Hey, props Nic. That's big

In more important news, I'm having girl
problems

DELILAH

Booooooo

MATTEO EMPHASIZED "BOOOOOOO"

NOAH

Thirding, it's Nic's night.

Someone help him with his problems
before he blows up the chat.

NOAH

Dude has so many problems, I'm not sure
there's enough time left on this planet
for that

Ignoring the rest of the messages that come through, I open Instagram, biting back a grimace when I note the thousands of notifications. Thank god for Pen handling this most of the time.

A cursory glance over the comments tells me enough.

The WTA account posted my match point from today, and Pen accepted collaboration on the post. When I scroll, I see no less than fifty comments saying the same thing as Jackson's co-broadcaster.

@bradley.grindz.1029: Wow, one 500 win. Big deal. Let's see her actually do well at a Grand Slam

@CallOfDoodieKing2576:   @bradley.grindz.1029 she literally can't, she's a choker

@bradley.grindz.1029:   @CallOfDoodieKing2576 what I've been saying, she's good until she has to close

There are plenty more like that, but the lump lodged in my throat is about as big as a tennis ball, angry tears heating my eyes. The flowers were a momentary balm for my insecurities. But even paired with the kind words from broadcasters and my friends, they're no longer enough.

And though I've worked so hard to rewire the habit this week, I throw my phone into my gym bag, change into spandex shorts and a tank top, and grab my room key so I can do what I do best.

fourteen

For the second time this week, Aleks stands outside the hotel gym, waiting for me. His phone is pressed to his ear, and when he notices me, he says, "Natasha, I've got to go."

"Get out of my way," I grit as I try to push past him.

He doesn't budge. "No."

"How do you always know when this is going to happen? Or do you spend all of your time standing outside of the nearest gym? What's your hits-to-misses ratio now?" I ask, hoping to get under his skin.

"I have a 100% success rate. Because I know you."

I roll my eyes. "Ante pali." *Here we go again.*

Instead of getting angry like I thought he might, he opens his arms. I stare at them for a few moments, pretending I don't understand what the gesture means, but the façade is cracking. I step into his body, resting my arms against his chest and my head in the crook between his shoulder and neck. It's comforting, each point of contact warm and safe, and smells of citrus and a spice I can't place. Clove, maybe? We fit in a way I wouldn't have expected, and when his arms wrap around me, it's everything I didn't realize I needed. The tears that threatened to fall earlier break free.

He gives me the few moments I need to put myself back together before saying, "How about we go for a walk, yeah?"

I nod, patting my face dry. The neck of his shirt is wet, and I glance away, embarrassed. "Okay," I say softly.

Aleks' eyebrows knit together, like it pains him to see me like this. He reaches toward me, perhaps meaning to wipe away the rest of my tears, but stops himself, instead turning to lead me back to the stairwell and outside.

Warm coastal air greets us, tinged with salt. The headlights of cars on Wando Bridge glow in the distance, steady enough to look like they're strung like pearls over the river. Crickets chirp as we amble toward the children's park near The Kingstide, where a wooden pier juts out quietly into the dark. Streetlamps cast golden pools along the sidewalk, the Sunday evening foot traffic slowed to a trickle.

"What gave me away?" I ask once I'm sure my voice won't break on the words.

"You looked like you couldn't get out of your head in the players' gym before your cooldown. Not as excited about the win as I'd hoped you'd be."

I sigh. "Press didn't help."

He grinds to a stop. "Did someone say something to you? Ask something in a degrading manner?" A muscle in his jaw ticks.

"No, not my press today. Though they were the usual

bloodhounds they tend to be. I saw the Tennis Broadcast with Jackson and Sam? Dan? He had a lot to say about my ability to win in big moments, and people online echoed the sentiment."

A soft breeze stirs the trees lining the quiet street, and we start walking again. "Sounds about right. Nobody can ever truly win anything with social media around, can they? Bunch of fucking trolls."

"I guess it just…it echoed what I was already worried about. That I'm not a closer. That I may never be able to win in those big moments. I mean, you saw me against Anya. And in Doha and Melbourne, if you watched those. I had opportunities, and I squandered them."

"Solnyshko, I do not give a single fuck what those mean-spirited, little-dicked individuals have to say about you. You closed today. You've done it plenty of other times. Just because it's a 500 doesn't mean you didn't have to work your ass off to win it." His hand brushes against mine, and I have to rein in the current that snakes through me. "In my opinion, winning those bigger tournaments often comes down to endurance. That's why I want to do extra conditioning this week before Stuttgart so we can make sure you're physically prepared for a Madrid final or an Italy final or a Roland Garros final. Or all three."

"You have more faith in me than I do."

"I have endless faith in you. You're utterly spec-tacular."

My head drops as I try to hide the blush warming my cheeks. Hopefully it's dark enough that he doesn't notice.

We reach the pier, where marsh grass hugs the rails of the boardwalk, brushing against it like gentle fingers.

Clearing my throat, I say, "My mother sent me flowers today."

"Yeah? Does she do that often?"

I shake my head. "It's never happened." Moonlight dances over the water. "I can't remember a time in my life where I ever felt seen by her or my father. Or anyone, really."

Until you.

It comes unbidden, hanging in the air, unsaid. Aleks shifts closer, like he heard it all the same. "And the flowers made you feel seen today?"

Did they make me feel seen? Not exactly. More like she hasn't entirely forgotten my existence, and that there are still things I can accomplish that will turn her head in my general direction. A newfound hope that things could change for the better between us. "I wouldn't go that far. But it's the first time I've felt like she was proud of me since turning eighteen."

Aleks hums, and when I glance at him, I can't figure out what the look on his face means.

"What?"

"Nothing."

"Aleks."

"No, it's just…I can't imagine not being proud of you for all the things you've achieved. But what do I know? I was proud when you tried sweet tea for the first time."

"You *are* surprisingly easy to please."

He lets out a derisive chuckle. "If only you knew."

"Huh?"

Shaking his head, he leans against the wood railing,

watching me. "Nothing. Speaking of sweet tea, what have you learned about yourself this week?"

My eyebrows furrow at the change in topic, but I say, "I like sunrise walks, sea bass, longan, and winning tournaments. And being sent flowers by my mother."

"Look at you. That's five whole things you now know about yourself, even if a couple are tennis related."

"Oh yeah. Watch out everyone. I'm so much more than a failed tennis prodigy."

Aleks tsks, bumping his body against mine. "Stop that. Each additional second spent talking about your mother's titles or where you were 'supposed to be' at this point in your life will result in a lap around the track added to your workout every day next week."

"Oooo," I say, wiggling my fingers, "I'm so scared."

"Fine, you'll be running extra liners instead."

My mouth snaps shut, and Aleks chuckles. He guides me back the way we came, the weight of the positives and negatives of the day lifting off my body.

"Did you ever do this? Lose yourself in tennis so badly, you needed to learn new things about yourself?" I ask.

"Where do you think I got the idea?"

I look at him from the corner of my eye, watching light and shadows play across his face. His smile is subdued yet more genuine than many he plasters on. He's so good at this, at pulling me from the darkness, that I have to wonder if it's not solely himself he's done this for, but his sisters and brother too.

"What sorts of things did you do?"

"One time, at a lower-level tournament, I told myself I

wanted to hit ten tweeners for the fun of it. Suffice to say, I did not win that match."

The image of him moving toward a ball with the intention of hitting it between his legs, then trying to do that ten times in one match, startles a laugh out of me. The subdued smile turns to that lit-from-within grin that takes over his whole face, like there's nothing he'd rather do than make me laugh. "Another time, I tried underhanded serves. My parents were *not* happy with me for that."

"Those aren't unrelated to tennis, but what did you learn about yourself?" I parrot his usual question back to him.

"That I enjoy tennis way more when I'm afforded the ability to be silly."

Smiling softly at my feet on the paved road, I ask, "What other sorts of things?"

"Why? Trying to copy my answers so you don't have to put in the work?"

I shove him. "This is what I get for trying to learn more about you. I should have known." I march away from him playfully, in far better spirits than before.

Joking. Messing around. Learning about myself just by existing beside Aleks.

"No, wait! I'll tell you!" His steps are loud behind me until he catches up. "I learned I like to draw. That if I actually apply myself, I'm sometimes good at it. That I prefer limeade over lemonade. That pineapple absolutely, unequivocally does not belong on pizza."

"I'll have you know it was a Greek man who invented that. Don't speak ill of my people." We cross the threshold of the side entrance of the hotel, moving toward the elevators.

"Not your people. Just their more questionable choices."

I hum, pressing the up button, then walk in as the doors open. Over the course of the ride, his expression changes, growing solemn.

"What are you thinking about?" The elevator chimes, and we walk toward my room, fishing my key card out of my bag.

"It's funny," he answers roughly as we reach my door, "that the best day of my life, the day I did the biggest, bravest thing I could possibly do for myself, gave me so much relief but ended so poorly for my siblings."

My step toward him is involuntary, as is the hand I set on his firm shoulder, my body moving before my brain processes. "If you want me to listen to you about not over-training, then you have to listen to me when I say you didn't ruin their lives by taking charge of yours. Granted, I don't have siblings and I'm not sure that even if I did, my personality would create these same feelings in me, but I do know that all your siblings are adults and equally capable of making decisions." My voice drops. "Have you talked to any of them about this? Maybe if you all came together and worked through it, you might come to a solution?"

It's weird setting aside my dislike for Anya. But if it means helping him appreciate that just because he's the eldest doesn't mean he's responsible for the way his parents are, that he doesn't have to let the guilt overwhelm him, eat him from the inside, I'll let it pass without too much thought.

Aleks shakes his head. "I don't like to talk to them about it. Nobody in my family knows why I left."

"Why?" I ask softly.

"Because they're still dealing with it. How selfish would it be for me to express relief that I got out when they're still in it? When they may not have the same ability to go against my parents' wishes, or haven't found anything else in life they'd want to do instead?"

I tilt my head, allowing his words to wash over me. I don't think it would be selfish, especially if it helps them, but maybe I'm not looking at it the way he is. Maybe I lack his unique perspective on the situation.

It frustrates me that I can't immediately find an answer to make him feel better when he's so good at doing that for me.

His serious expression is replaced by a smile. Not the one that lights his whole face, but the one he puts on to cover his true emotions. My hand drops as he steps closer, pressing me against the door of my hotel room. I'm rooted to the spot, staring back into his eyes. I should say goodbye, swipe my key card, and go to sleep but…

Maybe it's the roller coaster of a day I've had, or maybe it's that I haven't been touched intimately in months. Or *maybe* it's that the smallest sliver of me recognizes that our relationship has changed significantly in the last couple of weeks and the attraction I've been fighting is going nowhere.

"More importantly, are you sure you're still uninterested in my flirting? Should I dial it back up again?"

If it's a way to divert my attention, my body doesn't care, my heart skittering when his fingers brush against my hip. My stomach dances at his proximity, electricity flooding my brain at the prospect of sharing his air, his breath. I look away, over his shoulder, for the sake of plausible deniability. "Your will-he-won't-he act is giving me whiplash."

He leans forward, his lips brushing mine, soft and warm and featherlight, and I want more. A quiet sound not unlike a moan escapes me, my body forever betraying me in his presence. Aleks chuckles, his lips still touching mine. Still exchanging air. "Oh, solnyshko, if you wanted me to kiss you, all you had to do was ask."

I huff, disgruntled. When I can form words again, I say, "Keep dreaming. And you're only doing this to distract me from the conversation about your siblings." It's a win that I'm able to identify that. That I've learned enough about him, I can tell his intentions by which smile he wears.

He doesn't respond, simply takes the key card out of my hand and swipes me into my room, pushing the door open for me. I nearly fall backward, but his hand on my waist keeps me upright.

"Guess you'll have to be satiated by that, then." He squeezes my side once before he's gone, down the hall and into an elevator, winking over his shoulder.

fifteen

Five days later, after Harper, Sahar, and Noah have filed out of our apartment post movie, Delilah and I begin cleaning, returning it to its former glory. We right the L-shaped couch so it's centered along the wall, below the amalgam of odd art Delilah has accumulated over the years. At first, it felt like an eyesore in the space—though who was I to complain, seeing as it was her apartment first—but it's grown on me.

Tossing a blanket into the basket beside the TV stand, Delilah asks, "Do you want to watch terrible reality TV?"

It's an invitation that I so badly want to accept. It's been months since we've been alone in our apartment together, lazing on the couch after offseason days, watching braindead television. It's what we've been doing every night since I arrived in Orlando, but today was my rest day, and I'm too antsy to sit around anymore. Five days since the win, and I'm ready to be back on court, pushing for another title.

"Rain check. I'm going to go for a swim." Hopefully Aleks won't fault me for it. It's better than the gym.

Delilah pins me with an incredulous look. "Nic, it's dark out. Your bedtime routine starts soon."

"I have energy building that I need to dispel." I walk to my bedroom, searching my drawers for a bikini, sweatshirt, and shorts. "Be back soon," I call over my shoulder.

Unfortunately, my best friend is annoying in the best of times and refuses to leave well enough alone in the worst. She follows me. "You know, some might advise you that sex is a great way to dispel energy. Have you thought about that? Perhaps with anyone in particular?"

"Shut up, Del."

She stands in my doorway, eyeing the empty walls. She'd have lots to cover them with, but I'm not here enough to care what it feels like. My duvet is a dark green, with two matching pillows, and my mid-century modern wooden nightstands are devoid of knickknacks or personality. The only décor is a small bookshelf, which houses self-help books I've yet to read, the wilting flowers my mother sent me—still with no follow-up call in sight—and my trophies, my junior slam ones front and center.

"I'm obviously joking," she continues while I change, "but for argument's sake, let's say I'm not. Where do we stand on a romp with your sexy performance coach?"

Rolling my eyes, I shimmy into my shorts and toss the sweatshirt that sat on top of my dresser—after hours of packing and repacking ended with me not knowing what to do with it—over my head. The sharp scent of what I'm calling clove envelops me, followed closely by citrus, and being wrapped in it is almost as soothing as the hug Aleks and I shared.

Delilah watches me, her grin expanding until it takes over her face. "Oh, that's new! Whose is that?" She nods to where the sleeves fall past my hands, the hem of the quarter-zip covering the bottoms of my shorts.

I'm between a rock and a hard place now. If I take it off, I'll have to explain why I kept Aleks' sweatshirt; worse, I'll then have to explain why I've used it since he pulled it over me. But if I leave it on, I risk being seen in it. Clearing my throat, I shoot for nonchalance with the latter. "I don't know what you're talking about. This is my sweatshirt. I've had it for years."

"Oh right. Totally. Yes. Okay, sounds good!" Right as I believe I'm going to be safe from her pesky questions, she turns back around. "Oh, last thing. *Do* you have plans to hook up with your hot performance coach? We've got a pot going, and I'd love to win."

"You're a terrible gambler," I mutter.

"Lie. And you're deflecting."

"I was trying not to dignify it with a response. Of course I'm not going to sleep with him." At her narrowed eyes, I set my hands on my hips. "Why would I? We're going to be working together until at least the beginning of June. Doesn't seem like a good idea to start our professional relationship with a bang."

Delilah snickers, tossing her braid over her shoulder. "Even if you both clearly want to?"

"That's absurd." Too quick. I said that much too fast, and she's picked up on it.

"So there has been zero sexual tension since you began working together?"

"Do you really care this much about a bet?"

"No. I care this much about you. I want my best friend to tell me what's going on in her life."

Her words have the intended impact. With a sigh, I say, "Nothing has happened. At least nothing of substance." Delilah leans against the doorway, locking in for details. "There have been a couple of times where I thought we'd kiss. But this week has been back to normal, like nothing happened. And that's for the best because nothing should happen."

"But if it did?"

I shrug helplessly. "I don't know, Del. There's a reason I refuse to spend extra time with the people I sleep with."

"And what is that reason?"

Shaking my head, I grab my wallet, keys, and phone. There's not enough time in the world to detail the laundry list of issues I appear to have, as evidenced by the multitude of people who've found me strange and off-putting my entire life. "I'm going to go."

Delilah sighs. "I just want you to have fun, Nic. From what I've noticed, you haven't been hooking up with anyone lately, and that was, like, your one outlet. You're so…determined all the time, and it leaves little room for you to enjoy yourself. I think he'd be good for you."

Clearly I'm not operating as under the radar as I'd hoped.

I bite back a retort, trying so hard not to lash out at the one person in my life who's never deserved it. Softly, I answer, "I'll keep that in mind. Thank you."

"Do you want me to come with you?"

"Aren't you planning on sleeping soon?" She's been shifting her sleep schedule to prepare for Madrid in a week and a half, though I'm pretty sure Matteo being six hours ahead has also factored into it.

She shrugs. "Don't have to."

I smile gratefully. Or at least I hope I do. "I'll be fine, but thank you. Sleep so you can talk to Matteo in the morning."

Her cheeks pink, and with a wave, I'm out the door.

It doesn't take long to get to the state-of-the-art Olympic-size swimming pool on the Morozov Tennis Academy campus. There are very few people training in Orlando right now since the men are playing in Europe and the women will follow soon. Adding on the fact that it's Thursday evening, the pool is gloriously empty.

Chlorine worms its way into my nose, but the light refracting around the large room distracts from the near singe of it. I pull my sweatshirt and shorts off, tossing my stuff onto a nearby bench before easing into the pool. It's the perfect temperature, a comfort to my sore muscles.

Aleks has made it his mission to ensure that, though I'm taking my rest days (which, reluctantly, I have been), I'm also cursing him on training days. On-court footwork with Karolína to integrate our training, agility work on the field, lifting and recovery in the gym. I'm rarely this sore, and it's more welcome than I'd ever admit to him.

I wasn't lying when I told Delilah that things are back to normal. Aleks has backed off with his flirting once more. Marginally. The few times things grew tense between us, he smiled and told me, "You know what you need to say to change things," and continued what we were doing.

I've yet to figure out what he wants. On the surface, I understand that he wants to prevent me from burning out the way he did. But there has to be more to it than that, right? And does he flirt with everyone, or does it mean something? There's an unwanted (at least on my end) attraction between us, and I have no idea what to do with it. Probably for the best if, like I told Delilah, it goes nowhere.

My arms slice through the water, putting me into a meditative state. When I grab the diving block after a particularly tiring lap, pulling air into my lungs, a male voice says, "You're supposed to be resting."

I gasp loudly. My hand slips, and I fall beneath the surface for a moment, resurfacing with a cough as I attempt to get rid of the water lodged in my lungs.

As though I conjured him, Aleks stands beside the diving block with his arms crossed. His eyebrows are drawn, but there's a hint of a smile on his face, and I'm not sure I like it, whatever it may mean. The limited lighting lends an azure tint to his eyes and makes the locks of hair falling all over themselves appear darker.

"This is getting concerning. Are you following me? Stalking me?"

"No," he answers, running a frustrated hand through his hair. "Natasha got into a fight with our parents over her wanting to take a break, which ended with her in tears. I was at the gym and took her home but left my stuff behind. I saw you when I came back to pick it up. Figured I'd check on you."

An image of Oleg and Iryna Morozov ganging up on the shyest of their four children to the point of tears pops into my head. I imagine Aleks stepping in front of her, taking the heat like he always does, and it makes my chest ache.

"Is she okay?"

He nods. "Yes. She's at my apartment so she doesn't have to speak to them tonight."

"Good. Well, here I am. Didn't get enough energy out during my walk today. I'll go home soon."

"You're not supposed to be doing cardio today."

"It's not cardio. I'm doing a few laps so I can sleep tonight."

His eyes light, but he says nothing.

"Go away, Aleks. It's not like I'm lifting."

"It's still impacting your training. You're paying me to do a job. Let me do that job."

"Can you let me have *anything*?" I ask, a tremor finding its way into my voice. "This is the one way I can get my thoughts in check right now, alright? If I want a chance at sleeping, I need to quiet the voices that won't shut up. I've listened to you all week. I haven't done any lifting or boxing or anything outside of our training. Let me have this."

Pity dashes across his face, and I've never wanted to punch him more.

The expression is gone in a second, replaced with something wicked. "I'm going to grab you now."

"What? No! No, stop it!" He pulls me from the water effortlessly, which makes me angrier. I flail around, smacking his back and kneeing his chest when he throws me over his shoulder. "What the hell do you think you're doing?"

"Kidnapping you."

"You're crazy."

"Perhaps."

"Put me down, you *oaf*."

"Only if you agree to dry off, put your clothes on, and follow me."

"Sure. Or I could slice your carotid with my keys."

"Mm," he hums. "I like it when you're feisty." Under his breath, he says, "Though you're rarely anything else."

"Aleks, I swear to god I'll do it. Put. Me. Down."

"Now I'm certain I won't." He bends, probably grabbing my things from the bench, his left arm still holding me solidly to himself. A towel flies over my body. "There. Use that."

"Oh, yeah. Easy. I'll wrap myself in it while *being held hostage over your shoulder*." He's indifferent to the fact that the entire left side of his shirt is now drenched. Still, I refuse to use the towel in any capacity. I hope all the water transfers to him. "We can't take these towels. Put it back. And put me down, damn it."

His laugh vibrates against my legs, too close for comfort to where the sound travels low in my belly. "It's okay. I have an in with the owners."

"I'm going to kill you," I promise again.

"Got it. Understood. Though you should know those aforementioned owners are emotionally attached to me and probably wouldn't take too kindly to you bashing my head in, or slicing my neck, or any of the other murderous thoughts you're having about me in that pretty brain of yours."

I groan loudly, kneeing him once more but to no avail. Before long, we're in the parking lot and he's throwing a car door open and tossing me inside. I land with an unceremonious *ugh*, the towel, my clothes, and my wallet, keys, and phone heaped on top of me. Despite the force he's exhibited in the last minute, he gently nudges my legs out of the way before closing the door.

Soft leather and muted lighting greet me. It's surprisingly clean, though a half-empty bottle of Simply Limeade rests in a cupholder along with an unopened pack of Sour Patch Bites. In the back is a gym bag and a few folded T-shirts.

"This is a literal crime," I say when he slips into the driver's side, turning on the car.

"Even if I promise to take you somewhere you'll enjoy more than a facility swimming pool?"

My eyes narrow. "Is this a sex thing? Are you going to take me to a sex dungeon?"

Aleks chuckles, an eyebrow rising. "Are you saying you'd enjoy a sex dungeon more than swimming?"

"I—I—no!" With warm cheeks, I search for a way to reroute the conversation. "I'm just trying to figure out where you're taking me at nine fifteen on a Thursday."

"Somewhere you'll enjoy."

"*God*, you're infuriating."

"Does it make you want to strangle me? I'll admit, I like a little light choking action."

I whip around to glare at him. "Stop it."

Shrugging, he puts the car in drive and we're off. "I'm

simply telling you what I like so you feel comfortable telling me what you like. Figured it'd be good to get that conversation out of the way before the sex dungeon."

If my safety didn't depend on him focusing on the road, I would punch him right now. I really would.

"Aw, solnyshko. You're so cute when you're mad."

"Nobody in this lifetime has ever called me cute."

"Do you remember other lifetimes? Where people did call you cute?"

I rub the bridge of my nose between my thumb and forefinger, closing my eyes before I do something neither of us may recover from.

Deciding that the best course of action is to stop talking to him altogether, I put the towel to use, wrapping it around my body and bunching the sweatshirt so Aleks doesn't make out what it is.

After thirty minutes have passed, I eye him. "I have at least two weapons on my person. Killing me will be challenging."

He doesn't bat an eye, focus entirely on the highway. "That would be more believable if I weren't the one who dragged you from the pool. I know you have none."

"Anything can be a weapon if you try hard enough."

Aleks chuckles.

"Seriously? That's funny to you?"

"No. I'm just glad I'll never have to worry about your safety because I trust that, for you, it's true."

It's in no way praise, but a small smile works its way across my face. I turn toward the window so he can't see it, watching the expansive silhouette of undeveloped land fly by.

sixteen

A few minutes later, his phone rings loudly, startling us both. Anya's name flashes on the console screen, and though he declines the call, I glare out the window.

"By all means," I drawl sarcastically when the same ringtone plays a second time.

Aleks declines the call once more. "She's angry that I stepped away from her training. Been doing shit like this" —he nods toward the console—"for attention. She's fine."

I scan his features. For reasons unknown, though his siblings need him, I'm his priority. Taking me on a drive to prevent me from getting in extra cardio takes precedence over Natasha at his apartment and Anya's incessant calling.

It pulls on something inside my chest, a longing I haven't allowed myself to feel in years, outside of, perhaps, for my mother. A longing to be wanted and cared for and *seen*. And of everyone in my life, it's Aleks who's been affording me those things recently.

A rubber band snaps around my chest, tightening with

the realization that I might like him more than I ever believed I would.

"You know that conversation we had in Charleston? About how you don't want to tell your siblings why you left because you think it would be selfish?"

Aleks' gaze connects with mine, eyebrows stitching together. He nods.

"I've been contemplating it this week and…what if they believe they're alone in feeling the way they do? Natasha clearly is struggling with something similar, right? What if she thinks she doesn't have a choice? As far as she's concerned, you just fell out of love with the sport…" He's looking at me funny. "What?"

"No, I just…You're right. I've been going back and forth on it since you mentioned telling them. I'm just not sure how exactly to go about it."

"Oh." I'm surprised something I said held any merit or sway, since I have no experience with siblings or this kind of pressure. I nod. "Let her make an informed decision. Maybe if she realizes how similar her circumstance is to yours, she'll be more comfortable going against your parents."

He grins. "I thought you hated all Morozovs. Who knew you'd be such a sucker for Natasha?"

I roll my eyes. "I hate Morozovs who dedicate their lives to making me miserable. I also hate ones who talk shit about me and allow those words to end up in press conferences."

His hand twitches. "I didn't—"

"I know." I offer him a soft, reassuring smile.

"We're almost there. If your clothes are too wet, you

can grab a clean shirt from the back." His eyes drop to my lap, a cocky smirk on his lips. "Since you like my clothes so much."

Damn it. I curse past Nic for wearing his sweatshirt out of the sanctity of my apartment. "Don't flatter yourself. It was the first one I found." I refuse to give him the satisfaction of grabbing a shirt. If I have to partake in this activity wet and cold, so be it.

My phone buzzes a few times, and I open it to a wall of text messages from the girls.

SAHAR'S BAD BERLIN BAGELS

SAHAR

Nic, why are you in Cocoa Beach

HARPER

Blink twice if you need help!

DELILAH

When you said you were going swimming, I thought you meant at the facility???

Okay but actually can we have proof of life?

HARPER

Omg she's been kidnapped.

I'm fine.

Though I have, in fact, been kidnapped.

SAHAR

Exactly what someone who's pretending to be Nic would say

I sigh. "Now look what you've done," I mutter.

"What?"

"The girls checked my location and are worried."

"You could…tell them what's going on?"

"That would mean telling them I'm with you. When I should be asleep."

Aleks glances over, a curl to his mouth. "And that's bad because…?"

I ignore him, typing out three different versions of "I just needed air" before settling on *I'll be home soon. Go to bed.*

A few minutes later, Aleks pulls into an empty lot. The only light we have to see by is the moon and a flickering streetlamp. Beyond the lot is the vague outline of the ocean.

"What are we doing?"

"You wanted to swim, right?"

"Are you insane? You drove an hour so I could swim in the ocean instead of the facility pool?"

"You needed to take a few minutes to relax. To breathe. Which you did in the car on the way here, at least marginally, I hope. Now we can call this your one thing for yourself today."

I cross my arms, an affronted noise leaving my throat. "I'll have you know that I chose an artsy movie for movie night tonight, which led to me realize artsy films are *not* for me. And also led the girls to claim I was torturing them."

Aleks bites back a laugh, shrugging. "Okay, then it's a bonus list item. Do you want to get out or not?"

"It's not like I have much of a choice since you kidnapped me and took me an hour from my home."

His hand hovers over mine. "You always have a choice, Nic. Especially with me."

The look we share is meaningful, and even if I don't fully understand it, I nod. "Fine."

We get out and walk a few yards from where the waves crash against the shore. Aleks pulls his slutty little shirt over his head, tossing it to the sand, and though I've seen him bare-chested, it's jarring. His arms flex as he moves, and my eyes linger on the tattoo on his chest.

"Ready?" he asks me.

"Wha—what? I thought you were joking. We fly to Stuttgart tomorrow. I don't know about you, but *I* need to sleep. I have a routine."

Aleks walks until the water reaches his waist before diving beneath, his laugh booming. I follow, stopping when my feet hit the water. He surfaces, the moonlight casting a halo on his hair, his blue eyes dark as midnight. A wide, carefree grin splits his face. "In case I haven't made it abundantly clear, one of my favorite things to do is disrupt your routine. Keep you on your toes."

"You're the one who says I need to make sure I'm sleeping plenty for recovery!"

"Yes, but I also know you're going to go back to the facility and probably go for a run or something stupid, so I'm trying to tucker you out so you can fall into bed as soon as you get home. Get in."

"I'm going to have to showe—"

"Solnyshko, just get in."

I do, with a glare and a huff that make him smile. The water is the perfect temperature, and I move through it easily until I'm beside him, watching drops of water race down his body.

"Tell me what it felt like the first time you won a junior major," he declares.

With brows knitted, I meet his gaze. "What? You have plenty of majors, you know what it feels like."

Aleks shakes his head. "I know what it felt like for me. I know what it's felt like for my sister and my parents. But it's not the same for any of us. So how did it feel for you?"

I lift a palm through the water, then shove it down. "It's so cliché, but it was euphoric. A tidal wave of relief and disbelief and joy, all tangled together. Time slowed, and the crowd was cheering. For *me*. I felt so loved. It was everything I ever wanted and more." And why I feel like such a disappointment for going years without winning one.

His face shifts, his angular nose throwing shadows over it. If it made sense, I might categorize the look as affectionate. "I don't think I've ever heard you speak so much," he jokes.

I cross my arms, glaring. "I'm never answering your questions again, asshole."

Aleks chuckles. "I'm sorry, I'm sorry. Please answer my questions. You lit up brighter than the light of the moon."

"Considering I can barely see you, that's not very bright."

His smile wavers as he pulls me closer by the ties of my bikini bottom. I almost chastise him but stop when I note the downward tilt of his lips. "Winning for me was overpowered by relief. And hope that maybe I could relax, followed quickly by the realization that I needed to keep pushing for more. There was less and less joy each time I won until I hoisted the Wimbledon trophy and knew I was done."

"Quit the next day, right?"

"Out on a high note, they said."

The pieces of Aleks slot together—why he's so relentless in his pursuit of keeping my rest days rest days. He's mentioned not wanting me to become like him, but until now, the picture hadn't formed entirely.

He doesn't want my first major to be my last. The realization—which, if I were normal, wouldn't have taken so long to hit—pinches deep in my chest. "You care so much about others."

Aleks' eyebrows shoot up. "Oh. Okay. Is that a surprise?"

"Perhaps."

"A welcome one?"

I allow a small smile but don't answer.

"I know you travel the world for a living and you grew up in one of the most beautiful countries, but hopefully this view is a little more impressive than the walls of the pool room."

Squinting, I ask, "Are you trying to impress me?"

Aleks huffs a laugh, stepping closer. A thrill shoots through me when his chest brushes against mine. "I'm doing anything and everything I can to impress you. Sorry if my ways aren't orthodox or don't make sense to you."

I blink. "Why?"

"It's beneath you to play dumb, Nic. You know what I think about you."

"I'm not sure I do." A pause. "I think you're attracted to me. No," I correct myself, remembering the first time he saw me in a bikini, "I know you are. And that you believe I have the potential to be at the top of the tour. But I'm not exactly sure what you or anyone else thinks about me." Adults are so difficult to read. Kids are far easier. They say what they mean.

"You're already at the top of the tour," he murmurs.

"But you believe I can be higher."

He nods once.

"So, what?"

"What answer are you searching for? What do you want to hear?" he asks.

"I suppose the truth would be nice."

Aleks scoffs. "You don't want the truth."

What? What does that even mean? I take one step forward, the water sloshing around and between us. "Why do you really flirt with me? Would you do this with another non-family client? I thought it was a game before, but now I'm just confused."

He swallows. "I told you why I flirt with you."

"And that's the only reason?"

"I can't help it if seeing you fired up turns me on, solnyshko. I can be better at pulling back if you prefer."

My gaze drifts to the tattoo over his heart, right below his silver chain, and for the first time, I can make out the words. *For the love of the game.* I tap it. "Tennis?"

"It works for life too. A reminder not to take things too seriously." Another step toward him and a stuttered breath he tries to hide with a smile. "You ready to ask nicely?"

"Never," I whisper, my lips a breath from his. All it would take is a push from a crashing wave and we'd be kissing.

Aleks' mouth curls wickedly, and he hums. "That's too ba—"

I'd love to say I don't know who moves forward first, but it's me. My hands are in his hair, his lips on mine. His hands, hesitant at first, move from the outside of my thighs, one to the divot of my hip and the other into my half-matted hair, tugging me so he's in control. I relinquish, my chest falling against his, moaning at the firm press of his mouth, his tongue tangling with mine.

My hands roam over the muscles I've spent months trying so hard not to notice. Lean and muscular shoulders, arms, chest, abs. Valleys and ridges that deserve my full attention. The trail of hair disappearing into his shorts that shoots a wet heat between my legs, so powerful, my lower body grows weak.

He nips my bottom lip as my hand slips lower, and my head is nothing but static. Being around him quiets so many of the voices banging around in my head, but this silences them entirely.

Aleks tugs on my hair a little harder, pulling my head back so he can kiss along my jaw. I whimper when he gets to the spot where it meets my neck, and if he were anyone else, I'd be embarrassed.

The realization hits me like a freight train.

If he were anyone else, this would be fine. But he's not. He's Aleks, my most hated rival's older brother. Aleks, who might choose me over Anya today, but who probably won't weeks, months, years in the future.

Aleks, my performance coach. The man with whom I've spent a majority of my time the last couple of weeks, and if all goes well, with whom I'll spend a lot more in the coming months. No matter how kind he is, how hard he's working to keep me from his fate, no matter how attractive I may find him, I *know* this is a bad idea.

Gently, I push against his chest. Aleks takes half a step back, sucking in a ragged breath, a million different expressions passing across his face. Disappointment, I think. I can't discern any of the others.

When I finally gather a fraction of my bearings, I pant, "That…this can't happen again."

"Why not?" he rasps.

His gaze is so intense I can't hold it. I take another step back, my brain still scrambled like an egg. "Just…The moment got away from me. I don't hook up with people I have to interact with often. It's one of my rules."

"What are your others?"

I glance back up. His hair is out of sorts, whether because of me or the hand he's running through it now, I'm not sure. "No feelings. And no family members of my rival."

He grumbles unintelligibly.

"This can't happen again," I say once more, panicked. "Please. Let's pretend it didn't."

"I'm not good at that."

"I need you to be. So try."

He sighs, noticeably upset, and nods, turning toward the shore. We don't speak a word on the drive, and he hardly looks at me when we reach my apartment.

seventeen

I move about my hotel room in Stuttgart four days later, readying my clothes and bag for tomorrow's match and listening to my friends chatter on FaceTime. All three of them are training in Madrid in preparation for next week.

"I packed, like, twenty party outfits, and I'm still not sure it's enough," Sahar says as she spins around her tornado of a hotel room. She groans. "It's useless trying to go through all this stuff when we're going to fly out again in a couple of weeks."

"You don't think twenty is enough?" Delilah wonders aloud, her golden hair strewn about the pillow in her hotel room. "When do we go home? After Wimbledon, right?"

Sahar nods. "I *hate* packing for three months."

"But think of all the adventures we'll have. So many touristy things to do the next three months!"

"And it's entirely possible we'll go home at some point in that time." All three of us shoot Harper an incredulous look. She stands from the toilet, tucking a strand of dark hair behind her ear. "Alright, probably not. But it is *possible*."

The conversation devolves into the likelihood of that, and I open the article I was reading before the call. After I won today's match, reporters began talking about my chances at Madrid and Roland Garros, speculating that I'll make a deep run. The pressure bends my shoulders and my stomach churns.

"Niiiiiic," Delilah draws my name out like it's not the first time. "We can't see you."

Flicking back to them, I offer a halfhearted smile. "I'm here."

"How has training been?"

I shrug. "Fine."

Despite Aleks' claims that he's not good at pretending, the kiss hasn't made even a semblance of an appearance in more than my own thoughts. We trained as usual when we arrived in Stuttgart, and without Delilah, he took on the role of my hitting partner as well. Which means we've spent hours together, skirting around a subject that should probably be talked about but that I'm more than happy not to address.

Even if getting it—the press of his lips to mine, his groan, the rasp in his voice when I pushed him away—out of my head is near impossible.

"Just fine? I could get more information out of a mop," Sahar mutters.

"I don't know. Less fun without my usual hitting partners."

"Oh? Nic, that may be the nicest thing you've ever said to us," she answers.

Rolling my eyes, I hang up my kit—a dark blue dress with a small V cut at the collar and a matching pair of spandex shorts—set my shoes underneath, and put my packed bag beside them. "For that, I'm leaving."

"Nooooooooo," Delilah and Harper chorus.

"Wait I'm sorry, I was joking! Please!"

I laugh softly. "I need to get to bed."

Delilah sits up, pouting. "Fine. I suppose we'll survive."

We say our goodbyes. After doing my skincare and tucking the ever-growing list of things I'm learning about myself into my bag, I slide under my blanket and watch film.

An idea forms while scrutinizing my match against Anya when the camera briefly pans to Aleks in her box, and before I can get rid of it, I'm typing *Aleksandr Morozov match highlights* into the search bar. There are a lot of articles examining his decision to leave and videos of him from almost a decade ago right up until he quit.

Embarrassingly, I watch enough to fill an hour, and when I reach those later matches, I note the way his body curved, even during wins. How he always won with that fake smile instead of the one I'm so accustomed to, a sunken, unhappy quality to his face.

I fall asleep contemplating that fake smile but dream about his real one, fastened right on me.

～

WHETHER THE PRESSURE TO PERFORM CREEPS ITS WAY INTO my head or something else is wrong, I lose the first set of my match in a tiebreak the next day, barely scraping through the second to force a third.

It would be an embarrassment to go down in the round of 16. Worse to do so in straight sets.

During the break before the decider, I grab a towel and water bottle and walk to my box, where Pen claps excitedly, Aleks watches quietly, and Karolína sits forward, ready for a quick strategy session. "You've noticed Madeleine struggles with longer rallies, right?"

Wiping my face, I nod. "Almost every time, she makes a mistake or can't get to my down-the-line shot."

"Exactly. More of that. You're a much stronger player. Get up early and keep the momentum."

"What about on returns? Why am I struggling with her serve so much? And I'm making way more errors than usual." I've hit no less than twelve balls into the net.

"You're tight. Loosen up and play your game. Move your feet." She glances at Aleks, whose gaze I've been carefully avoiding. "Anything else?"

"Yeah, I think moving your feet more. Many of those net balls are because you're letting the ball get behind you. She learned how to harness your power over time, so make sure you're ready."

"Okay."

"You got this Nic!" Pen calls as I turn back to the bench. I wipe myself down one more time, take a long swig of water, and jog to my side of the court.

Get up early, I remind myself. This first game is crucial.

Unfortunately, that seems to be the opposite of what I'm capable of. Clearly, Madeleine had a good talk with her team, who've told her to get out of the longer rallies by rerouting the ball earlier than me, which means I'm often left on the defensive, running back and forth. It also means I'm hitting the ball on the run more, which leaves me with more mistakes than ever.

In an attempt to follow her lead, I cut off cross-court rallies early, but where I was able to place my down-the-line shots exceptionally in the first two sets, every time I try this set, they're a hair out. Before long, it's match point and I'm dizzy.

It's fitting that I lose a match point with a backhand into the net. Very in keeping with the disaster of a match I played. Madeleine is shocked, hands over her mouth like she won a major semifinal.

After our handshake, I shove my things into my bag and walk off the court to a cold goodbye from the crowd. My teeth grind together to stop me from crying. Or screaming. Or throwing something.

It's no surprise when, after cooldown, press, and a shower, I find myself in the gym. I told Karolína I was ready to watch film, but she said we'd look it over tomorrow to prep for Madrid.

My body is too run-down to punish too much, so instead, I find a corner of the empty players' gym, rolling my legs out while watching the match from start to finish. On points I lost, I make notes to myself about what I should've done better.

A ball I hit out after it landed on my baseline. *Move your feet better.*

A double fault that makes my gums ache from how hard I clench my teeth at the mistake. *Don't fucking hit a toss if it's too far to one side. Reset and try again.*

A volley into the net. *Move your damn feet and get your racket underneath it.*

It doesn't make me feel like any less of a failure, but it's enough to keep me away from the shark-like reporters and commenters on social media, all who, I'm sure, are talking about my disappointing loss and how this might mean I'm no longer favored to do well in Madrid next week.

It also keeps me from checking whether my mother has responded to any of my messages asking if she still wants to call and talk about Charleston. Or in general.

Aleks makes an appearance shortly after the first set, water in one hand and a suspicious box in the other. He says nothing, sitting beside me as I watch myself make mistake after mistake in the third set. There's no smile to speak of, just his messy hair and the warmth of his body closer than I should allow.

When the torture finally ends, I click my phone off and set it down. Both items Aleks brought are handed to me, and I take them, drinking half the water before opening the box to reveal baklava. Though Stuttgart has a large Greek population, it's something I never would have gotten for myself, his thoughtfulness a nail in the coffin of my depression. The gratefulness thrumming through me feels like something…more.

I hate being around others after a loss. The presence of someone important to me only feeds the monster in my head that tells me I'm not supposed to be here and they're bearing witness to that fact. And yet Aleks has now seen me after multiple losses, and his presence beside me isn't stifling.

After eating a piece, I say, "I played like shit."

Aleks doesn't answer, and I appreciate that he won't lie to me.

"I had, like, fifteen chances to get it together in the third set. Worse, I shouldn't have lost the first set to begin with."

"True," he agrees. "But you did."

I turn to him. "That's not helpful."

His smile is kind. "This sport is brutal, solnyshko. You play a tournament more weeks than you don't. One bad day can be the difference between an early loss or a title. Worse, you're losing every week, often to people you know you can beat. Matches you lose, you might have won half of the points in. How can you lose when you won half the points?" he asks rhetorically.

We're silent. Then Aleks pulls his shirt down to reveal his chain and the tattoo beneath it. He taps the ink once, a reminder. *For the love of the game.*

Quietly, I respond, "I don't love the game when I'm losing. I used to. It used to be about fun before the pressure of majors fell onto my shoulders. But now it just…"

He nods. "Now it feels like if you're not winning, you're worthless."

I sigh. "Yeah."

"You're so far from worthless, Nic. You go into each training session with your head held high, ready to take on anything Nora or I throw at you. You have one of the best backhands on tour, and when you're on, you're a sight to fucking behold. Your game is what makes the sport fun to people."

The words strike me in the chest, bowl me over. I hate that they make me want to reach out and touch him, hold his hand or some dumb shit like that. "Stop being nice to me. I don't know how to respond to it."

Aleks' deep chuckle rumbles, and he swipes a piece of the baklava. While he chews, I pick up my phone, which has been buzzing relentlessly.

SHOTS FIRED

HARPER

Next time, Nic!

SAHAR

Yeah, this way, you have a break before Madrid so you can kick ass

DELILAH

And since we'll all be in Madrid early, we can do lots of touristy things!!

HARPER

Ooo yes, good call, Del.

NOAH

Do we all have to partake?

AUSTIN

Yeah I don't want people looking at me like I'm dumb because I'm walking around with a map

SAHAR

Trust me, that's not why people will be looking at you like you're dumb

DELILAH

Also who still uses maps??

The messages continue pouring in. I'm about to click over to social media when Aleks sets a hand over my screen. "Stop. It's going to make you feel worse. Don't let the couch potatoes tell you how to play your sport."

"How else will I know what I, the next great Carmen Aguirre, should be doing to be as great as her?"

Aleks scoffs. "You're not the next Carmen Aguirre."

Standing, I cross my arms and say, "Wow, what a weird way to kick me while I'm down."

He stands too and steps in front of me, forcing me to meet his eyes. "Calling you the next Carmen Aguirre is a disservice to you. You blaze your own damn path." He brushes a few stray strands of hair behind my ear. "Calling you the next anyone pressures you to grow down one path. You have infinite places you can go."

"Where should I go next?" I ask quietly. It's a stupid question. I don't even know what it means.

But he seems to. "Wherever you want. You want to be a major winner? You want to be world number one? You want to get your pilot's license and spend your life flying around the world? Do it. If there's anyone I trust to do what they set their mind to, it's you. Because you're the first and only Nicola Vassilakis."

It is, maybe, the single nicest thing anyone has ever said to me.

And I allow that to be my reason for what I do next.

Gripping the fabric of his shirt, I yank him to me, the mouth I dreamed about last night meeting mine. He's so taken aback, his hand slaps the wall beside my head before he sinks into it. His tongue slips into my mouth, his other hand drifting to my chin, and suddenly everywhere we touch is unbearably hot.

I throw my arms around his neck, my brain fuzzy, and

when I push my chest against him, his groan reverberates in my mouth. The kiss turns half rabid, sucking and biting and moaning until he hits that same spot on my neck as the other night. Except this time, when I'm reminded how bad of an idea this is, I strangle the voice.

Because all my life, no one has prioritized my feelings unless they were paid to. And though I pay Aleks, he goes so far above and beyond: sitting beside me and commiserating after a loss, driving me to the beach to relieve my stress on a rest day, finding and buying me desserts from my country to make me miss home a little less, telling me how capable I am when I feel anything but. None of it is in his job description, and yet he does everything in his power to uplift me.

Aleks flips me, my stomach against the wall, his hand slipping under my tank top. Warmth zings through my veins, landing white-hot between my legs. "I still haven't heard the magic words," he whispers.

"Fuck me, Aleks. I won't ask any nicer than that."

I'm rewarded with a bite below my ear, a jolt at my spine when I feel him hard against my ass. "I don't have a condom, and I'm almost positive this is a crime."

I glance around, searching the ceiling. "It's well after midnight and there are no cameras over here. Did you see anyone?"

He pushes the strap of my tank top out of his way, kissing the skin it exposes. "No."

"I've got an IUD and I was clear at my recent physical."

Aleks groans against my skin, maybe at the notion of taking me raw. "Clear at my last physical and haven't been with anyone since," he rasps. It's all the reassurance I need to push against him.

His hand on my stomach slips beneath the waistband of my shorts and underwear, the pad of his finger brushing my clit. It's swollen and sensitive, and just the touch pushes a whine from my chest.

His chuckle is like gravel against my back. "If we're doing this, you're going to have to be quieter than that," he whispers beside the shell of my ear, his lips brushing the metal hoops. My head falls onto his shoulder, my neck bared for him, and when his finger travels lower, finds me soaked for him, he sucks in a sharp breath.

"You been wet and needy all this time? And you didn't think to ask me for help?"

"We were hardly at a place where I would have allow—"

I'm cut off by the finger he sinks into me, the tension in my spine humming to life anew as he pushes in and out, finds what works for me, and adjusts his rhythm until I'm writhing and panting and begging, my nails digging crescents into the flesh of his forearm. He smiles into the curve of my throat, kissing me softly. Aleks' finger brushes my clit once more, and the tension at the base of my spine explodes, blinding and all-consuming.

He doesn't give me a chance to catch my breath, pulling himself out of his sweatpants and shoving my shorts down just enough that I'm exposed. "Last chance to ask nicely."

"I…think we're…past that," I pant, straightening at the feel of his cock between my thighs.

"Fine. Then last chance to tell me to get lost before I

bend you over and fuck you 'til you see stars." I find the wherewithal to lift my head, turning so our gazes clash. He must glimpse in them whatever he was searching for, because all at once, his lips are on mine and he's pushing inside me. My body stretches to fit him slowly, and with every small movement, he groans.

"Jesus, fuck. It's obscene how wet you are."

I plant my hands on the wall, bending my hips. His hands find the divots of my waist, and he sinks all the way in, his groans guttural, primal.

"Once again, my fantasies never do you justice," he grinds out.

There is solely static between my ears, so much so that the words fly by me as if unspoken. The first few glides in and out are choppy, and though we're trying to be quiet, I'm positive it's not going well. "Aleks—" A moan. "More," I beg. What I mean is harder. Faster.

And because, apparently, he is a mind reader, his rhythm steadies and he speeds up. "Fuck, I'm not going to last long like this, solnyshko. You're so fucking warm and wet and"—he thrusts another few times—"too fucking perfect, Nic. That's what you are. Perfect for me."

I grab his right hand, guiding it to the column of my throat. He chuckles darkly, pulling our bodies flush. The pressure of his left hand on my hip intensifies, his thrusts accelerating. I'm so wet, it sounds absolutely filthy, our bodies slapping together until his rhythm turns choppy again.

"Where do you want me?" he asks, half frantic.

"Exactly where"—I gasp as he finds my clit with the

pad of his finger and circles me lightly—"you are," I manage, pitching over a cliff into my orgasm.

It's enough for him to let go, his thrusts growing slower and shallower as he follows me.

After we stop shaking, he pulls out of me gently. His chest remains pressed to my back, and he buries his fingers inside me, as if to keep his come in place before pulling my shorts and underwear up. Aleks' forehead meets my temple.

"The next time we do that, I want it to be somewhere I can both worship you and clean you properly. You hear me?"

Words defy me, and though I should tell him there won't be a next time, I know it'd be a lie.

So I nod, let him hold me while we catch our breath, and say nothing when he follows me all the way into my hotel room for another two rounds.

eighteen

The next day is a travel and rest day, our flight from Munich to Madrid quick. I make the mistake of allowing Aleks to sit next to me, which means the entire three hours are spent ignoring the smirks he shoots me, watching tidy fields and red-roofed villages shrink beneath fluffy clouds. The Alps rise in the distant blush of dawn, and when Aleks whispers, "Your legs still shaky?" I elbow him hard enough that he grunts and shuts up until our descent. We watch sunlight-warmed hills and scattered olive groves pass beneath us, his cheek nearly touching mine as he leans to get a better view.

That evening, after dinner with him, Pen, and Karolína—where we were interrupted on three separate occasions by his friends on the men's tour who happened to be eating at the same restaurant—he follows me to my room.

Initially, I think nothing of it. He has a strange, noble idea that he needs to deposit me in my room so I remain safe. Except when I open the door, he doesn't say goodbye.

"What?" I ask him.

"Oh, were you not giving me bedroom eyes at dinner?" His teeth flash, and I have to force my eyes away so I'm not reminded of them biting my inner thigh during our third round last night. He's *very* generous when he wants to be.

"You must have confused it with my *your friends are interrupting my dinner* face."

"They are awfully similar expressions." Aleks doesn't move.

"I'm not sure we should have a repeat performance."

"No?" He inclines his head. "Was it not to your liking?" The tilt of his lips tells me he knows it was one of the best experiences of my life.

"Aleks, we work together. I don't sleep with people I work with."

"By virtue of what happened yesterday, that's no longer true." I cross my arms, which makes him chuckle. "I'm just saying, things have already shifted, no? Why rid ourselves of the perks?"

"And that's all you want? Just hooking up and no expectations for anything else?"

Aleks' gaze glides into my room. "Of course. What expectations would I have?"

I mull it over, ignoring the twist of my stomach at his words. Before yesterday, it had been a while since I'd slept with anyone, my push into the top ten fueled by working so hard, I never found the time or interest. And if the way my body felt like it was gliding all day is any indication, it relieved some sliver of my usual stress.

Gripping the key card so it digs into my palm, I push

the door wider. "If we do this, we keep it on the DL," I say over my shoulder as we walk in. "It's stress relief to replace the extra gym work I'd do if you weren't watching me like a hawk."

"Happy to be of service."

The suite is the size of a luxury studio apartment, opening into a spacious living area with floor-to-ceiling windows overlooking Madrid's skyline. The light from a lamp I left on is soft as it glints off the coffee table, which sits in front of two linen sofas, facing a low entertainment console. On the right, the outer wall curves into an alcove, where my bed is tucked behind a partial wall, only visible when I take another couple of steps into the living area.

Taking off my heels and setting them beside my other shoes lined by the door, I pull my hair from the tight knot it was in at dinner and walk past the bed to the white-and-green bathroom, the tile cool against my feet.

"No cuddling after," I tell him, unzipping the dress and letting the silk slide over my body until it lands in a puddle. "Yesterday was a mistake."

"You'll have to forgive me if I fall asleep here and my arms happen to land on you."

When I turn, picking up the dress to put it into the closet, he's standing over the nightstand. It takes me a moment to realize he's looking at my list.

His eyes rove the paper, a soft smile tugging at the corners of his lips.

"That's private," I say, taking the few steps toward him and flipping it over. I should tell him that he might be right, though. That, for the first time in my life, I know things about myself that have nothing to do with tennis.

That I like strawberry lemonade, but not pink lemonade—something Pen always seems to have on hand, despite many of the countries I play in definitely not allowing the dyes in it. That I prefer nuts in pastries, courtesy of getting breakfast at a café with Karolína, who won't eat a baked good without them. That when I allow myself to pay attention to the reality TV Delilah likes, I do, though I'm loath to admit it, enjoy the drama.

That his training the last three weeks has allowed me to enjoy practices and matches more than I have in months.

But after last night, he's sure to have a big enough head, and by the smirk on his lips, I guarantee if I voiced any of that, it would only swell.

"I'm more shocked than anything that you've been listening to me." He turns, our faces inches apart. "It's such a rare thing."

His eyes drop, then flick back to my face before they widen and drop down again, taking in my lacy underwear and naked chest. The sound of his swallow is loud enough for *my* head to swell.

I begin unbuttoning his light blue shirt from the top, loving the way his breath stutters as my fingers ghost over his chain. "Don't get used to it."

"Wouldn't dream of it." I can tell it takes mental fortitude, but he drags his eyes to mine. "Can I touch you?"

My chest constricts, my lips turning up. "While I appreciate you always running it by me, my getting naked is a pretty good indication that I'd like you to."

"I'm a fan of enthusiastic consent." He lifts me easily, tossing me onto the bed. I giggle, excited in my anticipation, and it's a noise so foreign that we both pause for a moment. An affectionate smile spreads across his lips before he crawls over my body, pressing kisses to every bit of exposed skin.

"You were so hot in that dress tonight," he says against my stomach. "Next time, let me take it off you."

There it is again. *Next time* and the anxiety that accompanies the idea of continuing this. Rather than falling prey to the fears, I respond, "With how many times we've managed in the last twenty-four hours, you could hardly say I'm out of shape."

His eyes find mine while his lips explore the skin right above the hem of my underwear. "You know I never said that."

There's no time to think of a response, because he pulls the cotton aside and dives in, smiling when he sees my hands fisting the comforter. His tongue does alarmingly good work, and quick. It doesn't take long before I'm writhing and begging him to fill me with more than the tip of his finger.

Aleks listens, and by the end, half the pillows have been knocked off the bed and I've sent a prayer up that the walls are thicker than they appear for the sake of our neighbors. I'm so tired after, I don't even mind when he ends up under the layers of my bed with me, an arm around me as my heavy lids close.

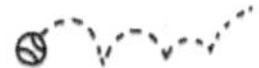

I WAKE, BLEARY-EYED, SOMETIME IN THE MIDDLE OF THE night, if the dark outside the large windows is anything to go by. Pushing aside the odd hurt pressing into my sternum when I realize Aleks has left, I stand and pull the thinner of my two curtains shut. I'll wake for my morning walk as the sun spills into the room.

"Shh, shh. I can't understand what you're saying, Tash. Breathe for me." Aleks' voice is quiet, scraping like gravel from sleep. I peer out the doorway cut into the wall and notice him pacing the hotel living area. The pressure on my sternum turns to relief, warm and soothing.

Leaning against the wall, I watch his shoulders hitch higher as he listens, the muscles in his back illuminated by city lights. The strange urge to hold him, protect him, overtakes me.

"I know. I think they're upset with Anya over her loss in Germany." A pause. "I know. He shouldn't have said that to you. That's unacceptable." Another pause. "Tash, if you want to quit, I support you." He sighs. "Of course I have regrets."

Aleks turns, still pacing. "I know it's hard. I wish there was something I could—" He cuts off when he notices me, a canyon carving between his brows. Does he not want me to hear this?

I recognize that he's been struggling to find the right way to tell his siblings, Natasha particularly, and I want him to recognize that I see him. That I know how hard this has been on him and that I'm here. I offer him a smile, nodding encouragingly.

Whether that translates, I don't know. But the tension in his face eases, and he reaches out, beckoning me. I pad to him without much thought, stepping into the circle of his arm. It drapes around me loosely, his fingers light in the divot of my waist.

It seems to be the encouragement he needs to say, "Actually, there is something I've been wanting to talk to you about." A voice on the verge of hysterics filters out of his phone, though I can't make out her words. "I was drowning, Tash. Tennis was all I'd ever been, but I didn't love it anymore. It wasn't fun. It became more a chore than anything else, and Mom and Dad's pressure was killing me. I had to get out. But I'm so sorry. My leaving did this to you and Dima and Anya. If I'd have stayed, maybe they wouldn't be taking it out on you. Maybe they'd look more favorably on you taking a break. They're trying to sink their claws in deeper to keep hold of you because if you leave too, they only have two more to keep the legacy going."

Aleks sighs, his weight shifting toward me. I place a hand over his where it rests on my hip, grazing a finger over his knuckles, up and down.

"I'm sorry I left you to deal with it. That I didn't tough it out to keep their attention off you. If you're open to it, I'd like to talk to the three of you this week since we're all in one place. Without Mom and Dad around. And if you still feel this way after you hear everything I have to say, I'll be there when you tell them you want out. I'll stay by your side and be strong so you don't have to."

He huffs a laugh. "Okay, Anya doesn't have to be involved. I can talk to her separately."

I hide my smile. Natasha might not be so bad after all.

"Are you sure you're alright? I can come to your room. We can watch cartoons like when you were little. Your choice of snack." Her answer sounds far less hysterical. Aleks stepped out of his comfort zone to make her feel better, and it tightens a fist in my chest. Pride sticks in my throat. "Another time, then. Good night. Hey, and no matter what happens, no matter what they say to you, you'll always have me, okay?"

When the call ends, he slips his phone into the sweatpants he either stashed here or went to his room to grab after I passed out.

"Do you want to talk about it?" I ask softly.

He shakes his head.

"Do you want to get back into bed?" I offer.

He nods, and I grab his hand, marveling at how much physical touch I've enjoyed the last couple of days as I lead him back into my bedroom. We slip under the covers, his thumb and forefinger stroking the soft fabric of the blanket I travel with.

"Sorry I woke you."

"Don't apologize."

"I'm glad I saw you when I did. I keep telling myself I'll sit down and talk to them, but then I chicken out. I'm scared of what I'll see in their faces if I look too long. Do they blame me for what they're dealing with? I don't know." His eyes drop from the ceiling, snagging on mine. They're so dark, I can barely discern where the blue ends and the white begins. "Maybe telling her over the phone was cowardly."

"Nothing about what you did was cowardly. Not then and not now."

The right corner of his mouth tips up. "When I saw you, I heard your voice telling me to stop lying. And I recognize it's going to be hard, but I want Natasha to be happy. If showing her what I went through provides her the courage to do the same, I want to be by her side, helping her get through to them."

My hand drifts toward his, slipping our fingers together again. "I'm really proud of you."

"I bet you just like that I'm listening to you, even as a voice in my head."

I squeeze his hand. "No." Though it is nice to know he thinks about me enough that I'm in his head. He sure as hell has a lot to say in mine.

He squeezes back. "Thank you."

We drift off with our hands nestled together.

nineteen

Delilah grinds to a halt in front of me two days later, so fast, I slam into her back. Matteo's arm stops her from falling, and in turn, prevents my own tumbling over her onto the rectangular stones of Plaza Mayor.

Like she doesn't even realize she nearly fell, she cries, "Guys! Look!" The chatter of our massive party quiets.

Taking a step back, I crane my neck to see the store she's gesturing at. A lit-up circular sign ensconced between hanging greenery reads Madrid Duck Store and features a giant rubber duck in the center.

"Can we go?" she asks Matteo quietly. Like he would deny her anything. He's already leading her inside the small shop, flipping his hat backward over his curly dark hair so he can nod at each one Delilah points to on the shelves lining the left wall. Harper traipses behind them, followed closely by Sahar and Noah, though the latter appears less impressed.

It's two days before the Madrid Open kicks off, and our final chance to spend an entire day exploring the many places Delilah and Harper chose for us from their list. We've seen the Royal Palace, a gothic cathedral, and visited every kitschy tourist shop one could imagine.

It's the most I've done in Madrid, and though I wondered if there might be something here that speaks to my mother's heritage, speaks to me, it's like any beautiful city I have no ties to.

"Do you need to head out now?" Aleks asks, standing beside me as Austin follows behind our friends reticently. The rest of our party—coaches, managers, family members—keep walking to a café down the plaza.

I check the time. "I can stay for a few more minutes."

My mother promised we'd talk about Charleston today, so I'm going to take a car to the hotel before everyone else. Though our calls have never lasted more than ten minutes on a good day, I'm hopeful that this time might be different. Maybe she'll compare it to one of her wins. Or maybe she'll have recommendations for places to visit while I'm in her hometown.

I step inside the duck store. Birthday ducks become Star Wars ducks become doctor ducks. Everything I've ever imagined, and many things I've never imagined, have been turned into a rubber duck.

"They have a tennis player!" Delilah says, holding one up triumphantly. It has a white visor and blonde ponytail, a racket tucked in one wing and a ball in the other.

"We should get matching ones," Harper adds, pointing to the male equivalent.

Sahar turns to me. "I don't think we're going to be allowed to leave here without at least one."

As she says it, I find a white duck with black cow spots

on it, a purple beak, and a yellow bell around its neck. "They might be on to something with these," I murmur in response.

Sahar picks up a snail, scrutinizing it from all angles with a smile that grows wider over time, if not a little mischievous. "Look at this guy. Doesn't he kind of remind you of Noah?" She holds it beside his face. "The resemblance is uncanny."

"I see it," Harper agrees.

"You're behind me. There's no way you see it," Noah says, flipping around.

A few feet down, Austin holds a pug up to Delilah, saying something that makes her throw her head back and laugh. Matteo watches them with a hint of a smile playing on his lips, his eyes tracking her movements. That pang I've grown used to hits, but it's not as sharp or deep.

Especially not when Aleks sidles up to me. "I wouldn't have pegged you for a cowgirl."

"What would you have pegged me for?" I ask, my eyebrows raised. "And be very careful how you answer."

Aleks' laugh is deep, little lines pressed beside his eyes, and the sound of it breaks out my own smile. We've spent the last couple of days training hard, getting dinner with Karolína and Pen, acting as though nothing has changed, then ending the night with our clothes scattered on the floor of my hotel room. It should be awkward, uncomfortable, should feel weird that our relationship has changed so drastically, yet it's the same as it has been since we started training together: easy and enjoyable, even when he pisses me off.

He points at one. "The hedgehog is cute. As is the unicorn."

"And here I was thinking you'd go for the penguin."

"It *is* a serious contender, I'll admit."

My phone buzzes in my pocket. In a panic, I whip it out, but it's just my alarm.

"Want me to come with you?" he asks.

I smile thankfully. "I'm good. You keep having fun."

After a moment's thought, I grab one of the tennis ducks in addition to the cow. Though I've been doing things to prove that tennis isn't all I am, it's still what I love most in the world, more so every day. They'll go nicely in my poorly decorated room in our apartment, and since I rarely buy myself anything on these outings with the girls, it'll also get its spot on the growing list on my nightstand.

I say my goodbyes with a small paper bag in hand, smiling when I hear Matteo talking Delilah down from buying ten to a more manageable eight.

The moment I walk through the door of my suite, I text my mother, turning on my ringer so I don't miss her response or call. I wait five minutes. Then ten. Then thirty. I prepare what I'll wear to train tomorrow, then tidy my room. Another half hour passes. After sending a second message, I sit on the edge of the tub, staring at myself in the mirror until my vision goes blurry.

It's been exactly two weeks since she sent flowers, and it shouldn't come as a surprise that the note saying we'd call was fake. If it was performative, who was she performing for? Was it her way of passing off her guilt? A bouquet of flowers that cost around $100 to make up for years of this?

I shouldn't be surprised. And yet, here I am, waiting for a call that, I'm growing certain, isn't coming.

When my phone does go off, it's a text from Aleks.

> **ALEKS**
> I'm back if you want company.

> I do not.

> **ALEKS**
> I'll leave my door open for you. 1832.

> Don't.

Nonetheless, when, an hour and a half later, I've still heard nothing from my mother, I end up in front of his room, noting the metal piece holding his door open.

"Idiot," I mutter, pushing through the door and closing it properly.

His suite is similar to mine. The living area is dark, though the light from the television in his bedroom is enough to see by. His back faces me, like he's sleeping, and I take a beat, considering going back to my room.

Before I make a decision, his arm lifts. "Get in here," he says when I don't immediately join him.

Sliding under the covers, I grumble, "I only came because I didn't want you to leave your door open all night and get killed."

"Aw, how sweet. Admit it, you care about me." Aleks' voice is raspy, like he was on the verge of falling asleep.

I scoff. "I do not. I'm just here to have sex with you."

"Alright, let's do it."

Neither of us move, and it takes me a second to realize

that the blanket I'm under isn't the one provided by the hotel. "Where did you get this?"

Aleks turns around to face me. "I noticed the one you had in your room and thought you might like one here if you came over. I figured it's a texture thing."

It's so simple, and yet it's everything. My heart swells so big, it might explode out of my chest and keep going, up up up like a hot air balloon. Throat scratchy, eyes burning, I don't shy away when he moves an inch closer. Because though I should, though I'm allowing myself to enter sticky, messy, potentially heart-wrenching territory, being around him is a comfort in so many ways. Like being with someone who knows you inside and out. Who knows what you're thinking without you having to say.

It's what I've wanted for so long, and it now feels like it could be in touching distance.

"What happened?" he asks quietly, as if he's already guessed.

"She didn't call."

"Did she give an excuse?"

I shake my head. "I wasn't even worth that."

"You're worth so much more," he says angrily. A moment later, he asks, "Are you going to keep trying?"

"I should, shouldn't I? She's my mom."

"I…don't really know the right answer to that."

Sighing, I sink further into the mattress. "Today was the first time I realized that all our calls over the years have been for her benefit and not mine. That they're more to assuage her own guilt over being a bad mom than to check in on how I'm doing." I need to stop caring so much. Focus on the circle of support I already have. "I just want to matter," I whisper.

"I'm terrified I'm going to leave behind a legacy of nothingness. No one remembering who I am or anything I did."

"Short of trauma-induced amnesia, there is nothing in this world that could make me forget you. Even then, I'm not convinced it would work." His mouth quirks. "I wouldn't know my own name, but I'd know the different shades of gray of your eyes. I'd know that when the right corner of your mouth dips down, you're about to give me hell. I might not remember anything about my own life, but I'd know you, solnyshko."

I'm fucked.

I'm so fucked, because instead of making me want to run with fear, the words make me want to burrow. To hide in his chest and never leave.

But at least Aleks seems equally fucked.

Things will change. Maybe tomorrow. Maybe next week. Maybe after clay season. I won't make it out of this unscathed, no matter when it happens.

But I can't bring myself to care right now. Not when Aleks is looking at me like I'm the planet around which he orbits. Not when he just told me he'd remember me through amnesia.

"Kiss me," I beg, and that's all it takes. He slips a hand into my hair, gently dragging my face to his until our lips press together in a tender caress. My hands fist the fabric of his shirt, pulling him over my body until we're slotted together like we were made for this and this alone. His arms rest against the mattress, holding his weight off me while he kisses a slow rhythm down my jaw, neck, and to my chest.

His fingers brush over the mati pendant on my necklace before he pushes up my T-shirt, continuing the path he's blazing until he reaches below my navel, where an intense heat uncoils, begging to be released. Aleks takes his time, sliding my shorts off slowly, like I'm made of porcelain and one wrong move might shatter everything.

Anything is possible at this point.

My underwear is next, at a pace so unhurried that I groan my dissatisfaction.

"Patience," he whispers against my inner thigh. I jolt at his warm breath, my body turning to pliable clay in his hands. His to hold and mold. Aleks chuckles like he knows it, licking from my clit down, his tongue painting the prettiest picture. At one point, I'm squirming so much, he has to pin me to the bed to keep me from twitching, my pleas growing louder.

Pleasure builds along my spine, his steady rhythm enough to bring me to the edge, and the moment he sinks the tip of his finger in, I'm gone. My vision goes black for a moment, my breaths irregular.

"You're so beautiful like this," Aleks says, kissing his way back up to my mouth. After a chaste kiss against my lips, he amends his statement. "You're so beautiful all the time. But particularly when you're begging me to make you come."

My eye roll is halfhearted. I throw my arms around his neck, pulling him closer, my fingers gliding through his hair. I slant my hips just right, and Aleks groans into my mouth, his kisses turning from sweet to hungry.

He rips down his sweatpants and boxer briefs, rubbing

himself against where he left me wet. "God, I don't think I'll ever get enough of this."

Aleks' mouth is on mine again a moment later, our moans meeting as he slides into me easily, filling me until I have to pull away and pant, my head thrown back as my hips rise to meet him faster. His chain smacks a rhythm against my collarbone.

"You take me so fucking well, solnyshko. *Fuck.*"

"A—Aleks can you—"

His thumb finds my clit before I finish the thought, his mouth against the column of my throat, kissing the spot that turns my whole body to jelly. Aleks finds a rhythm he likes, whispering against my skin. When it turns choppy, his groan visceral, he rasps, "Can you come again? One more for me, baby."

"I—I don't kn—" My breath hitches as he shoves all the way in, his thumb circling me so perfectly that I arch, my eyes closing with the pleasure that rocks through me. This time, it's slower, crashing in waves rather than zipping through me all at once.

"*Fuck,*" he moans again. "I'm gon—" His lips find mine, biting, his fingers digging into the flesh of my waist. He spills into me, and it's so intimate, I can't do anything but kiss him through it.

A few minutes later, after we've caught our breath, Aleks grabs a wet towel from the bathroom to clean me up. The smile on his face could rival the sun, his happiness so infectious, I find my own lips tipping up as I watch him.

"Stay?" he asks softly, his eyes midnight blue. "I'm hanging with Dima and Natasha tomorrow morning, but for tonight...?"

I should go, should stop getting used to falling asleep with his warmth beside me, but I'm sad and exhausted and tired of the aching loneliness. So I nod.

Once we're both clean and ready for bed, I drift off with his corded arm wrapped around my stomach. As I kiss unconsciousness, he murmurs something in Russian I'm too tired to question.

In the morning, I wake to an empty bed, a box of baklava on the nightstand, a paper tucked underneath it with a sketch of me, asleep with my hair strewn across the pillow. I smile, happier than I've been in a long time.

But when I check my phone, the perfect illusion of my life forming in my head cracks to the sound of Anya on the Tennis Broadcast, calling me a bully.

twenty

A re you joking?" The anger in my voice is not well leashed, and Pen's face twists. It was clear when we met in the hotel lobby that both she and Karolína had seen the video, but I didn't realize until I stepped into the practice court area of Caja Mágica that they'd also decided on a solution. Without me.

"It's an hour-long session so we can take videos and show that her comment didn't mean anything. We need to pivot before it's blown out of proportion."

I glance at Karolína, who's picking at her shirt, before turning back to Pen. "You want me to spend an hour pretending to enjoy Anya's company after she lied to the world about me? Again? I thought I was hitting with Valentina."

"Like Pen said, we're pivoting," my coach chimes in.

"Nic, I understand your anger, but if I told you at the hotel, you would have tried to get out of it. I spent over an hour convincing Anya's manager to do this, and it's your best chance to right the horrible things people are saying about you. If you come off like you *don't* hate her in these clips, I think we'll lose some of the heat."

I want to say I don't care what people are saying about me online, but that would be a lie. The various comments about how I've always seemed like a mean girl ate away at me on the drive here.

I hate that Pen's right. Hate that Anya weaponizes public opinion because she recognizes it's on her side. Hate that I'm going to give in to fix it. Like a puppet.

"Fine." Grabbing my bag, I walk onto soft, familiar red clay, the steady rhythm of rackets meeting balls sounding around me. Anya slouches on the bench, her father standing over her with his hands on his hips. I almost wonder if I'm about to witness the pressure Aleks has told me about, almost feel a modicum of sympathy, until her eyes lock on me and she sits up, smirking.

After I exchange hellos with her father, he steps away to talk to her coach.

The sound of my bag landing beside the bench doesn't even make Anya blink. She simply stands, her smile widening, and for the first time, I see the resemblance to Aleks. The blue eyes that light up, the slight tilt of the head when they smile.

"If it isn't the scourge of women's tennis, stealer of brothers and performance coaches, finally off her high horse."

Yeah, this is going to be a bloodbath.

"You're one to talk."

Anya scoffs. "All you have to do is look at our head-to-head record to know which of us needs help. I just didn't realize you'd stoop so low for a win."

Ire heats my blood. I can't remember hating anyone more. I so badly want to bite back, to point out how eager Aleks was to leave her and work with me. But that would make me no better than her and would throw him into more of an uncomfortable situation. "Hypocritical, considering you're slandering me on the internet. Has nobody taught you about libel lawsuits?"

Her eyes narrow at the change in topic, but a switch flips. The smile slithers back onto her lips. "Slandering? No." She shakes her head. "That doesn't sound like me."

The reason for her cloying demeanor becomes apparent when Karolína sidles up to us with Anya's coach and father. My coach observes us uncertainly.

"Ladies, we're going to do an easy hitting session. Pen wants shots of rallies and you two *not* killing each other while sharing a bench. Give me sixty minutes of pretend smiles, and this will all be over," Karolína reassures.

Anya shrugs, walking to the other side of the court and pulling a ball from her skirt. We line up at the service line and trade short balls over the net until we're ready to move back. After we've gotten warm, we shift to the deuce side for a cross-court drill.

Initially, Anya behaves like any other hitting partner, getting the ball back to me. The moment Karolína and Daria, Anya's coach, turn to talk, though, that changes. She hits balls on the line of the doubles court, and since we have to move back to the center each time, I'm chasing them down and breathing heavily long before she is, my back twinging with the effort. Her father, who watches us like a predatory bird, says nothing.

This is what she does, I remind myself. Psychological

warfare, Karolína would say if she were watching. Delilah told me she does it to get under my skin, so if I can put my head down for another forty-five minutes, I can get through this without letting her know she has.

Pen takes videos from beside me, shouting an encouraging "that's great" here and there. We continue the drill with our backhands, where Anya does the same thing: forcing me to work harder than her by hitting it as far out of my reach as possible. Before we expand to full-court rallies, Daria tells us to get water.

I try not to breathe too heavily when we get to the bench, but I'm not sure I succeed. Anya's still smiling like she's winning, which is absurd because you can't win at drills.

Ignoring Pen videoing us on the bench becomes difficult after she yells, "Nic, smile please! You want to look happy!"

"Hard to be happy when your parents can't stand you," Anya mutters.

My head whips around to find her eyes focused on her water bottle. "What did you just say?"

She bats her lashes. "What?" she asks innocently. "I said I'm so glad we're getting this break. I'm parched after the way you ran me all around the court."

The urge to stab her ratchets up. Pen tsks loudly, and I glance away. I won't smile, but strangling her would go viral, and that would be bad for a multitude of reasons.

Did Aleks say something to her about my parents? No. The notion disappears as quickly as it materialized. Which means Anya noticed it all on her own.

Heat rolls over my shoulders, nausea building in my

stomach. The sound of balls hitting strings is amplified, and I grip the mati pendant on my necklace.

I need this to be over.

Karolína approaches us, concern etched into the lines beside her eyes. "Full court, then we'll play a tiebreak and be done. Sound good?"

"Of course!" Anya answers brightly. She stands, grabs her racket, and heads back to her side of the court, her eyebrows coming together as her father begins talking to her in Russian.

"Karolína, I'm going to kill her."

"Really? You appear to be enjoying yourself." My eyes narrow. My coach laughs. "I'm kidding, Nic. It's obvious she's quietly needling you and trying to drive you crazy on court."

"So why aren't you doing anything about it?"

"Do you want your coach to step in and make it seem like you can't fight your own battles?"

She's right. I sigh. "No. But if *I* say something, Pen will tell me I'm being too heavy-handed for an hour-long PR hitting session."

At that moment, Pen hip-checks me. "That's because you'll yell at her, and that won't look good by anyone's standards."

"I'm going to hire a new agent slash manager," I threaten halfheartedly.

"Yeah, right. I'm the only person capable of handling your attitude, your schedule, and your socials." Picking up my racket, I fix the strings so they're perfectly aligned but don't respond. "I know you're mad at me, and that's fine. Just get through this session and your sponsor event tomorrow and I'll give you a break from PR shit, okay? I promise."

"Fine."

Anya spends the rest of the half hour running me around the court to the point that I barely get my racket on a ball, the session entirely useless. I should win awards for the number of times I ignore the urge to smack a ball at her head, cursing Pen.

By the time I've finished my session with Anya, another with Karolína, and am cooling down and recovering in the physio room, I'm still fuming. Aleks finds me there, and though I'm happy to see him, I refuse to show it.

Until this point, I've been able to keep the fact that he's Anya's brother mostly out of my mind, separating the two. Life has just begun to feel easier, whether because of our physical arrangement or the fact that I've been listening to him—not overtraining and doing things for myself that aren't related (or only tangentially related) to tennis—I don't know. But today was a reminder of all the reasons I didn't want this in the first place.

"Good workout today?" he asks.

I shrug. "Where were you?"

"Went to get food with Natasha and Dima, remember?"

Sitting up from the table, I tilt my head, hardly recalling his mention of it last night. "Oh. How was that?"

"I laid everything out for them. Dima told me not to feel guilty about it. That even without understanding my reasoning, it was proof he could leave if he needed. That he'd be okay too."

I offer a small smile, hoping he listened, that the knot of guilt is lessening. "I'm glad. And Natasha?"

Concern slips across his face. "She's going to retire and go back to school. Tennis has never been good to her. She wants me to be there when she tells my parents tomorrow."

"And you're going to be, right?"

"Yeah, I'm not sure what time, but I'll push for lunch so I can make it to your event."

"How do you feel?" I dig my fingers into my hip muscles.

His eyes flick to the motion before they're back on mine. "Good. I'm glad my experience can help Natasha. And Dima's words made me feel better too."

My chest crunches at the expression on his face, so like that of a child. I want to hug him, a new and surprising urge I've developed.

I'm still not sure we make sense at this point, still riled up from my hitting session with Anya, but he needs my kindness, not my uncertainty. So I smile again. "That's great, Aleks."

His eyes search my face before he asks, "Dinner or leftovers at the hotel?"

I don't even have to think, entirely uninterested in going out. "Leftovers."

I FOLLOW ALEKS TO HIS ROOM, A BATTLE RAGING IN MY head. A part of me recognizes we've always had a ticking clock on us. Anya only served to bring it to the forefront of my mind and expedite our end. The other part of me can't stomach the idea of going back to my dark room by myself, of falling asleep alone between sheets that smell like citrus and clove.

Aleks turns shrewd eyes on me as we step into his room, his door shutting loudly behind me. "You're upset."

"I…don't know what I am."

He takes a step forward, helping me slip my tennis bag off my shoulders. His hand hovers over my hip. "How was your day?" he asks quietly. "I heard you hit with Anya."

My shoulders slump at the mention of her. It's like a wooden sign directing me out of his room. "Did you know? About what she said yesterday on the Tennis Broadcast? And that we'd be hitting together?" Karolína and Pen decided without me; it wouldn't be crazy to think they told him before me.

"Not until Karolína texted me you'd be angry during cooldown today. And Anya…"

"What did she say?" I half demand.

He sighs. "Enough to know it probably didn't go well."

Anger flares through me. "She spends so much time trying to get into my head, it's a wonder she has any left to actually train. She spent the entire hour hitting balls to the far corners so I couldn't get anything back." I pause. "Then she had the gall to talk about my parents. I wanted to punch her right then and there, but the whole point of the session was to prove to the world that we *don't* hate each other."

Aleks watches me, his eyes drifting over my features. I remember again, suddenly, that this is his youngest sibling, the baby of his family. That, at the end of the day, she is his blood, and that means he will always side with her.

He glances away. "That's shitty, Nic. She shouldn't be talking about your parents. I'm sorry."

I blink at his apology. "What?"

"It's not right that she acted that way. I've talked to her before about the way she treats you, and I'd do it again if I thought it would help. I imagine she'd use my weakness for you to make it worse. Especially since she's mad I left her team to train you." Aleks sits on the armrest of one of the couches, gazing up at me. "That said, she's not…she's not the villain you think she is. You two, you're not so different."

I scoff. "You just admitted that what she did was shitty."

"And I stand by that. But you have to remember she's only twenty-two an—"

"I didn't act that way at twenty-two."

"She's not very mature. My parents baby her a lot, and despite the immense pressure she's under, she gets what she wants more than the other three of us."

"So she's spoiled, and that's supposed to make it okay?"

"No, no. Nic, that's not—" He cuts himself off with a groan. "I'm trying to explain to you why she is the way she is. Yes, she's spoiled. She believes she should have whatever she wants, even if getting it means being shitty to people, including her family. But she's under immense pressure, more so than Natasha and Dima because she's the most likely to end up in the Hall of Fame." He notices my expression. "I'm not saying she's doing the right thing,

I'm just saying she's working hard to be where she is. Like you. And the way she's treating you, I think, is a product of the way my parents treat her. She wants to be the best, like you, and she considers you one of her strongest competitors."

I take a few steps away from him. This is now the second time he's equated the two of us. Anya, who the world loves. Anya, who tennis fans would choose to support over me. Anya, whose brother admitted she was shitty to me while also humanizing her.

There it is. He *is* on her side. It was stupid of me to believe he'd set aside a literal blood bond for some person he trains.

"I should go."

"Nic, wait. I'm not taking her side, okay? It's not that black and white. I'm trying to help you see all the factors. To help you understand."

Pasting on a fake smile, I nod. "And I completely understand."

Aleks stands, reaching a hand out for me to take, trying to bridge our gap. But I'm angry and my bra is digging into my skin and I don't want his fingers on me right now, so I step further out of his grasp.

He deflates. "I don't think you do."

"Of course I do. She's your sister, Aleksandr." He flinches at the use of his full name, and immediately, I regret it. I know I'm lashing out. And I know it's stupid. But this is all proof that we shouldn't be doing this. The sex was supposed to last until it got complicated and, damn, has it gotten complicated. "I get it."

"This isn't...Nic, my sister made your day shitty, and I

want to help. Let me do that for you, please," he begs. "You were right before. Let's go back to not talking about her. Because I can't change who I'm related to, and right now, I just want to make you feel better."

"Aren't we being stupid to ignore that glaring issue?"

"I don't care if it's stupid. It doesn't change what's going on between us. They're separate entities."

Separate until they're not. Separate until we're playing a match in a major and he has to choose a side.

Separate until it matters most, and then I'm no longer his priority. Alone again. I must be tired, because all of these concerns come out as a tiny, plaintive "I don't want to be alone," and though it sounds like I'm talking about right now, Aleks finds the true meaning.

"I'll never leave you alone. For as long as you want me around, and probably longer, I won't let you be alone."

This time, when he holds out a hand for me, I don't back away. I pull my offending bra off through my T-shirt sleeve and toss it onto the couch, cracking a smile when his eyes widen at the motion, then slip my hand into his. I'm still angry, more at the situation than at him, but I'm exhausted, tired of fighting whatever my feelings for this man are.

So I stop fighting them, allowing him to curl around me. And when he whispers a promise of breakfast in bed before pressing kisses to my hair, I sigh, happy in his arms once more.

twenty-one

The first thing I register is a banging on the door, then Aleks groaning beside me. It feels like I've only been sleeping for a few hours, so I roll over and close my eyes again, barely hearing Aleks shuffling to the door and speaking to someone.

"God, Sasha, this place is a sty." I shoot up at the voice. A demeaning laugh. "Really? A bra? You're so predictable."

Everything about this is wrong. No one is supposed to know about us, least of all Anya.

"Mom and Dad want a family brunch. You're not answering your phone, and it may be the last day we can all sit down for a meal here before the tournament picks up."

"Anya, you can't barge into people's rooms. I'll come to brunch. Just get out."

For some reason, there's a tiny lurch in my chest, remembering his promise of breakfast in bed. Not that I expected anything, but it had been a nice thought as I drifted off to sleep.

Once again, I feel like an idiot.

"You don't want me to know that you convinced some Spanish rando to slum it with you? What do you care? I'm surprised you let her stay the night."

Not liking the way she's speaking to him, I stand and pad to the doorway of the bedroom, bleary-eyed.

"Anya, leave," he says firmly.

"Honestly, it's so like you. The three of us are getting shit from Mom and Dad if we stray from our routines, don't hit the gym enough, or miss any hours on the court, and you're here, hooking up with—"

The shock on her face when she turns and sees me is almost comical. Almost worth losing the element of secrecy.

But I'm livid and couldn't care less.

For her to treat him this way when he spends so much energy trying to make life easier for her? I don't fucking think so. I take another step forward, fixing my glare on her. "Don't talk to him like that," I say, my voice low and scratchy.

"You've got to be *fucking* joking." She whirls around to face him, and I can just make out his grimace. "Is this why you left my team? To fuck her? In a tour full of women, in a *country* full of women, you choose her?" She says something in Russian, angry and spiteful, I'm sure.

Aleks shoves a hand in his hair. "Can you plea—"

She flips back to me again, and again, it would be comical if not for the more pressing matter. "This is weirdo behavior, even for you. What, you can't get to me on court so you're trying to get under my skin by sleeping with my brother? Was stealing him from my team not good enough? Or was this always the plan?"

"You were asked to leave," I answer cooly, roping my hair around my fist before letting it fall. "Don't make me regret leaving you uninjured yesterday."

Anya scoffs. "If anyone needs to leave, it's you. We're about to have family brunch, and I can guarantee you won't be welcome there."

The barb lands closer to home than expected. Hoping to hide that fact, I tie up my hair, glancing at Aleks. His eyes are steadfastly on me, something tender in them.

"Could you excuse us please?" Aleks asks. The lurching in my chest is larger and more distinct this time, like I've been slapped. I turn to grab my things. "Anya," he says in a rush, "you. Can you please excuse us?"

The hurt is made blunt by relief, but it still sits heavy on my sternum.

His sister scoffs again, stomping out of the room, "It's not a bring-your-client-to-brunch kind of event," tossed over her shoulder. The door slams behind her, then silence.

"Solnyshko, I'm sorry. I—she walked past me and..." I'm grabbing my phone and room card, knowing that, while I might not have been the one to be excused, I'm about to be shown the door too. "Nic, look at me."

I do. He's wearing a pair of boxer briefs, his chest gloriously unclothed, abs on full display. In the light of mid-morning, they're truly something to behold.

I flick my eyes to his and nod. "You have to go. It's fine. It's an off day anyway. You should spend time with your family." The words feel thick as they leave my throat.

"I'm not—I'm just going to brunch. Natasha might tell them she's done this morning, and I want to be sure I'm there if she needs me. Plus, I need to stop Anya from running her big mouth. I'm still coming this afternoon, okay? I'll meet you outside the hotel."

For so many reasons, I have no ground to stand on here. I'm the one who's made it clear that we're nothing more than casual.

And yet that voice that tells me I'll never be someone's first choice, someone's priority, gets louder and louder. Not enough for my parents. Not enough for my yiayia when I had so many other cousins she needed to take care of. Not enough for the girls, who all have their own people, and certainly not enough for tennis fans, who find more sport in hating me than loving me.

I mean, I stood up for Aleks, and though he asked Anya to leave, he didn't exactly do the same. I know it's his family, I know I'm being unreasonable, but there's a nausea building in my stomach at the notion that our plans can so easily be replaced.

Resolved not to let it show, I nod, stepping past him. Right as I get to the door, I feel him behind me. He doesn't touch me, which I'm thankful for because I'm not sure I could handle it.

"We'll talk. I can tell you're in your head. We'll talk after, alright?"

Another nod, and I'm gone.

A few hours later, I finish Delilah's winged liner, blowing on it until it dries. "Done."

She stares at herself in my hotel room mirror, blue eyes shocked, her golden hair tumbling over her shoulders. She asked for a smoky eye, and though Sahar is the best of us at makeup, I have a steadier hand for liquid eyeliner.

"Wow," she breathes. "I look like a princess."

Harper moves away from the mirror, where she's applying mascara, wrapping an arm around Delilah's shoulders. "You *are* a princess."

Sahar is in my bedroom, I'm sure leaving it in a state of disrepair as she figures out what to wear, walking in and out of the bathroom in her version of a fashion show. "I don't know about you, but I'm a queen," she calls.

Pen typically puts together a sponsor event a few times a year, inviting my friends, our teams, reps from one or two of my sponsors, and any local celebrities she can find. They're not my favorite because they require more shmoozing than I'm comfortable with or capable of, but it's a chance to dress up, enjoy what a city has to offer with my friends, and it keeps my sponsors happy. Pen and Karolína are already there, setting up and meeting with them ahead of time.

I take my hair out of its clip, letting the straightened strands fall across my shoulders. Harper notes the pieces that land out of place, turning so she can right them. "I recognize you don't like when we talk about you," she murmurs, "but I have to tell you that you're the coolest person I know. I'm so proud of you and so thankful you're allowing us to celebrate these wins with you."

"It's just a sponsor event." I haven't won a thing yet.

"Winning isn't solely on court," Delilah adds. "Winning is standing up when you get knocked down. It's putting in the work when others in your shoes would quit. Your sponsors wouldn't be knocking your door down, begging to work with you if they didn't see how much of a winner you are."

"Exactly," Harper agrees. "You're a winner every time you step on a court. No matter what happens this tournament or on clay or this season or the next, you've been a winner. To so many people, but especially to us."

"I want to get in on this!" Sahar barrels into the bathroom, knocking Delilah into me. We all crash into the wall, my closest friends in the world giggling as we hold on to each other. "You're also a winner for your banging bod, insane backhand, and that glare you give Austin when he's pissing us off."

This time, I join in the laughter. My chest is warm, like when I drink liquor on an empty stomach. The warmth seeps through my body until I feel it in my fingertips and toes. I've spent a year and a half so sure I didn't fit into this group the way I thought I should, but they've loved me all the same. My own flesh and blood can't give me the time of day, but these girls have been hard at work showing me I'm not alone, even when I was sure I was, even when they were in another country or continent.

"Thank you," I whisper.

"Alright, we're crowding her. Back it up," Delilah says after a few moments. They do. Delilah holds her arm out to me, and I loop mine through it without hesitation.

We meet the guys in the lobby. A quick scan tells me

Aleks isn't here yet, and since we're running late and I need to be in the first car, there's no time to waste.

The car pulls up in front of a massive hotel, where we're led to a private elevator bank. When we reach the top level, the elevator doors part with a soft chime, a wave of orange and grilled seafood drifting in to greet us.

People are milling about, laughing, sipping from patterned glasses, pointing at the Madrid skyline. Harper and Delilah step out onto the tiled floor of the rooftop, pulling each other in two different directions as they fixate on things on opposite ends of the party. Matteo follows dutifully behind Delilah, and Austin, Noah, and Sahar brush past me on the way to the table nearest us, laden with food.

It's more people than I expected, the city unfolding behind them, Madrid's rooftops a sea of warm reds and off-whites. Soft lounge music hums, though not so loud that it drowns out conversation, and exposed bulbs float overhead, strung across polished wood beams. Oddly shaped modern furniture clusters around raised cocktail tables, where groups of people lean with their drinks and toothpick-skewered tapas.

Pen spots me, her elegant ponytail swaying behind her as she ambles in my direction. "There you are!" She waves me out of the elevator, and I realize the poor doorman has been sitting here, holding the doors open for me.

I step out, my green satin slip dress light against my skin. Pen touches the long gold earrings I've paired with the myriad of hoops adorning my ears. "You look amaz-ing," she says quietly. "I have two of your sponsors ready to talk to you. You just have to thank them for putting this together, and I'll handle the rest."

I reach for a skewered tapa, and she nudges me, her shoulder at the height of my elbow. "Not yet. You'll ruin your lipstick. Talk first, then food."

"I thought I was supposed to be enjoying myself," I grumble.

"Give me half an hour."

I sigh. "Fine. Where's Karolína?"

"Wowing the Stratosphere rep. Come on." Pen leads me toward a cocktail table near the back of the terrace, where three sharply dressed women stand, talking and laughing with my coach.

Zahra, the head of Stratosphere's athlete partnerships in Europe has her short black hair slicked back into a bun, white blazer and wide-legged black pants crisp and ironed. Tabitha, Pen's close friend and the social content lead, stands beside her.

Zahra spots me first, opening her arms for a hug and a kiss on both cheeks. "Nic! How lovely to see you," she says.

"Thank you so much for having me."

"Having you? I'm about ready to throw a hundred parties for you all over the world."

"Oh?"

Tabitha nods, eyes wide. "People were obsessed with how the clay line looked on you in Charleston." She raises a coupe glass with a slice of dried orange. "Pen's footage from your practice days did crazy numbers. That second-skin tank went viral, and we sold out more times than I can count."

"Oh, yes." My throat is thick, and I know I need to say more, but it's like my brain has stopped working. I glance at Pen, and her smile helps loosen the thoughts. "I liked it. It didn't shift when I served."

"Function *is* luxury nowadays," Zahra answers with a smile.

When the others laugh, I join them softly. Does that require a response?

Luckily, the third woman who was talking to Karolína hops in to ask, "How is your Madrid kit? Everything to your liking?"

"It's perfect, thank you."

Pen, probably sensing the imminent mayhem, slides in charmingly to talk about the fitting we'll be doing ahead of the French Open before the conversation shifts to content shoots. I nod politely and laugh when it seems appropriate, following Pen's lead, but most of the words float past me.

After a lull in the conversation, I scan the terrace. Right as I'm eyeing the elevators, they open. Aleks steps out in a crisp, collared white shirt, sleeves rolled to mid-forearm. His eyes find mine, and he smiles.

Relief settles into my stomach, immediately replaced by irritation that my body relaxes just by existing in his proximity.

"Nic, we'll let you have fun," Zahra says. "It's your party. Go mingle."

I thank them once more before stepping away. Aleks is beside me moments later. "Nic, I'm sorry. Brunch took longer than expected, and then they asked me to go through film for Anya. I didn't realize the time until after the cars left."

I shrug, grabbing a glass of water from a tray. "No worries."

Hoping for some quiet, I find an empty corner of the rooftop with a stunning view of the city, Aleks' warmth following me as I move.

"You're upset," he states quietly, resting his forearms against the tall wooden barrier beside me.

"No."

"You're obviously upset, solnyshko. I'm sorry I had to run out so fast and miss breakfast with you."

"How was the conversation?"

Aleks sighs, rubbing a hand along his jaw. "Not good. Natasha lost her nerve after a particularly nasty first few minutes. My father isn't the nicest in the morning. She's going to try again another day, but that doesn't matter right now. What matters is I'm sorry."

Taking a long sip of the cool water, I turn those sentiments over in my head. "You don't need to apologize. You don't owe me anything."

"No?"

I turn to him. "I think this morning is further proof that this is a bad idea. Yesterday, we flew through the conversation, brushed past the whole 'she's my sister' aspect of this like it wasn't massively important, but it is."

Aleks is already shaking his head. "But it isn't."

"You want to put a pin in the whole thing. Set it aside. Our one rule is that talking about her is off limits, but that's not feasible in the long term. It's not even feasible in the short term, clearly. Because I will play her again and again and again. I won't train with her, because that was a train wreck and I'm not sure it helped, but there will still be things she does on the practice courts that will get under my skin. I will still have mean thoughts about her that I'll struggle to stop myself from saying, and if you stand up for her the way you feel obligated to do—"

"Nic, she's—"

I hold up my hand. "And I understand why you feel that obligation, but either way, it only makes me angry. So if, instead, we keep this clear cut, that won't be a problem. Especially not if we part ways after Roland Garros."

Aleks steps closer, a muscle in his jaw feathering, and the spicy part of his cologne wraps around me before the citrus. His breath is warm, our faces inches apart. "You have no good reason to end this after Roland Garros. We've been doing great."

"It's a trial run, Aleks."

He scoffs. "If you say so."

"Aleks, she's your sister. You're beholden to run at her every whim. You'll have to make a choice when we play each other: her box or mine." He said he would sit in mine when we agreed to work together, but it's hard for me to believe that's true. "I mean, you watched film for her, so clearly being my trainer doesn't mean anything. And while we might not be doing more than fucking, I'm tired of being a second choice." I bite my tongue, but it's too late. The words are out there. I scramble to finish with, "I don't expect to be your priority over your sister. But I do expect to be a priority for my team members."

Because at the heart of it, that's true, right? Regardless of what we are (which is nothing), he is on my team, and seeing him sit in her box would be one more psychological weapon for Anya to wield.

Aleks laughs, angry. "You have no fucking idea, do you?"

I cross my arms. Is it so crazy to want my team members to want to cheer for me? "What?"

"From the moment you showed up at my parents' academy, your head down, your focus unwavering, I have been *obsessed*. What luck that I began training Anya right after that and got to travel to every country you did." His head dips, so close that we're now exchanging exhales. "I have searched for you in every room, in every city, at every tournament. I was ecstatic when you joined my sessions during offseason in November and bided my time, hoping, *waiting* for an opportunity to work with you. Because you are the most talented athlete I have ever seen and I wanted to be part of the reason you accomplished everything you set your mind to.

"The moment my parents told me you might need a new performance coach, I told them if you asked for me, I'd step back from training Anya. And I meant it. *You* are my priority. It's *your* box I will choose every single time when you play each other. And while I may have been gone today, it was only because I wanted to be there for Tash. I want to be free of this guilt. I shouldn't have gotten roped into film, but the minute I saw the time, I left, despite their appeals for me to keep helping."

"Aleks…"

"So, no, solnyshko. You will never be my second choice. And if you continue expecting me to choose her over you, I will take great pleasure in proving you wrong. Every time."

My heart stops. It's an absolute triumph that I haven't dropped my glass to shatter into a million pieces at my feet, my thoughts scattered. They're coming so fast, I can hardly parse them.

I didn't say what I did with the expectation he would tell me otherwise. Honestly, before this, I hoped to take those words back. But now...

"Oh! I'm sorry." Pen's voice sends a bucket of water over my head. I take a step away from Aleks, glancing at my manager. "I was going to have you talk to one more person, but I can come back." She looks between the two of us quickly.

"She'll be with you in a second, Pen," Aleks says, his voice hovering near gravelly. When our gazes clash, I realize his eyes haven't left my face. He drops his voice. "I'm sorry Anya found out about us. I know you didn't want it getting out. I'll figure out a way to make sure she doesn't tell anyone."

"Thank you," I answer softly.

He tips his head toward my manager. "Go. I'll find the guys."

I follow Pen on unsteady legs, Aleks' words replaying in my head over and over again, slotting together to form a picture, filling in gaps I never paid attention to. And when I'm forced to converse as though the world as I knew it didn't just tilt and drop me into another dimension, it's his voice I hear like a caress in my ear.

twenty-two

An hour or so later, Aleks finds me again. In a turn of highly uncharacteristic events, we've been sneaking touches as we mingle: his palm brushing against my back as he passes me with Noah, Austin, and Matteo; our fingers kissing when a large group of us head to the edge of the terrace to watch the city come alive.

I came into this evening sure that what we were doing was wrong, but his words scrambled my head so badly that the only thing my brain is telling me is to give in to him.

After Delilah makes a joke that leaves the group—my friends, Karolína, Pen, and a couple of reps—laughing, Aleks sidles up beside me, his eyes a warm, dark blue.

He nudges me. "Look at you having fun."

"I've decided it's okay that I'm not great at talking to people. I can enjoy being here without stressing about performing."

"Yeah, you can." Aleks releases a soft breath, his hand slipping into mine, squeezing, and letting go. "I'm so proud of you."

"And I haven't had a single thought about needing to leave early to hit the gym either. I'm practically a new woman."

"Nah. You always had this in you. Just needed a little direction."

A few minutes later, Harper, Sahar, Austin, and Noah say their goodbyes. The former three have matches tomorrow. Thankfully, due to our rankings, Delilah, Matteo, and I have byes the first round.

"Kick butt!" Delilah calls as they head to the elevator.

"We'll see you tomorrow, I'm sure!" Harper yells over her shoulder. "And thank you Pen and Nic and Strato for the best tourist bucket list night!"

We laugh and they disappear. Delilah sets her head on my shoulder.

"Tired?" I ask. "We can leave too, if you want."

"No, no." She nods to where Matteo and Aleks are chatting across the tiny cocktail table from us. "He's having a good time. I'm sure he'll be ready soon, but until then, I'm happy here."

Delilah's hair drops like a waterfall over her shoulders, where her lavender linen dress straps turn into a bow on either side. "I know Pen put this together, but thank you too. If you weren't the superstar you are, we'd never get to do things like this. I mean, none of the things on my and Harper's list compare to this view of the city." She moans. "And the food is to die for."

Though I had little to do with it, I smile, content to have these small moments with my best friend.

I took for granted the time we spent together last season—laughter in hotel rooms, dinners with our teams, flights together. And though that time has shrunk, getting to be part of their outings and witnessing the joy my friends derive from events like this lead me to feel some semblance of that same joy.

Like I was so caught up in tennis and all that it entails that I couldn't appreciate the things that were in front of me until I was forced to open my eyes.

"I'm sorry," I blurt out. Another uncharacteristic moment. The night appears to be full of them. Delilah eyes me uncertainly.

"Huh?"

Clearing my throat, I lean my side against the table, facing her. "Del, I'm sorry I'm so prickly. That when I first came to the academy, I tried so hard to push you away before you had the chance to leave. Even though that was never your intent. Thank you for including me in all of your touristy things and movie nights and game nights. Getting me out of my shell. I'm so lucky to have found a friend I love as much as you."

Her mouth drops open, and it's proof I don't say things like this enough. "Nic, I have a lot of friends, but none who are so exactly my opposite and who fit in my life so perfectly. It's been a privilege getting to force my friendship on you." She grins. "My two closest friends are the grumpiest people in the world, and I love it." She knocks her hip against mine, facing the boys. "And speaking of fun…"

I follow her gaze to Aleks. "What about it?"

"Oh, please! You haven't been having *any* fun since he joined your team?" Delilah wiggles her light eyebrows suggestively, and I hide a smile in my glass.

"Not sure what you're talking about. Though I will admit he's made training feel less like a punishment."

"Right. 'Training.'" She puts the word in finger quotes. "All I'm saying is, if something's going on, I'm happy for you. You probably won't want to talk about it, and you were nice to not push me about Matteo when we were first being idiots, but…" She shrugs, tossing her hair back. "I'm here. Whenever you need me."

And because it's a night of me acting strangely, I throw my arms around her and hug her tight. In the few hours we've spent together since the season started, our dynamic has been the way it's always been. Maybe I'm not her number one anymore, and maybe I never was, but a part of me believes she will make sure we're friends until we're in the ground. A different kind of soulmate than her and Matteo.

The four of us say our own goodbyes soon after, when an influencer Pen invited to "create a crowd" tosses a glass over the side of the barrier, then screams. All at once, Matteo and I were done with the evening and we converged, heading toward the elevators.

We arrive back at our own hotel, and Delilah and Matteo step out of the car holding hands. "We're going for a walk," my friend says on a happy exhale, and Matteo nods at Aleks and me before he leads her toward Fuente de Neptuno, where the Madrid evening folds over the square, casting shadows across stone façades and black wrought-iron balconies. The fountain glistens in the warm amber glow of the streetlights, and taxis idle quietly near the roundabout, scooters humming past in short bursts of sound.

Aleks bows beside me, holding out his arm. "And you, madame? Would you like to go for a walk?"

I glance at his arm for a few seconds before I slip mine through it. "No, but after all that fried food, I need to hit the little shop next door for some yogurt or kefir."

"I love the way you think."

When we get inside, Aleks grabs a basket and leads me to the dairy section, where I pick up a small white tub. "What does this say?" I wonder to myself, cursing my mother for not teaching me her language.

"Let me see." Aleks looks over my shoulder. "I don't know why I thought I'd be able to do this. My elementary level Florida Spanish is no match for this." He pulls his phone out.

"I guess I can get it and if it turns out to be cottage cheese, I can add it to my new things list."

"Yeah?" he asks distractedly, using a translation app on his phone to scan the tub in my hand. "I'm not sure you'd like the texture. It's great for adding protein, but I don't enjoy it." He holds his phone out for me to read. It is, indeed, cottage cheese. Aleks picks up another tub with the word *yogur* on it, and I nod for him to add it to our basket as I put mine back. He keeps his eyes on me as he does, a smile pulling at his lips. "So you've been keeping up with the list?"

"I can be a very good listener, Aleks."

"Just not for me?"

I shrug.

"Ouch." But he's smiling as he slips his phone into his dress pants and walks us down the snack aisle.

He was joking, but still I say, "I don't know why you

like me. I'm not..." I search for the right word. *Normal* comes to mind but I settle on "nice."

"So? I think we've established the depth of my love of your fiery ways. Plus, who needs nice? You're intelligent. Driven beyond belief. The hardest worker I've ever met. So incredibly talented. And a fucking smoke show. There are a million other things, but we'll fall asleep before I can list them all."

"It's more than that, though." I grab a bag of chips and turn it over to decipher what flavor they are. They're not typically something I allow myself to eat during the season, but what the hell? I've been doing lots of things I don't usually do. "I'm brash. Angry all the time. There's so much rage inside me and I lash out and I just..."

"Are you fishing for compliments?" His eyes smile, bright like when he's teasing me.

I roll mine. "No. I'm just saying. There's a reason I make sure I never do more than hook up with guys." Ignoring the domesticity of us right now, I finish, "It's easier that way."

"Easier how?" he asks gently.

Needing a moment to reorganize my thoughts, I toss the bag into the basket and check if anything else catches my eye. "Easier than allowing them to see all of me, I suppose. The parts I'm reticent to share with people. You know, the worst pieces of myself that nobody could like." They'd leave and take other pieces of me, maybe even the good pieces, with them.

"Honestly, no. I don't know."

"Come on, Aleks. If you saw every part of me, you'd run for the hills."

"What I said at the party may have scared you, but let's not pretend I didn't admit I've thought about you and you alone for the last year and a half. I'm not going anywhere."

Despite the warm flare in my chest, I don't voice the belief that his words are just that. Words. I can't fully trust them. We haven't even been working together for an entire month. There's still a chance he could see something in me and decide I'm not what he signed up for.

Going the safer route, I ask, "What about you? Why haven't you settled down with a pretty model or athlete?"

As soon as the words are out of my mouth, I realize it's not the safer route. It's the worst, most dangerous road in history, and not one I want to traverse. Imagining him brushing hands with someone else at a party in Madrid, following them around the city or leading them through a grocery store makes me feel legitimately ill.

Aleks' fingers find my wrist, and they pull gently until our bodies are flush in the snack aisle. Our eyes clash and hold. "Hadn't found anyone worth settling down with," he murmurs.

My heart beats a thunderous rhythm through my body. There's something unsaid, something left on the table. He must feel the thrash of my pulse in my wrist, because he glances at where we're joined and loosens his fingers.

"Does it bother you that I've stopped asking to touch you? Should I wait until you say yes next time?"

"No," I breathe. "There are times where I don't want to be touched, especially when I'm angry or overwhelmed and hot. But you do a good job of recognizing that." And recognizing when I need it. "It's getting easier to handle with the girls too."

Aleks smiles like he won the lottery. "Good." His gaze travels to my shoulders and the thin straps across them. "Now let's get you out of this dress."

"Aleks!" I say, shoving him.

He chuckles. "Mind out of the gutter, Vassilakis. I meant it's bedtime."

"Liar."

As we walk to the checkout counter, I press my fingers into my cheeks. They're warm and pulled taut with my smile.

twenty-three

By the time the quarterfinals roll around, I feel more rested than I have in a long time. My body isn't as sore as it would usually be a week into a tournament, and my mind is clear, voices of inadequacy quieting to a dull hum. I may be playing Emilia Kessler, world number one, but I'm prepared. On my best day, I can beat her.

The first set is a battle of sliding shoes and flat shots that I lose when my last service game goes awry. "You're tight," Karolína tells me before the second set. "Loosen up. Don't get anxious. Play your game."

So I do, sweat curling my hair around my face, my braid a mess. I play free, stepping into the court to force her to the corners with perfectly placed shots, a rush of adrenaline and joy in my veins again. By the end of the set, we're both breathing heavily, but I edge ahead and take it 6–3, pumping a fist to get the crowd rallied behind me.

Unfortunately, despite the cries of support from the fans, I get down early in the third and spend the next few games playing catch up. On her first match point, I fix my strings, slap the center of the racket against each heel, step forward, and whip my return with a beautiful cross-court angle that should get me back to deuce.

The crowd roars right as the automated system says, "Out." Bewildered, I glance back at the screen, where it shows the ball half a millimeter outside the line. My mouth falls open, frustration building behind my eyes.

It can't be. I worked so hard this month, did everything Aleks told me to do. This was supposed to be my tournament. My chance to prove Paris is a possibility.

But confirmation comes in the form of the umpire's "Game, set, and match, Kessler. 6–4, 3–6, 6–4." Emilia's fans cheer loudly, and when I drag myself to the net, she offers me a smile and an awkward hug.

It's January at the Australian Open all over again, this loss mirroring the one I suffered in the final. The world closes in around me. I wave goodbye, going through the motions of post-match press and recovery until I'm sitting in the women's locker room, my head tucked between my knees.

I don't know what to do anymore. To be ranked inside the top ten in the world but have no WTA1000 title…it's embarrassing. Any sense of belonging I've felt over the last month, season, year is wiped away. I might be good enough to be on the tour, but clearly, I'm not good enough to be the best.

My phone buzzes on the bench beside me.

CARMEN

I was away from my phone. We'll try again
another time.

I scoff. *Another time.* It's been a week and a half since
our planned call didn't happen, and now she wants to talk
another time.

Whatever.

This is probably punishment for not winning. Maybe
if I'd won here, the place she became *the* Carmen Aguirre,
she'd have more to say.

Maybe I should stop giving a fuck.

I sigh, clicking over to my socials. I'm hit with thousands of notifications, instantly overwhelmed by the
number of comments on posts I (Pen) have collaborated
with the WTA and other accounts on.

@bradley.grindz.1029: Once again, she can't close

@bradley.grindz.1029: get off the court

@CallOfDoodieKing2576: You should try pickleball.
You might actually win something there

@Steve843927413: get back in the gym! You looked so
tired. Have you even been practicing?

@G.money.sabertoothsfan: maybe instead of taking
all those photos on that rooftop, you should've been on a
court

There are more than I could feasibly read, my thumb flying through them until the door of the locker room opens and I jump.

"Nic?" Aleks calls. He's cracked the door, facing away so as not to look inside. "You done?"

Grabbing my bags, I stand and pull the door open. "Yeah," I answer quietly.

He scans my features but says nothing as we walk.

They might be trolls, but the people commenting are onto something. I've been relaxing too much. Partying too much. "I'm going to head to the gym. I have energy I need to expend."

"Nic, please. Don't do this. It's one loss. It doesn't define the season. You've been doing such a good job. How rested did you feel today? How good?"

I pin him with a glare. "Very. Lot of good that did me."

"Nic—"

"No, Aleks. I tried it your way and it didn't work. This was supposed to be my season. Instead, I'm losing to the same people. Feeling rested doesn't matter if I'm not winning big tournaments."

He scoffs. "It's been a month. These things take time."

That may be true, but if there's one thing I don't have, it's time. Anya and Emilia are in their early twenties, and every season, more and more young talent joins the tour and stomps down the competition. My time to win majors is dwindling, and I can't keep slowly tweaking and changing my approach. I need to get back to what was working for me at the beginning of the season and adapt from there. Work *harder* than I was then. Working harder is always the answer.

"I don't have time, Aleks. I should be seeing progr—"

"And you have! You *just* won Charleston."

"But I did poorly at Stuttgart and here. At least with my method, I was making it to major and 1000 finals. What do I have to show for my rest? A quarterfinal loss at a tournament I was favored to win."

I don't realize Aleks stopped until he jogs to catch up to me. Ignoring the disbelieving expression on his face, I tuck my hair behind my ears and march onward.

"Nic, that's not the answer. I promise you that. If you want to see more progress, you have to work with me here. Your overall fitness *is* getting better. You're stronger on court, your serve percentage is up, and you've never hit so many winners. All of that is because you're giving yourself the time to set your feet instead of hitting it flat-footed or on the run. And you've been having *fun* again. That's an indication right there that things are working." He steps in front of me, eyebrows drawn. "Let's train hard for Rome, then sit out Strasbourg."

I draw to a screeching halt, crossing my arms. "What?"

"It's a 500, and if you go deep in the draw, you'll be playing matches right up until the French Open starts. This way, if you take that week off, you have plenty of time to rest and refocus for the maj—"

"The matches I play at Strasbourg are practice. Why would I not play them?"

Aleks runs a hand through his hair, pulling at the ends. "I just explained why, Nic. You need rest, despite what you seem so dead set on believing. You need to take a fucking break. Pushing yourself past your limit isn't strength."

"Maybe it wasn't for you, but I'm not you, Aleks. And I'm not your siblings either." He flinches, and I want to pinch myself for being such an asshole. I didn't mean it the way he's taking it, but I'm on a roll and I'm tired of him trying to control what I do. I note Karolína and Pen waiting for us ahead, so I step around him. Over my shoulder, I say, "Stop trying to dictate what I should and shouldn't do."

"That's what you pay me to do!"

I shake my head, reaching my coach and manager. Aleks remains outside our circle, his hands in his pockets, his shoulders hunched.

Karolína takes in the state he and I are in, blowing out a breath. "Shall we go for dinner?" she asks kindly. She had nothing but positive things to say to me after the loss despite the two times I snapped at her in frustration when she was trying to be helpful in my box.

"No, that's okay. I want to hit the gym."

Her discerning gaze dissects me. "Is that a good idea? You've been doing so well." Her voice drops, gentle. "Don't punish yourself now."

"I'm not punishing myself. I just know I can be doing more."

We stare each other down. After a few moments and Pen's cleared throat, Karolína says, "I can't train a shell of a person, Nic. You are one of the most talented tennis players I've ever seen. Certainly the best I've ever coached. Please stop killing yourself over these losses. You have so much season left and years more to play. This is one tournament."

I glance away, hating the way the words mirror Aleks' sentiments. "I'll see you later."

"We're flying tomorrow. Meet outside the hotel at eight!" Pen calls as I leave, and when I look over my shoulder to reassure her that I've heard, I note Aleks slide into the spot where I was, hopping into conversation with Karolína.

Knowing things have shifted between us makes the pinching in my chest more poignant, but I assure myself this is a good thing. We were getting too cozy, the lines between what we should and shouldn't be doing blurring rapidly.

It's for the best.

WITH MY MATCHES FROM THIS WEEK, TODAY'S INCLUDED, loaded on my computer, I watch the footage, snuggling under my trusty blanket in my dark hotel room, alone for the first time in two weeks.

Lonely, my heart cries.

Stupid, my brain answers.

I ignore them both, picking out places where I should have done something else. Ran around a ball to hit an inside-out forehand. Moved forward instead of horizontally to force the ball back to the other side of the court faster. Followed through better on a backhand that sailed out.

My phone buzzes beside my computer, and every time, my stupid fragile heart hopes it's Aleks.

Instead, it's my group chat with the girls.

SAHAR'S BAD BERLIN BAGELS

HARPER

Don't worry about it, Nic. You've got Rome and Paris!!

DELILAH

You're an absolute tank

HARPER EMPHASIZED "YOU'RE AN ABSOLUTE TANK"

SAHAR

Let's just say I'm glad I'm on the other side of the draw from you in Rome

MAYA

My spidey senses tell me you're winning French this year babyyyyyy

And more from the big group chat.

SHOTS FIRED

HARPER

Who is flying to Rome tomorrow? Sahar is still in, so not her or Noah.

SAHAR

Boooooo don't leave without me :(

HARPER

That's what I'm trying to decide!!

AUSTIN

I'm still in bitchesssss. I'll be here at least another day

DELILAH

Matteo plays tomorrow so I won't leave
until the day after at the earliest!

NOAH

Sahar's going to win it all, so we'll be here
until the tournament is over

SAHAR

Awww I love your delusion

I like the first message so Harper knows I'll be leaving. Even if the rest of them stay behind, my focus is on Rome. The earlier I get there, the faster I can get used to the courts and conditions.

There's nothing from Aleks. *Good,* I remind myself. I flip my phone over before setting it on the nightstand beside the piece of paper I've been adding to almost every day. I fold it and tuck it under my phone so I don't have to see it. On-screen Nic from a few hours ago is pummeling an approach shot down the line and pumping a fist when it lands on the baseline.

If only she knew.

A knock on my door startles me. Did Aleks set aside his frustrations? Or is he here to tell me more about why I shouldn't play Strasbourg? I tug the covers off, stepping out of the bed and ambling toward the door. Karolína stands in view of my peephole.

When I open the door, she smiles at me. Kind and something else I can't put my finger on. "I figured you'd be awake," she says.

Stepping out of her way, I nod. "Wasn't going to be able to sleep without watching the match back."

Her eyes flit to the partial wall, behind which the sound of the match plays on my laptop. Her brows knit before she sits on one of the couches. "We haven't talked through our plan for the rest of clay-court season."

"What do you mean? I've always played all the tournaments during clay."

"What if this year you didn't? What if this year, we take the week after Rome to reset and recuperate. You'll have played two 1000s back-to-back. That's a lot of tennis, particularly when combined with a week for Strasbourg and the two weeks for Roland Garros."

I tilt my head to the side, hearing the echo of Aleks' words. "Where did that idea come from?"

"Aleks is worried about you, and I'm inclined to agree. You need the rest. He knows it. I know it. Pen knows it. Deep down, I think even you kn—"

A sea of thoughts drown out her words. I feel like someone's lit a match inside my chest and set it on fire.

He went behind my back. He took his concerns to my coach and breached my trust entirely. Control over my life, over my routines and my schedule, are things I hold dear, and Aleks has made a point to stomp all over that control. He's practically forced my hand by pushing my coach to approach me about this.

I'm seething, so much so, I miss the fact that she stopped talking. "Nic?"

"He shouldn't have said anything. Going over my head to you is…that's so wrong."

"He's trying to be helpful. He's worried about you," she reiterates.

"I don't care. I'm not a kid. I can look out for myself,

and I do. When he brought it up to me and I said no, that should've been enough for him to drop the subject. He shouldn't be enlisting your help to change my mind."

"Nicola," Karolína says so sharply, I flinch. She only talks to me like this when I've really stepped out of line, which in this case, is outrageous. "You played a tough match, then did recovery, press, and whatever else you forced your body to do in the gym, and instead of sleeping it off, you're watching film. Something we will do when we get to Italy anyway. You don't know how to rest, and eventually, that's going to be to your detriment."

"It's my decision, and I say I'm playing Strasbourg."

"It's *our* decision. We're supposed to work together to figure out the best course of action for you."

I cross my arms, a painful lump building in my throat. "So if I make this decision on my own, will you walk? Force me to scramble for another coach ahead of Paris?"

Her shoulders drop. "Of course I won't. I want you to win it almost as badly as you do. But I want—" She cuts herself off with a shake of her head, standing. "Never mind. It's been a long day. I'll see you in the morning. Try to get some sleep."

She opens the door, and just as she steps out, she says, "We care about you, Nic. All of this is because we care about you. We want you to win, but we don't want you to be miserable while you do it. I hope someday soon, you recognize that."

She doesn't wait for me to answer, the door swinging shut behind her.

twenty-four

I stare after my coach for what feels like minutes before I shut my laptop and climb into bed. Tossing and turning does nothing to help me fall asleep, and when it's clear there's too much fire in my veins to rest, I open my messages with Aleks.

Scrolling through our last few, I bite back frustration at what I've allowed us to become.

ALEKS

Come to mine tonight

Is that a question or a statement? I'm not a fan of being told what to do, especially outside of training.

ALEKS

Right, as if you like being told what to do DURING training.

Excuse the missed punctuation. Come to mine tonight?

What if I entice you with more baklava?

> Or you could bring the baklava here, since you've now left three of your shirts with me. I assume you need those back.

ALEKS

No, those were all purposeful. Wanted you to wear them.

Maybe use them to cover your scream when you're touching yourself alone tonight.

Plus I know you like me in my slutty short shirts more than those long ones.

> You don't know anything about me.

ALEKS

I know you're going to end up in my room tonight.

And I fucking did. That night, I slept in his bed, in his shirt, in his arms.

Seeing the messages fuels my anger, and I tap out *Are you awake?* before hitting send.

ALEKS

Yes.

Making a point not to throw on any of his shirts that I have, in fact, been using as sleep shirts, I grab my phone and wallet and head to his room.

When he opens the door, his hair is a mess, like he was tossing and turning as much as I was. He didn't care to throw on a shirt, his entire upper body on display, and his sweatpants hang low, well past the trail of hair that leads into the waistband.

"I'm not sure I'm in the mood for this tonight," Aleks says.

I hold up a hand. "I didn't come here to fuck you."

Aleks laughs, a hint sardonically. "I know, Nic. I meant I don't want to fight with you. Let's talk tomorrow."

"You went behind my back, Aleks. I have no interest in waiting until tomorrow to learn why."

He props the door open with a sigh. The room that felt lived in the last twelve days has been completely packed, all but one small suitcase lined up by the door. The door shuts, and he stands before me, eyes sad.

"I didn't—I wasn't trying to go behind your back. I just can't watch you destroy your life the way I did. I loved this sport so much. I loved the tour so much. And by the end, I hated it more than anything."

"What will it take to show you we aren't the same? You left on a high with the world's respect. You won a major the day before you retired. I'm still clawing for respect, and until I get it—"

"Until you get it, what? When you get your first major, will this be done? You'll stop overtraining and killing yourself?"

"I—"

He interrupts me again. "Why do you think you lost those finals this year, Nic?"

"Excuse me?"

"Australian Open, Doha, Indian Wells. Why do you think you lost? It's not because you're not good enough. On your best day, we both know you can beat Emilia and Anya and Valentina on *their* best days. So why do you think you lost?"

I grind my teeth, crossing my arms. I'm sure he doesn't need me to answer. It seems he's been itching to say this.

"Fatigue. You're working yourself into the ground, and I hate it. If you were to continue the way you have the last month and take an easy 500 tournament you don't need to play off your schedule, you'd have so much more in the tank for Paris."

"That's not your call to make!"

"I don't know how many ways I can tell you that I see the path before you—I *walked* the path before you—and it doesn't end well. You don't have to break yourself to be loved. Plenty of people love you for who you are right now, regardless of your titles. Do you not recognize that?"

"That has nothing to do with anything."

This time, his laugh is definitely sarcastic, tinged with anger or exasperation. "Of course it doesn't. Look, I want you to win a ton of majors as much as you do."

"Not as much."

"Just as much," he reiterates. "But I want you to do it over the next few years. I want you to be happy while you do it, and I do *not* want you to burn out and call it quits sooner than you want to."

I throw my arms up. We're going in circles at this point. "None of that gives you the right to go behind my back and try to make the decision for me. It doesn't matter how worried you are about me burning out or how kind you believe you're being—"

"It's not about me—"

"You're trying to undermine my choices because of your own issues. I think you care about me"—he turns

away, as if my questioning the fact is unfathomable—
"but I also think the experiences you had on tour and the
guilt you feel about your siblings is bleeding into our
professional relationship. Like since you can't control
what's happening with Natasha, you're squeezing the
reins with me. If you can't resolve that, this isn't going to
work."

Aleks turns back toward me, searching my face. He
looks flabbergasted, like I've gone too far or pointed to
something he didn't even realize he'd been doing. Am I
being unreasonable? Am I right for once? I can't figure it
out before he glances down.

Either way, nothing he's said makes me believe he
understands where I'm coming from, or that he feels bad.
I think I've said all I needed to until I remember the text
messages and the inexplicable emotions that have been
bubbling over the last few weeks.

I'd be a liar if I said I haven't allowed the idea of us
becoming more to drift through my head languidly as we
fell asleep tucked together. I'd be a liar if I said that all I
feel for him is casual, that it's simply because he's hot and
I appreciate what he and his body do for me. I'd be a liar
if I said I'd be entirely okay if I did this right now.

But it will be so much worse if I let it drag on.

Having something like this, raw and unwavering and
hot and comforting in equal measure…I don't know if I
would be alright if I let this go further only to lose it.
Lose him.

And therein lies one of our many dilemmas. I can't
hand him every piece of me because he'll take those
pieces with him when he leaves. And he will, even if he

claims he won't. I'm certain it would break me. It would hurt far more than the fissure growing in my chest now.

That kind of heartbreak—of believing I've finally been bestowed the thing I've secretly wanted my whole life only to have it ripped away when his sister needs him or when he sees some side of me he hasn't yet—it's the last thing I need right now, when I'm so close and yet so far from all of my dreams being realized.

"I think we need to end this," I say with more conviction than I feel.

Stop, my heart begs.

"What?"

"I'm so indescribably angry at you, Aleks. So we'll keep training, but right now, I think we need to…cut the other stuff off. I need uncomplicated, and that's not what this is."

"I know you," he whispers. "Even if you don't want me to. Even if you hate it; I know you. I know you're doing this not because you're angry, but because you're terrified. But you don't need to be. I know you want to belong, probably more than anything else in the world. And nothing in this world belongs more with me than you do. The way you feel about me? I feel it too."

My throat grows scratchy, my eyes warm, and I look away from him. I need to get out of this room. It's stifling and I can hardly breathe. "You don't know what I feel, Aleks. Stop pretending you do. At the end of the day, you believe you know what I need better than I do, and I can't have someone like that on my team. So we'll finish this in June like we said we would, and I'll find someone I can trust to take over."

"No, no, no." His hand reaches up, like he wants to touch me. Instead, he runs it through his hair, anguish pulling at the angles of his face. "Nic, no. Please, come on."

I'm halfway out the door. "We travel tomorrow. You should sleep."

And when I make it back to the lonely darkness of my room—the same lonely darkness I've recently found can be cut through by a former tennis player that lights up the room—I throw myself onto the bed and sob into a pillow like I haven't allowed myself to in years.

twenty-five

When we arrive in Rome the next day, I keep my over-the-ear headphones on until we reach the rental car. Even then, I don't speak to Aleks, who, to be fair, hasn't made much of an effort to talk to me either. Travel days are always rest days unless we're on a tight schedule, so the first evening, I reluctantly follow Karolína and Pen across the slick cobblestones of curved Roman streets, the smell of fried artichokes and tobacco in the air. The couple of times I glance behind me, to where Aleks has remained the entire walk to the restaurant Pen chose, I watch him drop cash into the cases of street artists, his eyes bright.

It makes me wonder if strength and conditioning coaching is what he wants, or if it's his way of staying in the sport, near his siblings. Which only reminds me of our conversation last night, which only makes me upset.

For the next week, I go through the motions of tour life without any of the joy I'd just begun feeling again. Hitting sessions with Aleks until the girls arrive, training with him in the gym and on the slippery clay courts at the club beside our hotel, Karolína watching and stepping in so their training is entirely aligned—medicine ball throws for rotational twist turned to perfect backhands, one-legged jumps for power turned to serves and explosive runs to the net. Film breakdowns in one of our rooms, both of them pointing out areas of improvement. When I go to the gym on my own in the evenings, Aleks doesn't try to stop me, but he does watch me hawkishly from across the room.

He's distant, often not in the best mood, and based on the fact that I watched Natasha exit a practice court with tears streaming down her face, I'm convinced they either haven't talked to their parents about her quitting, or if they have, it didn't go well. On more than one occasion, I contemplate asking about it, but we haven't exchanged a single word outside of my training, and I'm not sure we're in a place where he'd want to talk about it with me anyway.

My first match at the Italian Open, eight days after landing in Rome, is practically flawless. A near perfect 6–0 opening set and 6–2 in the second. Press and cooldown move quickly enough that I end the evening early, in my hotel room, staring at the piece of paper littered with things I've learned about myself this month.

It's crumpled from when I balled it up and tossed it into one of my bags the morning we flew to Rome. I haven't added anything to it since we were in Madrid, but just looking at it puts his voice in my head.

That's true of everything though, and the urge to text him, to make sure he's okay despite what may be happening with his family, is almost too strong to ignore. I toss my phone away so I'm not tempted and think myself in circles until I fall asleep.

The next morning, after a quiet breakfast with Karolína and Pen and a stretch in my room, I take the elevator down to the hotel gym to get a few sets of warmup in before my hitting session.

Except the elevator stops, doors opening to let Aleks in. It's not the first time we've been alone since that night, but the small elevator isn't big enough to handle the tension hanging in the air. Worse, Aleks decides to pull a button, and we come to a screeching halt, suspended twenty floors up. My jaw drops.

"Nic, come on. We need to talk through this."

"Are you crazy?"

"If this is the only way to get you to talk to me, so be it. It's been a week and a half, and I don't want your training to suffer."

I cross my arms, turning fully toward him. "Has my training been suffering?"

"Not necessarily, but you've been putting in more hours in the gym than I'd like, and I think you're tired."

"Oh! Thank you for once again telling me what *I'm* feeling."

"That's not—" A frustrated sigh. "Just tell me what I can say to make this right."

I take a step toward him. "No. It's not up to me to help you fix your mistakes. You've left my trust in pieces, and I don't see them coming back together easily. Evidently, you still don't believe I can make my own decisions since you want me to stop training outside of our sessions."

He swipes a hand through his hair, exposing a strip of his stomach, and glances at the elevator panel. So far, nothing has changed on the screen, which is alarming for a hotel that costs as much as this one does. "Of course I want you to stop training outside of our sessions, Nic! If it's going to impact the way you show up on court, it's my job to be worried about that."

"Get the elevator running again, Aleks."

"Or what?"

"'Or what?' Act your age," I snap. The anger that slithers through me is so familiar, and for once, I'm grateful for it. Maybe if I let it take charge, the ache in my chest at being so close to him will dissipate.

This time, he's the one who steps forward, our shoes toe-to-toe. His silver chain catches the light, reminding me of all the times it dangled over me as we—

No.

"Oh, I'm the one being immature?"

Peering at him through narrowed eyes, I ask, "What is that supposed to mean?"

"Why the hell did you hire me? What's the point of having a strength and conditioning coach to help your performance if you're not going to *listen*? What's my role here? Because I don't feel like your coach. You spend over an hour a day on unsanctioned training."

I scoff. "'Unsanctioned training?' Seriously?"

"What would you call it?"

"I don't know! It's not like I'm hitting the squat rack and maxing out my bench press, Aleks. I'm getting in some extra cardio so I'm ready for tough matches. I'm doing the exercises *you* want, just more often."

His head tilts. "Why are you mad at me, Nic? What are you really upset about?"

"Are you dense? I told you. You went behind my fucking back and practically told Karolína I can't be trusted to make my own decisions."

Aleks shakes his head, and it makes my blood heat. If there is a higher power, this man must have been created and sent purely to make me angry. "No. What's the real reason?"

"Aleks, you're pissing me o—"

"What's the real reason?"

"You made me trust you! After months of being sure you were no better than your sister, you came into my life and took care of me. Made me feel like I was your priority. Made me believe you wanted what was best for me. I don't trust easily, but you wormed your way in, then went behind my back. I've never let someone in so fast, and you..." I glance away, breathing heavily. "Restart the elevator before they send a search and rescue team after us, Aleks."

"No." His fingers hover near my chin, though he doesn't touch me. It's like a dagger to the chest. "If you believed I wanted what was best for you, why is it so hard to believe that me wanting you to sit Strasbourg out might be what's best for you?"

My gaze clashes with his. Over the course of the argument, we've gotten close enough that the smell I cling to in the shirts he left envelops me. "I'm not having this discussion again. Get out of my face." I set my hands on his chest, but my shove is barely more than a tap. My body's final betrayal where Aleks is concerned.

His hand grabs both of mine where they sit, the other slipping into my hair, pulling my lips to his. It's chaste, and when I try to deepen it, Aleks turns, resting his temple against mine, his ragged breaths beside my ear.

"What are you doing?" I ask, feeling cheated.

"We're not doing that until you stop being mad at me."

"Aleks, I'm not sure a day will go by that I won't be mad at you."

His nose below my ear sends a shock through my body, a bolt of warmth in the pit of my stomach. "Is that a promise?" he whispers.

"Wh—what?" I shift closer, desperate for *more*.

"I want you to promise to be mad at me every single day. I'll take mad over indifferent every day for the rest of my life," he says against the skin of my neck, the place he knows drives me crazy.

I hardly hear him, the need to be touched so dire, a moan breaks free of my throat.

He inhales once, then kisses my hair before backing away. His pupils are blown, a groove between his brows as he offers me a pained smile. "Don't worry. I've missed you too."

Rapid Italian through the speaker above us startles me away from him. I lean against the far wall, too stupefied to do more than stare.

"Sorry?" Aleks answers innocently. "We don't speak Italian."

"Do you need help? Has there been an emergency?" the man asks with a heavy accent and little patience.

Aleks takes me in, his grin turning wicked as he adjusts himself in his pants. "Don't believe so. You good?" he asks me. At my scowl, he says, "We're all good."

"Do you see a knob?" The operator is done with our shit. "The one that has been pulled up? Can you press it?"

"Oh, my bad. These elevators are a foreign concept to me."

The operator mutters something about Americans while Aleks rights the knob he pulled. The elevator jumps to life, and the man clicks off.

I finally catch my breath as the doors open to reveal the hallway to the gym. Aleks steps out, but I'm no longer in the mood for a lift.

"Aleks," I croak despairingly, shoving my body in the way of the elevator doors.

I'm tired of not knowing how he is. I can be mad at him *and* be worried. "Is everything alright? With Natasha and your parents?"

His expression shifts, darker. "Not yet. But it will be."

"Are…are you okay?" The elevator doors start to close before jolting open.

"Yeah, solnyshko." His lips tug upward. "I'm okay."

I nod, step back, and allow the doors to close between us. After clicking my floor number, I droop against the wall, wishing for the self-control I seem to have in spades in every other facet of my life.

twenty-six

Once again, I disappoint in Rome and Strasbourg, going out in the rounds of 32 and 16, respectively. I walk off the court in Strasbourg, beaten down and exhausted, my lower back flaring up again.

When I finish press, Karolína and I head toward the players' gym for my cooldown. Aleks is there, arms crossed.

After the elevator incident left me in a state of total embarrassment—both because I admitted far more to him than I meant to and because I'm sickened by how desperate my body was for him—I've been pretending nothing happened. Clay-court season is drawing to a close, then it's the shortest season of the year: grass. I don't have the bandwidth to unpack the complexities of our situation or to make decisions about whether this is sustainable in any way.

"I don't want to hear a single 'I told you so,'" I grumble angrily as the three of us step inside the gym.

"You won't," he reassures me softly. "We're just going to do a walk, roll out, and stretch."

Eyeing him, I wonder if he noticed my grimace after the serve I hit late in the first set, or if the pain in my back was obvious in my gait as I walked off the court. I tried so hard to hide it, sure I wouldn't hear the end of it if he noticed.

But Aleks has always been perceptive when it comes to me.

I step on a free treadmill, setting it to the speed Aleks recommends. Despite the fact that I played an evening match, the gym has players and their teams milling about. Once I get into a rhythm, I let my head drop, the crushing weight of defeat bearing down on every one of my weary bones.

This flare-up, all these losses, are they divine proof that Aleks and Karolína were right? That I should have sat this one out? I'm in more pain than I'd like to admit the week before my favorite tournament of the year. Obviously, if I hadn't played here and instead gone straight to Paris to train, this wouldn't have happened.

And if this impacts my chances of winning Roland Garros, I'll never forgive myself.

The first angry tear treks down my cheek before I can wipe it away.

"Hey, look at me," Karolína says. When I don't, she shuffles closer. "Nic, look at me."

I raise my eyes to hers, finding a concerned Aleks behind her.

"This doesn't mean anything, okay? You have five days to rest and prepare for Paris. This tournament doesn't define this season." She sets her arms on the treadmill, her chin in her hand. "I'm so proud of how far you've come this year and in the time we've been working together. You're at your absolute best so far and climbing higher each day. That title is as likely to be yours as any of the other women in the top, you hear me?"

I stifle a sob. "I'm embarrassed." And worried that I'll underperform. That I won't have figured out how to close when it matters most.

"Unfortunately, losing is one thing nobody in this sport can outrun. Every single player in the hall of fame lost more matches than tournaments they won. All of the greats faced defeat just like you have, and it doesn't make them any less great."

I nod, choked up, and we finish the last few minutes of my walk in silence before we head over to the area with mats. Aleks pulls out a foam roller for me to start on my legs while Karolína goes in search of Pen to figure out dinner for tonight and our travel plans to Paris.

Hiding my winces and grimaces appears effective, Aleks' face stoic enough that maybe he hasn't noticed. But when he has me lie on my back and lift my right leg so it's at a ninety-degree angle, then slowly pushes it toward me, I groan.

"That bad, huh?"

"You knew?"

"Of course I knew, Nic. I saw it after that serve. You played tight the rest of the match."

"Alright, alright. I get it."

He watches me as I bend my leg and pull it toward my

chest, hiding another wince. "I wasn't shitting on you. I'm worried about you."

"I'll go see a trainer."

Aleks holds his hand out to help me off the ground. My body aches in protest as we walk to the room connected to the gym, where on-site trainers work their magic on sore muscles and injuries.

"You don't have to come," I tell him before he pulls the door open. "Isn't Anya playing?" She was supposed to go on right after me, but she may still be on.

Aleks turns so he's facing me, eyes holding mine. "I don't care. I'm not on her team, I'm on yours. And I want to make sure you're okay." Affection softens the lines beside his eyes, and though the curve of his brow tells me he's worried, he smiles and opens the door for me.

The air in here is cooler, the smell of antiseptic strong. Bright, clinical lights reflect off white tile, and a row of padded treatment tables line one wall. A physiotherapist near us massages a player's shoulder, and another smiles when she notices us.

"Nicola, hi! Did you need help?"

"Oh, uh, hi. I have an old psoas injury that's flaring up."

She leads us toward a table near the back. "Which side? And is it your back? Your hip? Or the whole area?"

"Lower back. My right side."

She has me lie on the table and palpates, checking where the pain is before guiding me through hamstring, quad, and glute stretches. After another massage loosens it up, she hands me a bag of ice and says, "Be careful with it. Make sure you're taking a couple of extra rest days so it doesn't get worse."

It's a slap in the face I don't need, but I thank her and sit with the ice between me and the table back.

Aleks steps away to use the restroom, and I pull my phone out, reading my messages.

SHOTS FIRED

AUSTIN

Less than a week until Paris. We better be planning to go to at least one party

SAHAR

Are you here??

We've got five days until we play. What are you waiting for

NOAH

You know I'm in this group, right?

SAHAR

Oh, so now I can't party? When did you get so lame? Everyone else's coach lets them have fun

DELILAH

Sad I'm still in Italy :(

Matteo gave me puppy dog eyes so I'm setting the record straight that I would not rather be at a party in Paris than in Italy

HARPER

I'd switch with you in a heartbeat!

AUSTIN

Rude! I'll find a club we can hit tonight

Separate from the group, Delilah texted *You doing alright?* I type out a *yes, I'm fine* before I decide to be honest.

> **Not my best.**

I switch over to social media, swiping away Delilah's *Call later tonight?* when I notice the flood of notifications pouring in.

@Steve843927413: if she plays Anya or Emilia, she's done for

@bradley.grindz.1029: @Steve843927413 for real, did you see what Anya said about her?

Frowning, I open Google and search Anya's name. Her Wiki page comes up, along with news from Rome, where she lost in the final. A few of the articles are more recent though, one that's not more than a few minutes old. It's titled "American Prodigy Calls Out Greek Rival" and I have a sinking, angry suspicion I'm the rival in question.

As far as I know, things have been quiet since the bullying comment. The video Pen took seems to have done the trick in getting some of the heat off my back for my alleged bullying without me outright making a statement denying it—something Pen described as having the potential to make things worse. I'd hoped we were past this, but I shouldn't have underestimated Anya's immaturity.

Making sure no one is near me, I click the video and turn my volume up a few notches.

"Anya, you often play top ten players, but one person who keeps popping up is Nicola Vassilakis. Knowing she's been picked as a favorite to win Roland Garros, how do you feel about a potential meeting in the final?"

Anya shrugs, pushing her hair behind her ears. She's wearing the same Stratosphere shirt I often throw on for press since they send ten of them every few months, and for an irrational second, I wish I had another sponsor. "I'm not worried about her. She can keep poaching my coaches all she wants, but the pressure is clearly getting to her." Her lips curl. "She's distracted and sloppy, and she's been struggling the last few tournaments. I wouldn't be surprised if she's got a mental block that new coach can't fix."

The white-tiled walls close in on me, and I have to dig my nails into my palms to remind myself I'm in public. The quiet hum of the light above me grows louder, a buzzing in my ear. Heat rolls over my shoulders, joined by nausea. She doesn't know anything about my mental struggles, and indicating she does is despicable. Anya answers another question, but I click my phone off and set it as far from me on the table as I can.

In my periphery, Aleks walks toward me. Instantly, he recognizes something's wrong. "Nic? Does it hurt more? What's going on?"

Taking another few deep breaths, I type in my password and hand him the phone. When the first question has been answered, he turns to me, a wild look in his eyes. "I didn't—I don't have anything to do with—"

"I know," I answer softly. "I didn't think you did."

Aleks nods once before playing it again. He notices me cringe and lowers the volume, stepping away.

"This is my fault," he says after listening to it again, bridging the distance between us. "She's clearly bitter about you and I doing…whatever it is we're doing." He sighs.

"No, Aleks, it's not. You can't control what she says."

"It's not just that."

I meet his eyes, confused.

"My parents got worse after Natasha told them she wanted to quit. They threatened to cut her off, which means if she wants to go back to school, she'll have to find a way to do it without their help. She hasn't officially retired, but when she pulled out of Roland Garros, my parents were *livid*. It ended in a fight like our family has never had before. Dima and I were on her side, but Anya took my parents'."

He runs a hand through his hair. "I think Anya took it personally that I left to train you and am backing Natasha but am not willing to do more for her. The whole thing ended with Anya calling Natasha a baby and my parents so angry with the three of us, they wouldn't speak, especially to me. Like I've betrayed them for a second time."

"Oh, Aleks. I'm so sorry I wasn't there for you during all of that." *Fuck*, I'm so selfish. I spent a week and a half angry over what happened between us, barely talking to him, and all the while, he was waging his own war. "My anger…Clearly you were right"—I gesture at the ice on my back—"and I shouldn't have been so upset with you when you recommended I rest. More importantly, I should've been there for you while you were going through this."

"No." A shake of his head as he steps toward me. "You were right, Nic. I overstepped. I was frustrated about the situation with Natasha, and instead of dealing with it separately, I let it impact our relationship. So I wanted to get it handled before it bled into us again."

My chest constricts, so tight, I can hardly breathe. Any rage I felt about Anya's comments dissipates, replaced with something way too warm that I've been trying to cut off at every turn. Once again, Aleks is proving to me that I'm his priority.

"And is it? Handled?"

"It's getting there. I told Natasha I could cover the cost of any school that she can't. She's opposed to it, but I think it gave her hope that there's a way forward. As for my parents, they were angry after I quit, and that blew over eventually. I have no doubt this will too. Obviously, I have no clue what that looks like for Dima and Anya staying in it, but one battle at a time."

"One battle at a time," I agree.

Aleks chuckles, eyes lighting. "You're smiling."

I realize he's right, and there's no point in denying why. "I'm proud of you," I answer quietly. "You were so worried about telling them why you left, and now look. Natasha's going to pursue her dreams."

His expression turns pensive. "Yeah."

"And you? Are you pursuing your dreams? Or is coaching your way of staying close to your siblings?" The ice has numbed my back, so I pull it out while he contemplates.

"The oldest brother in me is glad I'm finally doing something worthy."

"Aleks…"

He chuckles. "You didn't let me finish. I love what I do, Nic. Getting to see how much our training has helped your game is so rewarding. I'd love to coach you to as many victories as you want, and when you're ready to retire, hopefully years down the line, maybe I'll coach another tennis player. Or work with athletes from other sports."

"As long as it's what you want."

"It is. Is it what you want? For us to continue working together?"

"I think there are things we need to figure out. My training has been far more efficient and I'm more confident on court. I know I wouldn't feel that way if it weren't for you so…we need to figure out the right balance. I need to dial it back one percent"—at his raised eyebrow, I laugh softly—"okay, five, and you…"

Aleks sets his hand on the table beside me. "Though a part of me feels to blame that you're hurting right now, like I should've stopped you before you could hurt yourself, I'm realizing I need to let go of what I've learned for myself and let you make your own mistakes." I roll my eyes playfully at the last word, which makes his grin widen. "So while I'd like to keep working with you and providing you with my thoughts on how best to move forward, I won't force you to bend to my will. I'm sorry I tried, and in the future, your word will be what we follow. I just want you to take mine into consideration."

It's all I need to hear to reach out and brush my fingers across his. "That's a good start."

twenty-seven

Though the high-speed train ride from Strasbourg to Paris is only two hours, we take the next day to rest and explore the city, my lower back sore enough that I wouldn't want to workout or practice anyway. I add to my old list by following Pen around Paris, enjoying places I've never been to and foods I've never tried. The afternoon is met with gold-framed mirrors and red leather at a Parisian café, fresh coffee and buttery croissants to sate us after the trip to our hotel.

Pen wants me to take photos for social media, so we stroll through gardens with tall, manicured hedges and vivid flower beds on the way to a restaurant with three Michelin stars, golden walls, long crystal chandeliers, and a waitlist booked out for a year—I have no idea what thread Pen pulled or who she knew to get us a reservation. When the chef comes to talk to us, Aleks and Pen keep the conversation alive, and the latter adds a photo with her to a shared album she's titled *Paris dump*.

The next four days, I have practice sessions with Sahar, Harper, and Delilah once she arrives before brief stretches with Aleks and film with him and Karolína. "We're emphasizing rest and recovery this week over pushing ourselves," he reminds me when I snap that I'm not fragile. It leads to a quiet apology and a continuation of the resistance banded clams.

In the evenings, while walking around the neighborhood in a large pack of us girls and our teams, Aleks' touch lingers—on my hip after I step into his space while a group passes us on the sidewalk, on my elbow when I'm too busy staring at my feet while trying to decide where to jump into conversation that I nearly walk into oncoming traffic, on my lower back, a brush of his fingers when we get sidetracked looking into a patisserie and need to catch up with our friends.

He started hesitant but grew emboldened when I didn't stop him, unbothered by the contact. So much so that, when he's not touching me, I'm finding reasons to be by his side.

We don't speak of any of it, especially not during the day, when we're hyper focused on the impending tournament. It appears to be something we'll address afterward, and with how much pressure I feel surrounding this major, I'm thankful he's giving me that.

The first time I step onto Philippe Chatrier, Roland Garros' center court, during the Round of 128, there's a buzzing in my blood. A sense of belonging, like my body is writing a song only the red clay in Paris can hear. I win in straight sets, dropping two games to my unseeded opponent. A couple of days later, I play another unseeded opponent, a crafty seventeen-year-old who worked her way up from qualifiers, and though she's able to keep up with my pace in the first set, I win 6–4, 6–1.

It's the most fun I've ever had on the court, and that excitement follows me into each point.

My third match is similar to the first two, and I'm grateful for all the tournaments I did well in this year. Because of them, I'm seeded high enough that the first few matches aren't against higher-ranked players. Though my back feels sore after a serve late in the second set, I end the match with a smile and spend the evening with a physio massaging the area, Aleks sketching by my side to keep me company while Karolína and Pen disappear to get us dinner.

"Would you ever want to do that for money?" I ask him when I see the one he just finished, a stunning image of me grinning on court that makes me realize how much better this tournament has felt.

Aleks shrugs. "Not really. It's like any other hobby, something I do when I have the time. Monetizing it might take the joy out of it."

It's such an interesting concept, I wonder what hobbies might interest me. A few minutes later, when I search what people are saying about me, he takes my phone away. But not before I see Jackson from the Tennis Broadcast talking about me being in peak form. It leaves a hint of a smile on my face for the rest of the evening.

Next, I meet my first seeded opponent in the round of 16. While it's not the best tennis I've played all tournament, my focus remains on getting the ball to her side of the net, forcing her to run back and forth across the court until she's too tired to get the last ball back. My winner average is down after I leave Court Suzanne Lenglen, the secondary stadium, but I get the job done in two scrappy sets and celebrate getting into the second week of the tournament with dinner with the girls, the guys, and Aleks, all the while aware I'll face world number one Emilia Kessler in my quarterfinal in two days.

Going into the second week, I listen to Aleks and only train when he allows me to, handing over my laptop before bed so I can't watch film late into the night.

When I step onto Philippe Chatrier on Tuesday, the buzz in my blood ratchets up, begging—no, screaming—for me to finish this. To do what I haven't been able to do all year.

It's a hot June day, and though I train in the humid hellscape that is Florida, my lungs burn and my body aches more than they have the last week of matches. After scraping by in the first-set tiebreak, I lose my footing and drop the second set 1–6. It's a grim meeting with my team during the break before the third set, but I wrap a cold towel around my neck and press it to my face, downing half a water bottle and an energy gel as Karolína runs through what I can improve upon for the deciding set.

"What are you going to do?" she asks before I leave.

"Step in a foot farther during her second serves." She holds up a finger and nods encouragingly. "Play to the corners a few more shots before trying for the winner." A second finger. "And focus on my footwork." Three fingers up.

"You got this, Nic," Aleks adds from beside her with a proud smile.

Emilia is unsurprisingly formidable, an opponent I can say brings out my best tennis. One who makes me a better competitor. And with Karolína's pointers, I pull ahead. During the third game, I step in for two of Emilia's second serves, which gives me the break I need. In the sixth game, I hit cross-court shot after cross-court shot, wearing her down until she's struggling and the opportunity for perfect winners presents itself. During the eighth game, I jump to my toes as soon as the serve sails off my racket, ready for her return, and because of that, I beat her in the decider 6–2.

I drop to a squat, my hands covering my face in genuine, unrepressed shock and jubilation, my heart racing, the knots in my stomach unraveling so completely that I feel indestructible.

Beating the world number one is never easy, but even less so on a stage as big as this, with German fans who have traveled here to watch her screaming for her at the tops of their lungs. It occurs to me as we shake hands at the net that her massive fan base didn't factor into the match this time. It was just me, the clay, and the determination to do something I haven't been able to.

I leave Roland Garros' largest stadium with my head held high, new fans metaphorically assembling behind me, awaiting what I'll do in the semifinal.

Once again, we celebrate with dinner, and I do a truly commendable job of listening to Aleks, getting a massage from physio, doing a long, recovery-focused cooldown, and waiting to watch film until the next day. I barely remember to check for messages from my parents, and when I do, right before I fall asleep, I see Aleks' *I'm so unashamedly proud of you, solnyshko* and feel so warm, I have to remind myself I'm not allowed to knock on his door and fall asleep in his arms until after this tournament is over.

In the semifinal on Thursday, I meet an unseeded French player, who has battled her way through multiple top-twenty opponents, including Valentina Ortega, last year's champion. To describe the crowd as difficult to manage and plain rude would be an understatement, and yet I find once more that I'm able to overcome it. When I hear them cheer, "Blanche! Blanche! Blanche!" I pretend they're saying, "Nic! Nic! Nic!" It's invigorating, so much so that I have more aces than I have all tournament combined. I win 6–2, 6–4, and though I'm being booed in spectacular fashion, I smile politely at the fans and congratulate my opponent on an amazing run. After everything, I end up on the floor of the players' gym, staring into space in disbelief because for the first time in my adult career, I'm in the French Open final.

My team and friends each take turns squeezing me, and though it's not entirely comfortable, I accept their hugs and praise with a nod, hardly hearing them.

Two major finals in a row, two major finals in a row, two major finals in a row. The words play over and over in my head. I may have lost in Australia, but clay is my home, and I won't, *can't,* let this chance slip through my fingers. The pressure builds in my chest, tight and uncomfortable, until later that day when I learn who my opponent will be.

Anya Morozov.

My eyes find Aleks' first when the match on the television in the gym ends with Anya screaming, "Let's go!" to the crowd. Suddenly, the balloon grows heavier, filled with doubt, and Aleks takes me aside, his fingers soft against my right hip.

"Breathe, baby. Breathe. That's it," he says when I finally listen, taking air in and out, my shoulders rising and falling.

"It's Anya," I say miserably. "I…"

"Can beat her. That's it. That's the only thing I want to hear out of your mouth right now." He drops his head so we're the same height, his bright blue eyes forcing me to latch onto them. They're earnest. "I have never seen you play the way you have the last week and a half. I mean that. And you know that I've watched you for over a year. This is the best you have ever been. The past is the past. Your record means nothing. You beat Emilia after losing to her in Melbourne and Madrid. You can beat Anya to win your first major."

After taking another couple of calming breaths, I step into his body, my head falling into the crook of his neck. That I ever believed he would choose to sit in her box when we played each other was a disservice to him. Immediately, I'm enveloped in the warmth of citrus and clove, and his arms wrap around me loosely, like he wants to give me the option to step away whenever I need.

But I don't need to, and I certainly don't want to.

"What if I don't? What if I can't?" I ask. I hate how scared and small I sound. It's so unlike me, and yet fitting that it's in his arms I feel safe enough to voice the terrible thought.

"Nothing changes. You still got to a second major final, and your first in Paris. You're still the strongest player I've ever had the pleasure of watching. You move up a few spots into the top five, where you've always belonged, and you play your heart out for the rest of the season. With my help, of course, to tell you when you need to take it easy. It's not the end of the world, solnyshko. It's a game." He adjusts us so he can tap his chest with his index finger, where his tattoo rests. "Remember?"

"'For the love of the game,'" I whisper.

"Exactly. I know it doesn't feel like it right now. And I know it won't, no matter the outcome on Saturday. But it's a game. And you'll have plenty of time to collect your titles after. Alright?"

I nod but don't step away from him. We haven't held each other like this since before our fight, and half of the tension in my shoulders lifts. "I've missed this," I admit quietly.

Aleks squeezes me. "Me too. Let's get through Saturday, then I'll make it my mission to be your full-time happiness incubator."

I chuckle, his own laugh rumbling against me. Karolína calls me hesitantly from the doorway of the players' gym, and my surroundings come back to me. Tournament staff stand a few feet away, looking away from us as though, if they make eye contact, they'll catch fire.

"Okay?" he asks as I step away. It's weighted heavier than the one word it is.

"Okay," I answer, hoping it conveys just as much.

Karolína, Aleks, and I spend the evening on recovery

and all of Friday watching film, coming up with a strategy for how I'll get over my biggest mental and physical hurdle.

I promised myself not all that long ago that I would be hoisting a major trophy soon. And despite the self-doubt that flits into my mind here and there as we prepare, I mean to keep that promise.

twenty-eight

Because the universe is set on building as much tension as possible between us, Anya and I warm up in the same room. I face Aleks, who stands against the wall, and behind me, Anya trains with her performance coach and parents, facing the opposite wall. Every time Aleks drops a ball in my periphery for me to catch, I imagine her eyes burning holes in my head.

"Focus, Nic."

"I am," I grumble.

Aleks laughs. Karolína puts a few freshly strung rackets in my bag. When I take a sip of water, glancing over my shoulder, I note I was right: Anya's glaring, her eyes bouncing between Aleks and me. Their parents, too, are watching us, though her father quickly barks something at Anya and they all return to her warmup.

"Focus," Aleks reiterates, though his eyebrows pull together like he witnessed his father's ire. "Stop looking behind you. Don't let her get into your head. That's a huge part of her game plan. Play your game, ignore her and the noise and everything else. Focus on your tennis. You'll be unstoppable."

I set the bottle down. "For once, I'm glad you know her so well."

He laughs again before handing me a jump rope. I begin hopping, running through my five key points for today—get my first serves in for some free points; if I have an opportunity to put the point away, do so effectively or she'll find a way to do it first; do not get caught with flat feet; stretch the court and be prepared for shots with a lot of angles; and finally, don't let her get in my head.

Right around the time my heart rate reaches its max and my body is warm, we're led to the entrance of the court. My name is called, and for the second time this year, I step onto court for a Grand Slam final. There are cheers from the crowd, people swinging Greek flags, and I wave, keeping my headphones over my ears and taking in the large letters that read "Victory belongs to the most tenacious" in English and French across one of the stands.

I'd like to believe that, at least today, that's me.

Our warmup moves at light speed. Anya is on her best behavior now that the eyes of millions are on her. When it finally comes time to start the match, every cell in my body awakens. My blood hums, singing to the clay and Philippe Chatrier in a language foreign even to me. I bounce a ball one, two, three, four times and slap it into play.

Anya gets it back, a winner down the line. She pumps her fist, and the hum of my blood turns to an angry sizzle when she stares right at me, the crowd behind her. My next serve is out, my second serve too easy. She hits another winner.

"Slow down," Karolína calls from my box. "Take a breath."

I blow on my hand, accepting two balls from the ball kid. I breathe in and out deeply before bouncing the ball four times and slapping it into play again. This time, she hits it right at me, and though I'm able to get my racket on it, it's a high ball that lands inside the service line. Anya attacks it easily. Three winners in three points. It's so demoralizing that I wind up double faulting away the first game, holding back a frustrated scream.

Don't let her get in your head, says a voice that sounds like Aleks. *Don't let her know you're upset.*

Still, I lose the first set 6–1 and end up in the bathroom during the break, trying to use deep breaths to settle the rock in my stomach and the frustration in my veins. I can't—won't—lose the next set. I have fought tooth and fucking nail for this. Years and years of struggling through the tour, then an injury and another few years with mixed results. I fought so hard through it all, and I'm not letting it slip through my fingers the way it did in Melbourne, Doha, and Indian Wells this year.

Forcing the tears to remain at bay, I breathe in deeply, then breathe out. Deep breath in, deep breath out. I splash water on my face, pat it dry, take another couple of deep breaths, and jog back onto the court, my face neutral. It's a new set. The first set was a different Nic. This set is mine.

Tossing my towel in a bin on the edge of the court, I look at my box. Karolína stands, clapping. Beside her are Pen and Aleks, and behind them are Delilah, Matteo, and Austin.

All six of them wear encouraging smiles and yell various versions of *you got this*. I can't remember the last time my box was so full, like I have a big family backing me, just as I've always wanted. And though Harper and Sahar left Paris to train on grass, I know they're watching my match carefully too.

"Remember the game plan, Nic! Come on!" Karolína nods optimistically.

I grab my racket and head to the court. Anya is serving to begin the second set, so I align my strings properly, hit the center with the heel of each shoe, and drop into position. Her first serve is tough, but I get it in, and when she runs me to the far side of the court, then back and forth and back and forth, I finally take advantage of a ball in my strike zone and hit a winner down the line.

My box screams louder than the rest of the crowd, and not for the first time, I mentally thank Aleks for getting my conditioning to where it needed to be for this match.

We go back and forth on deuce a few times before she drops a ball inside the baseline again and I put it away, breaking her serve for the first time today. Relief sighs out of me. It may only be the first game, but it's a bit of momentum I desperately needed and harder than it sounds against Anya's strong serve.

The next few games, we hold serve, battling hard until it's 5–4 in the second. The crowd heavily favors

Anya, but I ignore it, especially when Aleks cheers for me so loudly that Anya glances over at him, her expression contorting. She may have the crowd, but I have him, and because of that, for once, I might be getting in *her* head.

My first serve is an ace. The next is out wide, and though she gets her racket on it, her return sails long. The next is another ace. Set point, I bounce the ball four times, toss it in the air, and hit it so hard, I feel it in my back. Her return is a perfect winner, and I wince at the ache near my hip. I need to win this set so I can take a medical timeout and have the physio come on court.

Bounce, bounce, bounce, bounce. Toss, slap it in the air. She gets it back to the center of the baseline, and I run around it, smacking the angled forehand with such a high velocity that it bounces inside the service line and hits the wall before she can get into position.

"Come on!" I yell, letting the booming claps of the crowd in, letting them take residence beside where my heart beats a wild rhythm. The tide is shifting. At the very least, they want this to go to a deciding set.

We're even now, just a set until one of us is crowned this year's Roland Garros champion.

I make eye contact with Aleks, who grimaces, like seeing that I'm in pain hurts him too. Calling for a physio, I reset one more time, taking the painkiller she offers me and sinking into the massage until it feels a little less tense.

If I win this, I'm taking that fucking break Aleks keeps talking about. Hell, I'll take it even if I don't.

"Your range of motion may be inhibited," the physio tells me, her neat, slicked-back ponytail swinging as she puts things back into her backpack. I nod my understanding and head back to the court for the final battle.

I return well the first game, but she holds serve. I hold in the second game. The third is hers and the fourth mine, back and forth holds of serves until we're into the third-set tiebreak, my back begging for reprieve.

Ten points is all I need. Ten points, and I can have everything I've wanted for years.

Anya double faults the first point of the tiebreak, slamming her racket on her leg three times in a way that will certainly bruise later. I hit two perfect first serves, an ace and a ball she returns out.

My head keeps rushing to *seven points left*, but I force my thoughts to *one point at a time*. Anya wins the next two, screaming after I hit a ball outside the baseline. I win the following three. At 6–2, Anya hits a drop shot that brings me sliding toward the net, and when she gets it back, I tap the ball out of her reach.

I pump my fist for the crowd, many of whom seem to be backing me now. I revel in the noise until I notice Anya gesturing at me while talking to the umpire.

She has to say it four times before I hear her. "Her racket went over the net. That's not allowed!"

I'm 99% sure my racket didn't, but I look at the woman in the tall chair. She says something in French, then repeats it in English, "Anya Morozov is requesting a video challenge."

The crowd quiets as I pop onto the screen. My racket makes contact with the ball right inside the plane above the net, and when it switches to slow motion, it's clear my racket never crosses over.

"The racket stayed on her side. Vassilakis' point. Vassilakis leads seven points to two."

Anya stomps a foot, the smug expression she wore the whole first set replaced with anger. "What! That's not fair! I want to watch it again."

There's a collective murmur in the stands, perhaps Anya's fans realizing she's on the edge of a tantrum. At this point, it's poor sportsmanship to imply that the umpire was wrong, particularly when we've all seen the replay slowed down.

She's trying to delay. I've got the momentum and I'm three points away from the trophy. Walking away from the net, I grab my towel, wiping my face, arms, and grip down. I hear Karolína somewhere, telling me to decrease my serve speed, but the rush of my blood overwhelms the words.

Focus on your game, Aleks' voice says in my head.

So I step up to the baseline, and after Anya finishes throwing a fit, receiving a warning from the chair umpire that only serves to make her more angry, I bounce the ball four times and hit my prettiest ace yet, right up the T.

Anya screams, this time in anger, stomping to the other side of the court. Each time we've played over the last few years, I've allowed her to get into my head. It's no wonder I've struggled to beat her. The crowd, too, I've allowed into these matches, but when I tune back in, I realize the loudest chant is my own name.

Our roles at Indian Wells have been reversed. *Finally* I understand what it's like to have a crowd rooting for me to win a major title. And it comes as a blinding realization that I don't care.

This is for me. For the love of the game.

Four bounces, a toss, a smack of my racket, and her return slides into the net.

I'm one point away. My hands shake, my knees too, and if the buzzing in my head weren't deafening enough, the crowd is.

One more glance at my box gives me everything I need. Six people rooting for me. In every way that counts, these people are my family. More so than my parents, who couldn't be bothered to come watch me play. I've spent so long trying not to let the great Carmen Aguirre down, trying not to let the people who used to love me down, that I've failed to focus on the people who matter. The people who have been by my side through all my lashing out, through all my anger, through my good and (admittedly more common) bad moods. Tennis may not be a team sport, but I'd be nowhere without my team and friends.

I step into the court, swinging my braid over my shoulder and adjusting my strings, slapping my racket against both heels before getting low. Because not only am I doing this for me, I'm doing this for them and all the hard work and long nights and time away from their families they've poured into me.

Anya serves down the T, and I hit it back, cross court. She smacks the ball down the line, and I slide over to hit another cross-court shot, forcing her to run as much as she's forcing me to. We're both immensely tired. We're both breathing heavily. And when she hits another ball down the line, I power my way to the ad side, setting my racket as I move and hitting the world's prettiest backhand despite the way it makes my back spasm.

"Jeu, set, et match, Vassilakis," the umpire says into the mic. The crowd bursts.

I did it.

I'm too floored, in absolute disbelief. My racket drops out of my hand as tears fill my eyes. I don't know when, but I fell to my knees, and now I slide so I'm lying on the red clay that I love so much, staring at the roof of the stadium, tears streaming down my face.

It's everything I've wanted and more. It's where I triumphed so many years ago as a junior, and where I was growing concerned I would never win again. It's the biggest tournament on my favorite surface, and I've done the thing so many people have accused me of being unable to do.

I closed. I didn't let Anya into my head. I played my game, and I beat the world number two. If I thought the crowd was deafening before, this is…

Absolutely insane.

I can barely see through the tears, but I stand and walk to the net, shaking Anya's hand. I'm too happy to care that she squeezes too hard, too overjoyed to notice that she says something under her breath. I shake the umpire's hand as well, thanking her.

Some people dedicate thousands of hours to the pursuit of this feeling, and after years of believing I was a failure, believing I peaked at seventeen, I've done it. When I glance at my box, Aleks is the first person I see. He's screaming into cupped hands, waiting for me to look over at him. Our eyes meet, and it's clear how proud of me he is.

It reminds me that I'm allowed to go to my team. With the help of staff and security, I race up the stands to my box and throw myself into Karolína's arms.

"My beautiful girl," she says into my hair. "My determined, beautiful girl. You did it. Of course you did it." She's choked up, tears leaving trails on her face too.

"Sorry," I say as we pull apart, realizing I'm covered in clay from lying on the court. "I got sweat and clay all over you."

"Get over here," she answers, pulling me back in. When she finally lets me go, I enter into a group hug with Delilah, Matteo, and Austin, their overlapping congratulations overwhelming enough that I have to step away, thanking them.

Pen is next and stops screaming and jumping long enough to hug me, though her phone is still recording. Always working on my content.

Aleks is last, and for a moment, I just stare at him. Then, without thinking, I launch myself into his body and kiss him. It doesn't last more than five seconds, his arms wrapping around me, his head dipping against mine.

"If this is to get back at my sister for the way she behaved in this match, I'm going to have to protest a little."

Delilah snickers behind me, and I shove at his chest. "Can you not ruin this moment please?"

"Nothing could ruin this moment, solnyshko." He takes my hands in his, where they sit on his chest, squeezing. "You're fucking incredible."

"A group picture!" Pen yells. "Quickly, before she has to go back for the ceremony."

I smile my widest, happiest smile, tears dried along my cheeks, and when Aleks wraps an arm around my waist, pulling me against him, I realize how right he was.

I was looking for love in all the wrong places. No need to search it out, wish for it, or bust my ass on the court for it.

It's right here, and it was already mine.

twenty-nine

The evening is a whirlwind of mandatory media and photo ops, Karolína, Pen, and Aleks hovering around me at every turn. It's so late by the time all is said and done that I'm staggering to my room, my muscles aching and my calves begging me to get out of the heels Pen's friend-who-is-also-a-stylist put me in, the red-and-black bodycon dress so tight, it's become a second skin.

But I have a couple of important things I need to get done before I can go to bed.

The group message has been going off incessantly, so I step out of the heels, groaning at how good it feels to be flat once more, and swipe through them quickly.

SHOTS FIRED

DELILAH

MY BEST FRIEND IS THE FRENCH OPEN CHAMPION

HARPER

NIC I'M SO PROUD OF YOU!

SAHAR

I feel like I'm going to need to bow the
next time I see you

HARPER

Agreed, you're too cool for us.

NOAH

Insane match, Nic. Huge congrats!!

YOU LIKED "INSANE MATCH, NIC. HUGE
CONGRATULATIONS"

MATTEO

Congratulations, Nic.

AUSTIN LAUGHED AT "CONGRATULATIONS,
NIC."

AUSTIN

Dude's a robot

But seriously, was so cool to watch from
your box today

Will be replaying the way the crowd
cheered for you over and over in my head
as motivation to get myself one of these
babies

Maya texted me separately, many variations of congratulations typed in all caps, not a single one without a typo. She then sent a video of her and Cooper in front of the television, jumping up after the final point and screaming excitedly.

I thank everyone before switching to my messages with Delilah.

Did you find it?

DELILAH

Heck yeah I did!

1 image

The goods have been secured. I'm en
route now

Why are you talking like that?

DELILAH

Can you please let me have my covert ops
mission just this once

A few minutes later, after I've changed out of the dress
and into a pair of Stratosphere shorts, a tank top, and
Aleks' quarter-zip, which, sadly, no longer smells like him,
a complex knock sounds at my suite door.

I open it to Delilah, who wears all black, including the
hood over her head. She's hunched over, hiding the paper
bag in her hand. Matteo stands behind her, his curly
brown hair messy and his hands in his sweatpants pockets.
He looks completely out of place and simultaneously
perfect beside Delilah, who he watches with the softest,
kindest eyes.

"Dear god," I murmur. "Don't you have a match
tomorrow?" I ask him rhetorically. The women's final is
always played on Saturday and the men's is Sunday, which
means Matteo will be on court in less than twenty-four
hours.

"I wasn't going to let her walk around the city on her
own at this hour," he answers gruffly. "Plus, I sleep in
before late matches."

"How about a little applause for your best friend, who

found comparable limeade and Sour Patch Bites in Paris when everything should be closed?"

Instead, I pull her into my arms, squeezing her once.

"The goods! You're squishing them!"

I start drawing back, but she crushes me tighter to her. "I'm kidding. If you're willing to give me a hug, I'm taking it. Aleks and his strange cravings can wait." Quieter, she says, "I'm so proud of you, Nic. So unbelievably proud of you."

There it is. Joy in the place of the uncomfortable longing that used to live in my ribcage when spending time with my best friend.

We step away, and I dab below my eyes. Apparently, I'm now someone who gets misty-eyed in front of people after years of hiding frustrated tears. I chalk it up to the long two weeks I've spent here and take the bag from her.

"Thank you so much for doing this."

"Anything for you." Delilah beams. "Good luck! I leave early Monday morning, so I don't know if I'll see you before then..."

"If you're here tomorrow, there will be space in my box for you," Matteo chimes in softly.

"Assuming I'm not dead tired after press, I'll be there."

Delilah nods, and they head toward the elevator, but she turns back. "Don't get too randy in public spaces!"

Matteo picks her up easily, carrying her to the elevator while grumbling about bedtime. I'll have to thank him for that later.

After putting on a pair of socks and slides, my feet too sore for anything more than that, I grab the crumpled sheet by my phone, my wallet, and the paper bag and make my way to Aleks' room.

I didn't think to check if he was awake, but luckily, the door swings open moments after my knock.

His smirk is wide, his hair is disheveled, and his eyes sweep over my messy bun, photo-ready makeup, and his sweatshirt.

"Coming in?" he asks in greeting.

"Actually, I was thinking we could go to the roof."

He grabs his things and follows me. "You should know that if you're planning to kill me, I have two weapons on my person."

"You wouldn't hurt me," I answer seriously.

There's a beat where he digests this, then, "And yet you've made no such indication that *you* wouldn't hurt *me*."

I roll my eyes, stepping into the opening elevator. I select the top floor and swipe my access card. It took Pen a long and charming phone call to convince this hotel, who sponsored my stay while I was here, to allow this.

The doors open to a view of the city, the Eiffel Tower shining brilliantly straight ahead of us. There are blankets and pillows on a raised platform, and I watch Aleks realize what's happening.

If the last nearly three months have shown me anything, it's that Aleks spends too much of his time worrying about others. His siblings, his parents, me. His days are full of bettering other people's lives, to the point that I'm not sure he stops to think about his own. After everything we've been through, I wanted to be the person who makes him feel special.

Want to be that person.

"Nic, what…?" he trails off quietly, eyes snapping to mine. "Did you do this for me? When did you find the time?"

"I have the best friends and team in the world. And of course I did this for you." I glance down. "You deserve it and more for all you do."

"Can I hug you?" he asks, but before he can finish, I step into his arms, my hands slipping around his neck and into his hair. I inhale, my favorite scent wrapping around me like I'm home.

"Thank you," he murmurs into my hair, kissing me before leading me to the blankets. We settle into them, stars twinkling above us. When I look at him again, he's staring at me with a soft smile. "Hi," he whispers. "How do you feel?"

"I…I'm in shock? Unbelievably happy. And so tired. I got asked so many stupid questions during media today too, and…What?" I ask when his smile widens.

"Nothing, I just missed getting you to talk. We've been so focused on training that we haven't done this in a while." Aleks shifts closer, like he's drawn to me. I feel it too, but there are a few things I want to talk about first.

"Anya. Was she…"

"Spitting mad? Yeah. She's probably still throwing a tantrum. If we're quiet enough, we might be able to hear it. But I don't want to talk about her."

"But we need to. Because if we want to move forward, I don't want that over our heads. I want us to be on the same page about everything."

"Everything, huh?"

"Aleks."

"Fine. What's there to talk about?"

"Let's say we were to start dating. What does that look like with your family? And a few years down the line?"

He's too happy to answer, pulling me to him. We kiss, his hand cupping my jaw, until I lean away. "Aleks, please!"

"Sorry, sorry. I don't know how I'm expected to not kiss the new French Open champion when she looks this good and tells me she wants to date me." At my pointed glare, he raises a hand in surrender. "Alright. If we were to start dating, I would tell my family. My parents would be cool about it, when they eventually talked to me again. Dima and Natasha would congratulate me because I'm sure my obsession with you is obvious. Anya would throw an absolute fit. Then I'd tell her that I don't care what she thinks. If she wants any sort of relationship with me, she needs to grow up and make nice with the woman I love. At least off court."

The word pushes inside my chest, sighing happily around my heart. This time, it's me who kisses him. He mumbles something into my lips, and I ask, "What?"

"You didn't let me finish."

I fake a beleaguered sigh, nodding for him to continue.

"And down the line, when I begged you to marry me, she'll have hopefully matured a lot and will accept you into the family, if not as a sister, then as someone she's indifferent to."

My eyebrows rise. "We aren't even dating and you're talking about marriage? That's a bit of a jump, no?"

"Oh, solnyshko. It's going to happen. It's not a matter of if, but when."

I blow out a breath. The notion is terrifying, especially since this would be my first real relationship. But with Aleks, I'm optimistic. "Then I guess I'd have to be good with Anya's indifference."

"Really? You wouldn't try to bash her skull in if we went on trips with my family?"

"I make no promises. But for you? I would do my absolute best."

Aleks laughs. "In my dream world, you two get along off court, and on court, you continue pushing each other to be the best you can be. Because at the end of the day, rivals are the people who shape us into our best forms. Maybe not emotionally, but certainly our games. One day, when you're going into the Hall of Fame, maybe you'll even thank her for being that push."

"That is light-years away and very best-case-scenario, but I see what you're saying."

My phone lights up beside me. Carmen Aguirre Vassilakis' name flashes on the screen, and Aleks scoffs, perhaps at the absurdity of her calling or of her being in my phone under her full name. "You can take that. I know it's what you've been hoping for."

Shock registers on his face when I decline it.

It's strange not needing my mother's approval anymore. I've spent a quarter of a century wishing for her to care about me, and now that she does…

What does it matter? She hasn't been here for my trials and tribulations, why should she get to be here for my wins?

I shrug. "When I was being passed around my box, I realized I'd been searching for the wrong thing. Or rather, searching in all the wrong places for something I'd already had. I have everything I could ever want or need right now. I don't want to spoil it with a cold congratulations and a promise to talk to me that she doesn't mean to keep." His lips tilt down at the idea. "I have something more important to discuss."

I finally open the paper bag. Delilah included a bottle of champagne, which I set between us. I also place his limeade and candy in front of him.

Aleks glances at it, surprised, then at me questioningly.

"Aleks, I'm brash. I'm easily annoyed. I'm angry a lot, and it's often unwarranted or a product of a lot of factors both in and out of my control. I struggle to allow myself to feel things, and I'm terrible at being vulnerable. A part of me is certain I'm unlovable, and there are going to be days where I test you, want you to prove your love to me even when it's unfair. I might lash out for fear that you'll stay long enough to see something you'll run from. In every conceivable way, I can't imagine I'd be a good partner. And yet I love you. And I'm selfish because I want you to love me despite all of that."

"Nic, I just said I love—"

"I know, I know, sorry," I say, swiping at a rogue tear. "I practiced this speech like fifteen times and didn't account for you saying it first. Anyway, you once told me that nothing belongs together more than I belong with you, and I'm inclined to agree. So if you believe we can handle whatever your sister throws at us and fighting when we don't agree on my training and the thousands of other factors that could come up, I'd really like to do more than fuck you."

Aleks' head tilts. "Is that what you practiced?"

"No, but you made me lose my train of thought and that's the best I can give you right now."

"*God*, you're so cute." He cups my jaw once more, tilting my head so I'm staring into his eyes. "Nic, it's okay that you're brash. I love when you're mean to me. I'm your cross-court rally, showing up for you always and breaking your walls down."

The words startle a laugh out of me. "That's the most absurd and corny thing you could have said."

"Maybe so, but I realized it when you were wearing Anya down today. It's true. I don't care about the bad days as long as you spend them with me. And I don't care if you snap at me, as long as you kiss me later when you're feeling better. Every time you think I'll falter, I'll prove to you again and again that I love you. I want to spend my life traveling the world with you, helping you reach your full potential, and one day—and this might scare you—raising a couple of mini-yous. If you want." He clears his throat. "I know that's a lot to throw at you right now, but just so it's on the table."

"It's not a lot," I whisper. It's a life I've always been sure I wouldn't get to have. A life I was certain no one would want to stick around for. But Aleks makes me believe it could exist. That we can, someday down the road, have kids who are loved and prioritized by both of us.

I may not be easy to love, but Aleks has made it seem effortless.

"Can I kiss you now?"

I move out of his hold, pulling out the crumpled piece

of paper. "No. Eat your candy. I have one more thing to say." Handing it to him when I realize he's not eating, I continue, "I want you to know I took this seriously. Because of you, I've learned so much about myself outside of tennis. I'm more than Nic the tennis player. I'm Nic, lover of sunrise walks and hater of sweet tea and artsy movies, among other things. So thank you for sticking with me and helping me despite everything I threw at you. And while I'm going to continue learning about myself, the one thing I want to do every single day is love you."

He drops the paper and scoops me into his arms, pulling me over his body, our mouths melding together. His hand slips into my hair, and I groan in protest when he pulls away. Somewhere, the champagne, limeade, and candy have been knocked over.

"I'm glad I've gotten to know you along the way too." His gaze drags over my body. He grins. "*All* of you."

"God, Aleks. You ruined it."

But I kiss him again, hard, because I can and because I love him so much, the thought of not kissing him makes my chest tight.

I've always found uncharted territory daunting. But for the first time in my life, I allow myself to sink into it. To welcome the embrace of the one person who refuses to be cut by my jagged edges.

Wholly safe and profoundly loved at the center of someone else's universe.

2 YEARS LATER

ALEKS

I set the massive vase of flowers on the wooden dining table in the kitchen of our rented villa in Naxos, the thick cream envelope with Nic's name on it on display in front of them and a big box of kourkoubinia beside it. When I glance through the open doors, I catch movement in the hanging wicker chair.

Nic leans back, her tanned skin covered only by a blue bikini, her bare feet brushing the air as the horizon spills open behind her. Wavy brown hair, which she hasn't gotten treated in the last year or so, catches a breeze, reaching toward the salt of the Aegean Sea below her as if to become one with it.

I reach for the sketchbook that has become a shrine to her, pulling the pencil from the metal hoops that bind it. Pages upon pages of sketches of her on the court, in a swimming pool, sleeping in hotel beds. I flip to an unused one near the end and get to work.

"It's been three days of lying in the sun, and my sock tan has gone nowhere," she says to her phone, where Delilah, Harper, Sahar, and Maya are squares on her screen.

The girls share a laugh before Harper says, "And it never will. We'll have pale feet for the rest of our lives." Nic's laugh joins theirs, a dripping of warm honey from her lips, and I find my own pulling up.

"It's true. I don't play nearly as much anymore and it's still there," Maya adds.

"How—feel—career—Wimbledon," a choppy voice sounds from her speaker.

"Del, babe. Where are you, and why is your service so bad?" Sahar questions.

There's shuffling, then Delilah's voice. "Sorry! I was asking how it feels to have a career Grand Slam." Last week, Nic won Wimbledon for the first time, which means she's officially won every major at least once—a career Grand Slam.

French Open the first year we worked together. US Open later that year. A repeat performance in Paris the next year. And this year, a win at the Australian Open and at Wimbledon.

World number one and a 5-time major winner. Pride builds in my throat again, as it's been doing often the last few months when I contemplate how far she's come. From struggling to win at multiple 1000 tournaments to winning titles left, right, and center.

She's unstoppable, resilient, and an absolute inspiration. Tennis fans love her fire and determination, rooting for her at every tournament like she's always wanted. I don't know how I got so lucky to be pulled into her orbit, but each day, I thank her for grounding me with her gravity. Loving me as deeply, even if it is in her own quiet way, as I do her.

Helping her achieve her dreams has been the most rewarding thing I have ever done. Screw my titles. Witnessing how a change in her training plan can make a world of difference to her on the court injects a euphoria into my veins, and it's further proof I'm getting to do what I love with the person I love.

"Kind of hard to believe, I guess? It's this thing that you want your whole life but that has always seemed so far out of reach. Then suddenly, it's right there, and I…" She shrugs, staring past the bright blue pool and padded daybeds to the sea, a relaxed smile on her face. "Surreal is the only word."

"And now you can take a break! You could skip hard-court season and still go to the finals."

She laughs again. "Not even Aleks could keep me off court for that long. I'd be clawing my way back."

Nic turns, her gaze clashing with mine and locking, her lips climbing when she notices me watching her. Her eyes flick beside me to the flowers, and she stands.

"Seriously? Here I was thinking the sexcation would last until the end of the year. Is little Aleks not up to the task?" Sahar asks as Nic pads to me.

"Little Aleks is doing just fine. Thank you for your concern, Sahar," I reassure her.

"Oh, phew. Hi, Aleks. Noah misses you."

I chuckle. "I miss him too."

"Who are these from?" Nic asks me, setting her phone

down. The four faces of Nic's closest friends stare back at me.

Handing her the card, I finger the velvet box in my pocket and walk behind her, pretending I'm going onto the terrace. But instead of stepping out onto the stones, I turn and drop to one knee.

Hopefully Pen is walking onto the terrace as planned, ready to take photos and videos from afar with Karolína by her side. This week-and-a-half break from the tour is as much for Nic's team as it is for her, and though she's a private person, she'll be glad to celebrate this moment with them.

"Aleks?" Nic asks, her voice breaking as she flips the piece of paper over. It details how proud of her I am, talks about the smallest fraction of the reasons I love her, and asks her to turn around. Which she's not doing.

"Right here, solnyshko."

"Aleks, wha—" She cuts off when she turns and sees me, her gray eyes light. Luckily, that means she's happy and not that she'll be threatening a vase to the head in the next few seconds.

Always a good start to a proposal.

"Bye, Nic! We love you. Hope you have the best night," Delilah calls over the phone. The four of them helped me pick out the pear-shaped diamond and emerald inlaid stones beside it.

"Use protection!" Sahar's voice joins in. "Or don't, whatever you want."

Harper laughs. "We'll celebrate when we're all together." They click off, and there's silence.

A salty breeze sifts through Nic's hair as her eyes water.

Her expression will be seared in my head for the rest of my life; it's a moment I'll sketch for decades and still never get right.

"Aleks…"

I grin, my own tears choking me up. "Hi, baby. I had a long speech prepared, but I know how impatient you are, so I'll give you the letter I wrote later and just say this: I am hopelessly, wildly, irrevocably in love with you, Nic. I have been privileged enough to watch you grow, both on and off the court, and I can say with all the certainty in the world that you are the most amazing, determined, passionate, gorgeous person I will ever know. I admire everything about you, from the furrow in your brow when I wake you, to the fact that you're about to lead the charge to help other athletes by talking about the pressure you fought through after your early success, to the look of genuine disbelief on your face when you win a title, though I never doubt you.

"I sometimes can't believe I'm the person you've chosen to wake up next to every morning, but if you'll have me, I'd like to be that person for the rest of our lives. So, Nic Vassilakis, will you marry me and be the most beautiful bride the world has ever seen?"

Her mouth opens, then closes, then opens again. A second later, she's flung herself into my arms, my grip on the velvet box tight as she wraps herself around me and kisses me. "Yes. Of course, yes." Another kiss. "If that was the short version, I can't even imagine the long version." I pinch her, and she laughs against my lips before kissing me one more time. "Screw you for making me cry. But god, I do love you."

I push to a stand, taking her with me, and when her feet are back on the ground, she stares at the ring in awe. "Did you pick this out yourself?"

"Why? Do you think I wouldn't be able to pick out your dream ring on my own?"

Nic giggles, my favorite sound in the world. It's so rare to get one from her, so hard to earn that I relish it each time, victory warm and soft, dancing in my chest. "I didn't say that."

Taking the ring out of the box, I slip it onto her finger. It's the perfect fit, and after she watches it twinkle in the sunlight that pours into the room, I weave my fingers through hers and pull her into my body. "You're right. I had to send a lot of photos to the girls. Natasha helped too. She's excited that you're going to be a part of the family."

Tash and I got closer after she left the tour. I'm helping her pay for her undergraduate degree, and though she's a few years older than most, she's made lots of friends. Still, we talk twice a week about what she's learning and the college experience she always dreamed of.

Nic leans back, her eyes on mine, brows halfway to furrowed. "Yeah? You told your family?"

I nod. "Dima says congratulations. My parents too." After a couple of weeks, they calmed down and met with the four of us for a family talk. Natasha and I explained how the pressure bent us to the point that we no longer loved the game, and though they've struggled to ease up, they realized if they do want more Morozov legacies, they're going to have to take a different approach with

Anya and Dima. "They're excited for the wedding. I don't have the heart to tell them we're going to have a small ceremony."

"We are?" she asks, bewildered. "Have you planned everything and I missed it?"

Laughing, I kiss the tip of her nose, which is rosy from her time in the sun the last few days. "No, but I know you want to keep it small. Believe it or not, I do know you."

Nic smiles softly. "And Anya?"

A month after Nic and I started dating, Anya tried to stir more shit up in the press, and I told her in no uncertain terms that I was very much in love with Nic and that she wasn't going anywhere, no matter what Anya did. Since then, things have grown less hostile. They play each other often, trading wins and majors and pushing each other to play their best, but with new kids aging up, they have plenty of other players to worry about.

"She heard from our parents. Texted me that she's glad I'm happy, which was a surprise." I lift Nic a couple of inches in the air. "Who knows, maybe you'll move from indifference to best friends."

Nic snorts. "Highly unlikely." She pauses. "But I will make every effort not to threaten to hit her, whether to her face or to you."

"I'll allow one a month."

"A month? How ab——" Her eyes cut behind me. "Pen! Have you been there the whole time?"

Setting Nic on her feet again, we turn to look at her manager and coach, who can't hide their watery grins. In many ways, along with the girls, we are her family. She hardly talks to her parents and only on her terms despite her mom now wanting more of a relationship. Pen and Karolína are the two people she spends the most time with beside me. It felt fitting that they be here.

"Duh! When Aleks told me he was doing this, I knew we would need photos. They're not great, but they exist," Pen says, which means they're going to be absolutely breathtaking.

Nic leaves my side to hug both of them, and after a quick, quiet conversation, we agree to meet tomorrow for a celebratory lunch.

Pen and Karolína make themselves scarce, and Nic and I change for dinner. Before we head out, we stand on the terrace, staring at the water crashing below, glasses of champagne in hand. Nic grabs my other arm and wraps it around her waist, and I rub the silky fabric of her blue dress between my fingers before splaying my hand across her torso.

"What should we toast to?" she asks me quietly.

"To the future Mrs. Nic Vassilakis Morozov?"

She laughs. "Or to the future Mr. Aleks Morozov Vassilakis."

"I'll drink to that." I clink my glass to hers, setting my lips beside her ear and whispering, "To us. And to that new weapon you can threaten me with for years to come."

She wiggles her ring finger, biting her lip. "And to the slutty little shirts that finally did me in."

acknowledgments

I want to say a huge thank you to my sensitivity readers Gigi Zarbi, Anastasija White, Nina Kauffman, and Marianna Cardenas. Your dedication to ensuring I handled these important topics with care is so appreciated. Any mistakes made are my own. Thank you to my alphas—Marja Graham, Miah Onsha, and Lisa Couch—for always helping me find the big picture pieces that weren't working in my early draft. Thank you to my betas—Janelle The, Cindy Nguyen, Haley Warren, and Brooke Novotnak—for helping me fine tune this story.

Thank you to Rachel, my guardian angel, for being the best editor and champion of my work.

Thank you to Miah and Laura for finding the little things, as always! Your attention to detail is forever incredibly appreciated.

To my bestie gals Marja and Miah—I'll say this every single book. I would be lost without you. I love you forever.

Thank you to my and E's families for believing in me. To E—I'll never be able to thank you for everything you do for me, but I hope to keep trying. I love you endlessly.

And last but certainly not least, thank you, dear reader, for picking up this book and taking a chance on me. Your support means the world to me. I hope you enjoyed reading Nic and Aleks' story as much as I enjoyed writing it.

about the author

Vai Denton is an American author, romance enthusiast—especially if sports are involved—and book lover. She has spent much of her life struggling to find her identity between her two cultures, using books as a sanctuary. Her hope is that her stories provide readers with the escape she once sought. In each of her books, you can expect swoony, healthy relationships that will have you kicking your feet.

If she's not reading or writing about love, you'll find her playing tennis, watching football, Pride and Prejudice (2005), or any number of her favorite romcoms with her two cats and fiancé.

If you'd like to contact Vai, find her on instagram @vaidentonauthor or via email at vaidentonauthor@gmail.com